LIFE WITH A
STAR

LIFE WITH A STAR

JIŘÍ WEIL

With a preface by

PHILIP ROTH

Translated from the Czech by

Rita Klímová with Roslyn Schloss

Northwestern University Press
EVANSTON, ILLINOIS

Northwestern University Press
www.nupress.northwestern.edu

Originally published in Czech under the title *Život s hvězdou*. Copyright
© 1964 by Mladá Fronta, Prague. First published in English 1989 by
Farrar, Straus & Giroux, Inc., New York. Translation copyright © 1989
by Farrar, Straus & Giroux, Inc. Preface copyright © 1989 by Philip
Roth. Northwestern University Press edition published 1998 by
arrangement with Farrar, Straus & Giroux, Inc. All rights reserved.

Printed in the United States of America

10 9 8 7 6 5 4 3 2

ISBN-13: 978-0-8101-1685-6
ISBN-10: 0-8101-1685-5

Library of Congress Cataloging-in-Publication Data

Weil, Jiří.
    [Život s hvězdou. English]
    Life with a star / Jiri Weil ; with a preface by Philip Roth ; translated
from the Czech by Rita Klímová with Roslyn Schloss.
        p. cm. — (Jewish lives)
    ISBN 0-8101-1685-5 (pbk. : alk. paper)
    1. Holocaust, Jewish (1939–1945)—Czech Republic—Prague—
Fiction. I. Klímová, Rita. II. Schloss, Roslyn. III. Title. IV. Series.
PG5038.W4Z313 1998
891.8'6352—dc21
                                                                98-31022
                                                                CIP

♾ The paper used in this publication meets the minimum requirements
of the American National Standard for Information Sciences—
Permanence of Paper for Printed Library Materials,
ANSI Z39.48-1992.

PREFACE

I first heard Jiří Weil's name in Prague in 1973, where a survivor of a distinguished Jewish literary family told me Weil was one of Czechoslovakia's best writers. When I got back to New York I met a translator who, it turned out, had translated two Weil stories, perhaps the only translations of his work into English. I read them and was stunned, not solely by the horrors they described but by the elemental means that served to communicate Weil's hatred for the Nazis and pity for their victims. They were stories conceived in rage and tears, then told with the matter-of-factness of the journalist and the disarming simplicity of the family anecdotalist. I thought of Isaac Babel. Weil's animating emotions were harsher and less ambiguous than Babel's, and, from the evidence of those translations, Weil appeared to have been by nature a colloquial storyteller rather than a relentlessly self-scrutinizing stylist of the minimalist persuasion. What he shared with Babel was the ability to write about savagery and pain with a brevity that in itself seems the fiercest commentary that can be made on the worst that life has to offer.

From what I have since learned through various sources about Weil's life and work, there are other resemblances to Babel. The two were born only six years apart, Babel in Odessa in 1894, Weil near Prague in 1900. Both writers were Jews and knew it. Both read Russian and knew Russian literature—in 1928 Weil received his doctorate from Prague's Charles University for a thesis on Gogol and the English novel. Both became literary victims of socialist realism and political victims of Stalinism (and Stalinist anti-Semitism). And each lived through his lonely years as a writer and a man, unpublished, unread, withdrawn, and silent—and, by party stricture, unmentionable in literary circles and classrooms.

In the mid-thirties Weil wrote *From Moscow to the Border*, a polemical novel that partly grew out of what he had observed of Soviet totalitarianism while he was working in Moscow, in the Czech section of the Comintern publishing house, during the early years of the Stalinist terror. A citizen still of the Czech democratic republic, he could not be put to death for his disenchantment, but his comrades' attacks were severe and they were renewed with the postwar publication of *Makana the Father of Miracles*, *The Harpist*, and *Life with a Star*. The last was considered by the Communists a "decadent" example of "pernicious existentialism."

In the early fifties Weil was expelled from the Writers' Union; he had already incurred expulsion from the Party for writing *From Moscow to the Border* (which did not stop him from writing its sequel, *The Wooden Spoon*, a manuscript that remained unpublished for some thirty years before it appeared in 1970 in an Italian translation). In the late fifties Weil was made director of the Jewish State Museum in Prague—with the thaw, and thanks particularly to the effort of Nobel Prize poet Jaroslav Seifert, he had been readmitted to the Writers' Union—but he is said to have lived a retiring, isolated, unhappy existence until his death from cancer in 1959.

Volume 1 of *The Jews of Czechoslovakia* designates *Life with a Star* "the outstanding Czech book published between 1945 and 1948," that is, the brief period of relative freedom between the end of the war and the Communist takeover. "This work," it continues, "whose title alludes to the Star of David which the Jews were forced to wear on the street during the Nazi occupation, is the story of the effect of Nazi anti-Semitic measures upon a humble Czech citizen of Prague." (A similar description might serve to summarize a later Czech novel of some quality, *Mr. Theodore Mundstock* by Ladislav Fuks.) When the Nazis entered Prague, Weil pretended to kill himself. Hidden illegally in the city—and believed by the authorities to be dead—he was able to survive the occupation. These harrowing experiences furnished the inspiration and probably much of the story for *Life with a Star*.

His last book, *Mendelssohn Is on the Roof*, also deals with Nazis and Jews, and most readers consider it his other major work, after *Life with a Star*. Published posthumously in Czech in 1960, it is reported to have taken Weil fifteen years to write. An S.S. man has orders to remove the statue of the Jewish composer Mendelssohn from among the statues of musicians that ornament the roof of the Prague Academy of Music. Since he does not know which one is Mendelssohn, he decides to take down the one with the biggest nose. This turns out to be the statue of Wagner. The novel proceeds from there.

—PHILIP ROTH

TRANSLATOR'S NOTE*

Throughout the book, the unnamed "they" are the Germans, who occupied Czechoslovakia from March 1939, when the protectorate of Bohemia and Moravia was established, until the end of the war in Europe, in May 1945. The city is Prague, the river that runs through it the Vltava (or Moldau). During the occupation the Nazis made the Jewish Religious Community of Prague, the prewar center of religious affairs, the self-governing administrative body for all persons considered to be Jews according to the Nuremberg racial laws. In fact, this "self-government" was a fiction, and the Community became the instrument of the Nazi genocide of the Jews. All Jews were required to register with the Community and, starting in October 1940, with a Central Office for Jewish Emigration directly subordinate to the Gestapo. This central office was located in the elegant Stresovice district in a villa confiscated from a wealthy Jew. In addition to controlling the Jewish Religious Community, it administered all aspects of the lives of Jews and issued orders for the organization of transports to various concentration and extermination camps in occupied Polish and Soviet territories.

The Community was charged with drawing up transport lists of approximately 1,000 to 1,200 people each. Those called up were sent to a makeshift wooden building that had served as an annex of the Trade Fair Palace and, because it had been used for an exposition of radios during the last trade fair, was known as the Radio Mart. The building had not been in use

---

* For a detailed account of the Nazi genocide of Czechoslovak Jews, see volume 3 of *The Jews of Czechoslovakia: Historical Studies and Surveys*, published by the Jewish Publication Society of America and the Society for the History of Czechoslovak Jews (New York, 1984). The information in this note is taken from there.

for several years and lacked plumbing, ventilation, and heat. Here Jews scheduled for transport were "processed," a procedure that usually lasted three or four days.

In November 1941 the Germans decided to create a special camp for Czechoslovak Jews, which they claimed would only be a ghetto, a place where Jews would have self-government and be given work. For this purpose, the northern Bohemian town of Terezin, about thirty-five miles from Prague, was evacuated. Named for the Austrian Empress Maria Theresa (and known to the Germans as Theresienstadt), it had served as part of the Austrian fortification system since 1780. By the late nineteenth century, however, it functioned merely as a garrison. During the German occupation, the so-called little fortress was used as a Gestapo prison and the greater part of the town as a concentration camp. The promise of a meaningful Jewish administration proved hollow; Terezin actually served for most of its inmates as a place of transit to extermination camps in the east, principally Auschwitz after the spring of 1944. Of the over 75,000 Czechoslovak Jews deported to Terezin, about 57,000 died in other camps, more than 6,000 died in Terezin, and only about 9,000 survived.

LIFE WITH A
STAR

1

"Ruzena," I said, "at this moment people are sitting down to well-set tables. There are flowers in vases. Plates clink, and steam rises from soup bowls. People begin to eat. They cut their meat with their knives and pick it up with their forks, they wipe their mouths with napkins and drink beer, and then they rest, contented, everywhere, in restaurants and in homes."

Ruzena could not answer. She was not in the room, she was not with me at all. I didn't know what had happened to her. I hadn't seen her for a long time. Perhaps she was not on earth anymore, perhaps she had never even lived.

But I spoke to her. I had to speak to someone. I cooked my food on the drum-shaped stove. I was cold because the stove didn't warm the garret, the doors and windows didn't close tight. My attempts to seal them with old socks didn't help. I had cleaned the stovepipe twice. I was tired, dirty. I was in despair and it was lunchtime.

"Ruzena," I said, "people are drinking coffee now, well, maybe not real coffee, but they are sitting somewhere warm, after a satisfying lunch, and I am freezing, Ruzena, and I am hungry."

The garret was full of smoke, perhaps from the little stove, perhaps from the cigarette I was smoking. I had rolled it from imitation tea, most likely made of strawberry and raspberry leaves. I refused to smoke hops. They made me sleepy and gave me a headache.

"Ruzena, people are lighting up cigarettes, blowing clouds of smoke, and listening to the radio. They had their lunch some time ago and now are looking forward to their afternoon snack. Soon they will be drinking coffee with milk; they will have rolls with their coffee. How long has it been since I last had a roll?"

I had to talk to someone. I was alone, quite alone in the icy garret full of smells and smoke. I had to restart the fire. I blew into the burning embers, afraid the fire would go out again; I only had a few matches. I was alone in a small house on the outskirts of the city, dressed in a dirty track suit. A mattress lay by the stove; an overcoat and a single suit hung in a recess in the wall.

I had burned the bed and the wardrobe. I had burned everything I could because I had no coal and because I didn't want to give them anything. They would not get anything from me, not even the old socks I used to seal the windows and doors, or the curtains that I used as rags to clean the floor, or the furniture that had already been swallowed up by the stove. I didn't yet know what to do with the mattress. I had to sleep on something. It would be cold on the bare floor. I also didn't know what to do with the washstand. It was made of hard wood that I didn't have the strength to cut up, and it had a marble top. I threw it into the garden to break it, but it didn't break and it lay there crushing the grass. I intended to burn the mattress as soon as they tried to do something with me. I would find some way to destroy the washstand, and the only thing remaining would be an old broken coffee table. Yes, I didn't burn it on purpose, even though it would have been easy; it was only made of thin bamboo sticks. The coffee table had to stay. When they came to confiscate the furniture they would find nothing but cracked walls, an empty garret, the broken-down stove, and, in the middle of the room, the coffee table; this useless piece of furniture would reign over the room.

"Ruzena," I continued, "you aren't listening to me. You seem to be mending socks or stockings. You're thinking about the film you saw. It was a silly film, Ruzena; it's not worth thinking about. It was a Czech film about love and a blue veil. I saw the posters and could figure the whole story out immediately. I saw stills from it too, in some window. A fat young woman plays a double part in it; sometimes she laughs and sometimes she cries.

"You would do better to tell me how to cook my lunch on this stove. Look, the fire doesn't want to burn. You were always smart, you always knew what to do in every situation. 'Run away, Josef,' you said. 'You will have a terrible life. You are all alone and people who are alone have a bad time when things get difficult.' "

I did not run away. I was afraid to cross the border. I had no one who would go with me. I was alone and there was no one to advise me. I was afraid they would catch me at the border. I would not have known what to do in a foreign country.

I blew into the fire and looked at the ceiling; there was a damp circle there that kept growing, and when it rained hard, water dripped from the place where there was a hole in the roof. I knew the place well; I myself had smashed the tiles with an ax during the summer, when I was all alone in the house and wanted it to fall apart. I wanted it to be in ruins before they did something with me. Now in the fall it was bad when it rained hard and bad in the winter when the roof was covered with snow.

My water didn't want to boil. I put some bones in it, nice big bones that I had to break up with an ax so they would fit into my pot and that I was able to scrape some meat off. I wanted to make a stew with it. I hadn't eaten meat for a long time and I craved it. I imagined myself biting into a piece of pork; it would have a crisp crust that would dissolve on my tongue. Or I would tear off a piece of beef with my teeth; I would have a big piece and it would be all mine. But I had no ration cards for meat, I had no money to buy it on the black market, and I didn't know who would sell me any. I could only buy blood; I was allowed to buy that. I could make a soup out of it; at least it was a little like meat.

In the early afternoon I had stood in the butcher shop. The blood must all have been sold because I didn't see the blue enamel pot on the counter, but I stood there anyway. Perhaps they had a little left somewhere. I held on to my soup pail and waited.

"Mr. Halaburda," I said, "do you have a little blood left?"

"Sold it all this morning," the butcher answered. He was chopping off pieces of nice meat. I looked at it longingly. Such beautiful red meat. I wondered how it would taste grilled. Yes, that would be a steak. Long ago I too had eaten such meat; yes, sir, I had eaten a lot of steaks.

I lingered in the shop and watched the butcher clip ration cards and sell portions of meat. I didn't know what to cook the next day; I had counted on getting the blood. I had already cooked the barley groats—I couldn't very well eat them dry. Often I had done just that, but now I couldn't swallow a single groat when I was looking forward to the blood so much.

"Mr. Halaburda," I pleaded, "you know I'm not allowed to shop in the morning and I would very much like to buy some blood."

"Tell you what, I'll sell you some bones. You can make soup with them."

I was happy about the bones and I told myself I would make myself a festive lunch. The bones were big and beautiful and had scraps of meat on them.

I went home, put down the bones, and began to cut wood. I had to split off splinters from a dry piece of wood I had kept from the bed. It had lasted a long time. I would hack away at it with the ax, my hands freezing. I wore old woolen gloves that my fingers stuck out of. But I always managed to chip off some splinters.

Then I sat close to the stove and put the pot on, but I had no water. I had used it up washing my sooty hands, so I had to go out to the pump. I had smashed the feed pipe during the summer, soon after I made the hole in the roof. I said to myself at the time that people might be willing to live in a wrecked house but they wouldn't want to live without water; they certainly wouldn't want to do that. The water seeped into the ground and a lot of it was wasted, but the house wasn't mine and I didn't pay for water.

I took a water can and went to the pump on the corner. There was ice on the ground and my feet slipped; my hands burned from holding the handle so tightly. The water ran slowly, reluctantly, but I managed to fill the can. I hauled it back. Icy water splashed on my hands. I had to warm them over the stove.

"Ruzena, it's half past two and I still haven't had lunch. I looked forward to it so much. This morning I just drank black water and ate my dry bread and then I sliced some of my lean cheese. I got up late—I have to get up late, you know, because the room is so cold. At the sawmill they promised to sell me a little wood, but as you know, this stove swallows up wood, and coal won't burn without it."

I remembered that I still had the frame from the bedsprings. I ran down to the cellar. Even if the fire in the stove went out, I had to get some wood. The ax probably dented each time it slipped on the wire springs. But when I came back, the fire had not yet gone out. I put more wood in the stove and only then the water began to boil a little. I sat by the stove and I felt warm. I knew that when the fire went out I would lie on the mattress, in the sleeping bag, with a book in one hand, and I would read, and then, when my fingers grew numb from the cold, I would stick out the other hand. I would read until my eyelids began to droop and then I would sleep for a long, long time.

But sometimes I can't fall asleep. I keep rolling over in my sleeping bag, overcome by fear, strangled by it. I want to cry out in terror. This happens when I am scared that they will come to get me.

Or it occurs to me that they will call me to the Community

and send me into forced labor. I have already been called up once for registration. They didn't send me, but the next time they will. They are only saving their own skins; they would have to go themselves if they didn't send someone. What if I only weigh 102 pounds, they don't give a damn. They sit in their warm offices and it's all the same to them what happens to Josef Roubicek, former bank clerk, because there were and still are so many other Roubiceks.

I couldn't sleep, so I tried to read, but the letters swam before my eyes. I shivered with cold and with fear. I would like you to be with me at this moment, Ruzena. When you came to see me we used to sleep together on the wide sofa; you made coffee in the morning and brought it to me. How wonderful the coffee smelled and how fresh the rolls were. You would sit by me; we drank together and then I lit a cigarette and lounged in bed for a long time while you washed in the bathroom. I am sure you would drive away my fear now.

I ate the soup made from bones, picked out the marrow, broke the hard bread into the soup. I enjoyed the stew very much even though I made the gravy without any fat and I couldn't see the meat. I had a butt from a real cigarette, and I mixed it with the dry tea leaves and had a good smoke. I was warm. I forgot everything. I knew I was at home. The bare walls were pleasant; I even loved the damp circle on the ceiling because it was still mine.

"Thank you, Ruzena," I said. "Thank you for keeping me company. I had a good lunch and now I'm warm. It's a good thing you taught me how to cook at the summer cabin."

Ruzena did not answer. I sat in the darkness. I didn't want to get up and turn the switch on, but the red-hot coals from the stove glowed in the darkness. I looked at them and smoked the leaves I had mixed into the large butt.

2

That day I dreamed of the woods. I walked and walked with Ruzena in the woods. We didn't know the path well. We didn't have a map with us, but we didn't care. We marched on, laughing, saying the woods must end somewhere. But suddenly the path petered out, the woods darkened, we no longer saw the sun. I was suddenly full of fear that we were lost in the woods. I threw down my knapsack and lay in the moss and Ruzena bent over me. She reproached me for something. I didn't understand her. She talked about pots and a kettle. I didn't remember any kettle or pots, and I was telling her that her friend Mana was treacherous and was spreading gossip about her.

"Ruzena," I cried out, "you don't love me."

Suddenly the kettle Ruzena was talking about was there. It was made of copper and was all shiny. I had seen one like it long ago, at my grandmother's, when I was small, and now I wanted to tear it down from the wall. The kettle was huge; it got up on its feet and began to march directly toward me. Ruzena disappeared and I was alone in the woods with the kettle; my feet were numb and the kettle marched on, only now it had changed into a huge drum. Someone was beating on it violently and yelling, perhaps the drum itself was yelling. Then it suddenly dissolved. I began to wake up and then, fully awake, I heard someone at the door calling my name: "Rou-bi-cek, Rou-bi-cek." I couldn't climb out of my sleeping bag very quickly, and the voice at the door continued to yell. It had to be someone who had the right to yell that way. I struggled from the bag, and finally I was out of it and opened the door. I was in my track suit. I didn't have to get dressed.

"Are you Roubicek?" asked the man at the door. "I might as well have yelled my lungs out. You don't have a bell. Were you asleep or what? Here is a notice from the Community."

"Excuse me, sir, do you know what they want?"

"I just deliver the mail."

I had only my track suit on and I was cold. I ran up the stairs, and along the way I read the notice. I was ordered to come at nine o'clock. There would be no time to boil water for coffee. I wouldn't be able to warm up a bit by the stove. I would have to wash in icy water and, all cold, walk out into the freezing day. I didn't feel like getting out of my track suit—it was warm—but I had to wash. The water seemed to burn me. I cut myself a piece of bread and some of the cheese.

"If I had a thermos bottle," I said to myself, "I could have heated some water yesterday and have something to warm my stomach with today. That would make for a much better ride downtown."

I had owned a thermos bottle long ago, but I had broken it. It was a good thermos bottle. I used to take it on picnics and I had stuffed it with moss, but it had fallen from a chair and broken.

I shivered with cold at the back of the streetcar. I walked from one end of the car to the other while it was empty, and then I stamped my feet, which were quite numb. My socks had holes in them and I wore light tan summer shoes. I was so cold my eyes teared. I longed to warm up a bit with at least a cigarette, but I didn't have one. I hadn't had time to make one from fake tea. I couldn't warm up in one of the cafeterias downtown because they all had NO ADMITTANCE signs.

I ran through the streets, glad that it would be warm in the office. I walked through the corridors and looked for the person who had sent for me. The building had four stories. It was full of people. They climbed the stairs back and forth, up and down; they pushed through the corridors and waited by the doors. They ran around noisily, and none of them could tell me anything about the room I was supposed to report to. Everyone was intent on seeing to their own business. They were irritable and unfriendly. They seemed to look at me angrily, as though I was one more person who would want something, who would make requests and leave less for the others. I went up to the fourth floor, walking behind people who were rushing somewhere, and I thought, These people are surely going to the same office as I am. But they were stopping by a small window, where they each received a cup of tea that they stirred with a spoon attached to the counter by a string. I got in line and waited my turn.

"I'd like some tea," I said to a fat woman who was pouring it out of a large pot. Next to her stood a man who looked at me carefully.

"Section?" he hissed at me.

I couldn't answer. I didn't know what section he was referring to. I only wanted some imitation tea, warm, with no sugar, so that I could wash down the bitterness in my throat.

"Don't you understand? Which section do you work in?"

"I don't work here. I wanted some tea."

"But I'm telling you, this is a canteen for employees only."

The people who were standing behind me were pushing impatiently for me to go, but I stood there not knowing what to do. I kept looking at the large pot of tea, at the beautiful steam rising from it, and I had to swallow my saliva.

"Move," they shouted at me.

I left the window and looked at the people who were shouting at me. They looked healthy and full of bureaucratic eagerness. They pushed toward the window as if they were fulfilling some important mission.

Yes, these were all clerks, so someone would be able to tell me where the right door was.

I chose a man who was drinking his tea slowly and who seemed old enough, and I showed him my notice.

"You have to go to the second floor. That's where the registration office is. There's a big sign downstairs, can't you read?"

I stood in front of the door on the second floor. There were a great many people there and I thought about the word "registration." I didn't like words with foreign origins; they were always threatening. I had already filled out lots of questionnaires and answered bagfuls of questions. I always smiled, embarrassed, when I was asked, "What do you live on?" As if I myself knew what I lived on. Once I wrote "on assistance," but that was not true. I didn't receive assistance from anyone, and on the last questionnaire I wrote "this."

The people standing behind me in line were quiet; they spoke to one another in whispers. I asked the man next to me how much longer we would have to wait.

"It's a pretty long procedure and then you still have to go to Stresovice."

"Stresovice" was the word I was most afraid of. It meant an authority that could do as it liked with me, a mysterious office where people walked on tiptoe. Many who had entered there had not come back, and those who did come back lay . . .

I was hungry, but now I had forgotten my hunger. Only the bitterness in my mouth remained. I waited quietly.

"Ruzena," I said to myself, "I often had to wait for you too. I always waited quietly like now, even if I didn't know whether you were coming, but I waited anyway. I knew you wanted to come, if only you could, because you loved me. I saw nothing of what went on around me when I waited for you. Perhaps I was all alone on the street, but perhaps people were walking all around me and streetcars were rumbling through the street. Only when you came did things begin to move again and I became aware of the shop windows, of people walking about; I heard the sound of the streetcars and car horns then."

The line moved ahead slowly. Three people entered whenever three left. I tried to forget the dirty corridor and my tiredness.

I first met Ruzena on New Year's Eve. I didn't have a party to go to. I had made a date to go out somewhere with Frantisek Stejskal, who had the desk next to mine at the bank. We had been to a number of places where we would sit down for a while and have something to drink. We weren't drunk, just in a good mood. I don't even know how we came to be at Pokorny's. It was a cross between a bar and a dance hall. They had a lousy jazz group, but they also had one attraction, a violin player who swung the violin over his shoulder and played it on his back; then he'd lie on the floor, throw the violin up in the air, and catch it. People liked his act a lot.

The place was full. I didn't feel like staying, but Frantisek saw a friend. We sat down at his table. I was told his name was Jarka Pospichal. There was a young woman sitting next to him; Frantisek introduced her to me as Jarka's wife, Ruzena. I looked at her and wanted to say something pleasant. I was in a good mood. She was tall and slim. She didn't look like a married woman; she had very lively eyes.

I paid no attention to Jarka Pospichal, who seemed quite drunk. I learned that he was a bank clerk too, that he worked for a small savings bank. I was looking at Ruzena when Jarka—completely ignoring us—suddenly began to jabber away. I didn't listen to him but kept staring at Ruzena instead.

"Let's dance," she said, as if we had known each other for years. We pushed into the tightly packed crowd, pressed against each other, because the dance floor was full. I got dizzy, and in the middle of the dance I told her, "I love you, Ruzena."

"I love you too."

And as she said it, it became the truth and she could not have said anything else.

"Move," someone yelled at me from behind, and only then did I see that there was a space in front of me and I was in the dirty corridor again and I felt the bitter dryness in my mouth. I took a few steps forward and leaned against the wall. The faces I saw looked greenish and contorted. I was alone again.

I looked around. There was nothing to focus one's attention on, just the dirty corridor and a sign on the door that I couldn't read. I didn't want to keep looking at all these people.

When we came back from dancing that time we were a bit high, but Frantisek and Jarka didn't notice us.

"Ruzena, you're married," I said.

"Does it matter?"

"You come from the country," I said, without knowing why.

"Because my hands are rough?"

"No, I didn't mean it that way." I began to stumble over my words and she laughed.

"But you're right, I do come from the country. Jarka and I went to school together."

I told her that I came from the city but that I had always been alone. I told her all about myself in the midst of the noise of the music and the dancing, how my aunt and uncle had taken me in, how they reproached me for every penny they spent on me, and how they soon got rid of me by getting me the job I had at the bank.

Ruzena was quiet. I didn't know if she was interested in what I was telling her. When she got up, we squeezed hands. Then we all went to a cheap tavern for tripe soup and coffee. It was almost morning. The place was full of people drinking beer. We had to sit at a table with others. Someone played the accordion. Frantisek and Jarka stared stupidly at the table, falling asleep over their glasses.

Ruzena and I sat next to each other and didn't say anything. I wanted to tell her this was all silly, but somehow I forgot everything and instead I kept still. The dawn was gray when we said goodbye, the sidewalks were muddy, and the roofs were dripping. I looked at Ruzena as she walked off with Jarka. I was alone again and I went home slowly.

"Your turn." Someone pushed me from behind.

I went through the door and gave the clerk the notice I had received.

"Roubicek, Josef," he read slowly. "Sit down."

3

I had to answer questions and the clerk dictated the answers to a typist. The interrogation took a long time and it seemed as if the questionnaire would never end, but suddenly I stopped being afraid and felt like laughing at all the effort being wasted on one Josef Roubicek, for whom no one had ever shown any concern. I had become important, too important. They wanted to know everything about me, they measured and weighed me, they wanted to examine my whole past.

"We're finished," said the clerk. "Be at Stresovice tomorrow at 9:50—on the dot."

I was no longer cold. I was only hungry. It was almost noon. I didn't know what to make of the long interrogation. I asked, "Perhaps you'll at least tell me what all this means. I live on the outskirts and I don't know about anything. What will happen to me?"

"I don't know anything either, and if I knew, I couldn't tell you. Those are our orders, from above. This is a registration and it concerns emigration."

So they would move me, not that I had any objection. I would be glad to move anywhere, even if I didn't know what I would do elsewhere. I had no skill except sitting at a desk and adding up columns. I would be glad to move away from my drum-shaped stove. I could burn the mattress, roll up my sleeping bag, and go to some other country.

I didn't feel like leaving the building for the street. I knew I would have to make the long trip by streetcar, and at home I would have to start the fire. It always took me a long time to get warm and to cook my food. I had a half day before me and didn't know what to do. I was tired, but I knew I wouldn't be able to sleep, because I would keep thinking about Stresovice.

I walked down the stairs slowly, and I was close to the exit when someone called me. I recognized Karel Wiener. He

wasn't really a friend. We had met several times at meetings
of bank employees. He worked at a fancy bank and he always
walked like he thought he was special. I didn't like him, but
I acted friendly. At least he would keep me in the warm building a little longer.

"I wouldn't say you look well, but then who looks well
nowadays?"

I looked at Wiener. He had on a worn overcoat and no tie;
under the coat I could see a pair of rumpled trousers, and he
wore leather snow boots. But everything was made of the best
material, and his cheeks were ruddy.

"What were you doing here?"

I told him. He gave me a funny look.

"Well, who knows, maybe it will be good for something.
Here a person never knows what to do. One can think how
smart one is and go right ahead and do something silly. Or
one gets into a mess, and it becomes the only way out. Although I must tell you that none of those clerks seems to be
eager to go to Stresovice. They send people like you, who
don't have pull. Well, they won't get me to go there, so they're
sending me to Lipa."

I knew what Lipa was. It was a farming estate that they'd
also wanted to send me to.

"Rudolf Fantl killed himself."

"Killed himself? How?" I asked. Fantl was Wiener's friend.
He had worked for an export firm. He had lots of money.
Wiener once told me he had taken a car trip with him.

"He committed suicide. He couldn't take it. He got a visa
to go to South America; he was able to get all the necessary
permissions, but then the war started. He took some cyanide
and that was that."

"Is cyanide good?"

"The best you can use. It works immediately."

We were standing at the entrance; people were passing us
on all sides. There was a crowd around the doorman's booth.
People were asking the man questions, and he shouted at them
from his small window.

"Good job, being a doorman. He sits in a warm cubbyhole and yells at people. But he's also the first person they meet up with when they come here. Let's go somewhere."

"I don't have any money." I had only a few coins, which I had to keep for the streetcar and for bread.

"Don't worry, I'm inviting you."

We went to a tavern near the building. It had plain kitchen tables and rough chairs and an ADMITTED sign on the door. The place was crowded, full of people nervously fidgeting around in their chairs. Wiener ordered soup and potatoes with gravy. It wasn't good food, but I was hungry and it was warm in the tavern. Wiener seemed to know a lot of people. He whispered with them. I overheard scraps of conversation: "They have geese at the cemetery."

I was tired and sleepy. I couldn't understand how geese had come to be in a cemetery, but I didn't care. I sat in the warmth and grew drowsy. I didn't even notice that Wiener was no longer at my table.

"Wake up." He poked me. "You can't sleep here or sit for too long. I've already paid. Let's go."

I thanked him and said goodbye.

"Here are two cigarettes for the trip home."

They were real cigarettes.

At home I started the fire and made some coffee. I had bought some imitation sausage. It looked more like bologna. I didn't know what they had made it from; someone in the shop had said that it was made from river crabs and others that it was made from yeast. I didn't particularly want to buy it.

This time I couldn't talk to Ruzena; she was somehow too far away. They had probably driven her off and chased her away in that dirty office, when they were spelling out my name and pressing me for unnecessary dates and numbers. So I talked to Death.

I am sitting between bare walls next to a broken-down stove; I am eating awful bread and a loaf made from river crabs. They came by sea, somewhere in China. I have nothing left. They have cornered me here and I have nowhere to go. They want to take away this bare room, which rain drips into, take it away from me; they don't even want to let me sleep on the bare floor and read the same books over and over again. They will drag me off to a foreign country and maybe kill me there. I do not believe they will allow me to live. The people who were crowding around the offices were frightened. Wiener was sorry for me. He bought me lunch out of pity, he gave me cigarettes out of sympathy. My dearest, is it difficult to die? I would not have asked Ruzena; she would have laughed at me. But I do not want to talk to Ruzena. Whom am I talking to? I am talking to you. Who is that, you? I am calling you, yet I do not see you. But you are female. For once I would like to sleep quietly. Could you, unknown, terrible, bring on sweet slumber? Answer me! I locked myself between these walls, but they still want to take me away from here. That is why they interrogated me and wrote everything down. Maybe they think that you too like to have everything put in your accounts. And what if I came to you without their help, without their papers? Perhaps you have a wedding ring made of cyanide for me? What if I swallowed that wedding ring and remained lying here, in my sleeping bag, if I ceased to be Josef Roubicek? Would I mess up their accounts? But no, I would not mess up anything. They would just throw away my folder. They would carry me down the narrow staircase here. They would bury or burn me. But I have nothing, not even cyanide or a wedding ring from Ruzena, or one from you, you stranger— you woman. How could I get it? What did they say? It is here; it is in Prague.

We had been talking for some time, Death and I, but she was a very inattentive companion.

"A country," I said to myself. "There must be such a country. The sun will shine all day there. I will walk the streets of its city, past beautiful shops filled with goods; there will be shop assistants behind the counters and they will call to me, 'Come, Mr. Roubicek, choose. We have everything—ham, real coffee, clothes made of English wool, the best cigarettes, chocolate-covered strawberries.' But I will pass them by indifferently. No, I no longer need anything. I have everything I need in my beautiful apartment, with modern furniture, central heating, and a bathroom. I am in a hurry to meet Ruzena and I cannot spare a minute. She is expecting me at exactly 9:50. The most I can do is buy flowers wrapped in tissue paper. I will carry them as a sacrament. 'That's Roubicek,' I will overhear people whispering among themselves. 'Which Roubicek?' 'Oh, you know, the director of the bank, the great financier. Haven't you heard about the deal he pulled off at the stock exchange?' Ruzena and I will sit on the thick upholstery of the car and I will casually give orders to the chauffeur. 'Where are we going, Josef?' Ruzena will ask. 'To the seashore, to France; we'll go via Paris and you can buy everything you need there.'" But the fantasy was not a success. I could not imagine a rich Roubicek or the boulevards in Paris. I saw Stresovice and the beastly faces in uniforms.

I tossed about in my sleeping bag for a long time before falling asleep.

I awoke early, before dawn, switched on the light, and started to cook breakfast. I had to go to Stresovice, and the clerk had told me to be there exactly at 9:50. "I'm giving you a late appointment because you live far out, but you better be there at 9:50 or there'll be hell to pay."

I did not enjoy the coffee at all, or the paste made of Chinese river crabs, even though I knew that I would have to wait a long time in Stresovice and that I would be hungry. But I lit a cigarette. It was one of the ones Wiener had given me. I had been sorely tempted to light it the day before, but I saved it for the morning, before I went to Stresovice.

I stood in front of a large villa. It was an ordinary villa among many others, but still it was different. We stood on the street; nobody spoke or even whispered. My feet grew numb from the cold as we stood in front of the gate. I saw their policeman. He stood in the doorway with his feet planted apart. He seemed to be looking over our heads, but we knew he was watching us. To the left there was a garage. I had heard about this garage. They used it to lock up those they wanted to beat up; we were in the street and close to the garage.

At this moment Ruzena is leaving home to go shopping. I thought of her walking in felt boots with a shopping bag, smiling into the frost with narrowed eyes.

"You see, Ruzena," I said, "now I am waiting for them to move me out. I am waiting in front of an awful place and I don't know what they will do with me in there. And yet I didn't want to run away with you to a foreign country."

That day we were sitting in an outdoor restaurant above the city and Ruzena said, "Josef, let's just take a few things and leave. We'll get along somehow over there."

"But what will we live on? We'll die of hunger in that foreign country of yours. I don't know how to do anything except add up columns in a bank, and I don't know any foreign languages."

"That doesn't matter. We'll make a living somehow. What are you afraid of? We love each other."

I was afraid. The city was spread out before us. I was born here, I knew almost every street, I had my own café, my movie house, my newsstand and tobacco shop. I didn't want to go anywhere else.

"But, Ruzena, it's impossible."

"I knew it, Josef. I don't know how to beat this fear out of you. But think about it. Otherwise we won't get anywhere. Jarka won't divorce me and I can't run away from him. You know how it is between our families. We both come from the same town, where people know all about one another."

I was angry because Ruzena had said that I was afraid. I was afraid, but I didn't want to admit it.

"But if we leave, it will be the same thing."

"No, you don't understand. If I ran away, then that would be that. I would be gone once and for all. But if I live with you here in Prague . . ."

I didn't understand Ruzena, and I didn't want to understand her. I didn't want to go away, although I myself didn't know what to do. We loved each other but we always had to meet in secret. It was difficult, the constant deceit, lies, evasions. It wasn't the right way to live—because we did love each other.

"Let's not talk about it anymore. But someday you'll be sorry!"

I was afraid then. I thought Ruzena wanted to leave me. She understood me.

"No, I don't want to leave you, but what if I have to . . ."

But then she kissed me and we forgot about everything. We went downtown through winding alleys. We stopped often to kiss; we stopped kissing only when we came to well-lit streets.

We had been waiting for a long time. The gate opened and we all surged forward into the courtyard, where an official of the Community with a yellow armband urged us on. Because we were all freezing, we were glad to go in, past the garage to the back door, but there we had to wait again. We turned in our notices, and the official with the yellow armband let people in according to the times their appointments had been set for. Now we were even stiffer from the cold. We were almost inside the building, and the garage was only a stone's throw away. In the courtyard there was a man in uniform and he looked at us.

It began to snow.

4

Snowflakes were falling down my neck. It was very quiet. No one spoke. We stood before the door. Behind it was an official with a yellow armband who would let in three people at a time, according to their appointments. The soldier stood under the projecting roof of the garage paying no attention.

It was my turn at eleven o'clock. I was very cold and numb. The official with the yellow armband motioned me to enter the office. Inside were more people with yellow armbands. Typists were rapidly banging on typewriter keys. I had to answer questions. The questionnaires were even longer than the ones they had filled in at the Community. I spoke quietly and the noise of the typewriters drowned out my voice. Everyone spoke quietly and walked as if on thin ice. There were no guards, unless some were hidden in the house. They were invisible; they could enter the office at any minute.

Then we were herded into a large room where a number of people sat behind desks. I was sent from one desk to the next. "Jewelry," one official barked at me. "I don't have any," I said. "Gold," rattled a second. "I don't have any," I said. "Savings deposits," hissed a third. I went from one desk to the next. They asked about mortgages, life insurance, real estate, bank accounts, treasury notes, stock certificates, lottery tickets. These were all financial assets I knew about from the bank, but now they seemed unreal and nonsensical because I was expected to have them.

I went through the whole room and everywhere I said, "I don't have any." The people at the desks didn't look at me. Perhaps they were not even people but machines, each of which asked the same question for the hundredth time. They placed forms before them on which they would cross something out or write something in. I didn't know whether I was answering correctly when I said "I don't have any," but I really didn't have anything except a watch, a very ordinary steel watch, which they didn't ask about. Finally I advanced, along with some others, to a closed door, before which stood yet another official with a yellow armband. It seemed to me that in front of this door the tension was even greater, because I noticed that the official too was afraid. We entered singly. As I entered I saw a man in uniform. He sat at a desk set apart behind a wooden barrier. He had his legs crossed and he stared at the wall opposite him. I had to hand the form they had filled in for me to an interpreter, who passed it on. The man in uniform looked at me as if he had seen me before. He seemed to look at me for a long time, intently, so as to preserve my features in his memory. He put the papers on the desk and made a mark on them. Then he said *"Fertig"* impatiently. I left the villa by another door. I walked quickly, with a few other people, to the streetcar station, and when the streetcar came, I sat down in the second car. I heard people talking again, ordinary talk, and the words "Hannah is learning to be a seamstress and Fred is taking saxophone lessons" came to my ears. These were people I had been in the villa with, and everyone seemed to be learning something or wanted to learn something. They were excited, as if their lives depended on learning something.

I felt left out because I wasn't learning anything and didn't want to learn anything. They spoke of carpentry, of repairing shoes, of gardening and various crafts that they were already working at or intended to work at. I envied them because somewhere they would be smoothing wood with a plane or soldering pots. I didn't know how to do anything and I didn't know if I would be able to learn anything.

"Josef, you're all thumbs," Ruzena used to say. "You can't even hammer a nail."

Sometimes I did have to do various jobs, when it was necessary—mend the canoe or make a fire between two rocks. I also learned to cook, but I knew that others could do such things much better. I never did a very good job of them.

The people I was with at the registration center had got off the streetcar one by one; I was the only person left. Other people had come and spoken of various things or read newspapers. I paid no attention to them. It was almost noon; everyone was in a hurry to get home, and I had to think—and think hard—about the fact that it was snowing. I wanted it to stop. The snow was my enemy.

I had to clear the sidewalk in front of the house where I

lived because policemen walked the streets and measured with their eyes the space that had to be cleaned. They had also learned to yell.

I had an old wooden shovel that constantly had to be put back together again and a worn-out broom; if it snowed all day and the snow formed drifts, it would be very difficult to shovel with my fingers sticking out of torn gloves and my stomach rumbling.

And my hunger! Ruzena had once said that I didn't know how to take a big bite out of a slice of bread and that I was too choosy, but that wasn't quite true. I thought of food only if it was really good; otherwise I paid no attention to it. I read the newspaper during lunch, and sometimes I didn't even know what I was eating.

But now, when Hunger came, I did begin to think about food and I began to look into grocery stores. I would stop in front of butcher shops that I had always rushed by before; now I would look at the pieces of raw meat.

There were signs everywhere, even in restaurants where they served potatoes with gravy, in shops, taverns. Even Hunger had learned to yell! I paced with him, back and forth, but he was more persistent.

Then he slowly settled down. He probably became used to me, so that there were times when he didn't make himself heard. I was weak. Perhaps Hunger loves weakness; perhaps he wanted to see me humiliated. But I didn't bargain with him. I was just glad he behaved himself. I was afraid I would wake him.

I knew very well that he would wake and demand attention when I was shoveling the snow because he didn't like my working. He only wanted me to lie still, not move about and disturb his sleep.

Suddenly I was standing with Ruzena again on a slope in the mountains, and the wind and snow whipped our faces. We had to push hard to make headway. Ruzena's cheeks were red from the wind, and snowflakes were melting on her face. We came out of the cabin feeling warm. We put on our skis in the shed. There was no one on the slope; the weather was bad but we wanted to go out. I kissed Ruzena on her wet cheek. She had a beautiful, slim body in the ski suit. She laughed when snow fell down her neck as we kissed. I laughed too. We had a hard time making headway against the wind. We were out of breath when we entered the forest; it was quiet there. We skied down and laughed when we picked up speed. We stopped only when we got down as far as the hotel. We took our skis off and stamped our feet for a long time to shake off the snow. We ordered coffee and ate large slices of bread spread thick with butter.

"Don't you think," said Ruzena, "that it would be wonderful if we could be together this way all the time, set our faces toward the sun, climb up the hillside, and ski down into the valley? I managed to steal these few days; I told Jarka that I was going to the mountains with Eva, but what if she comes back early and meets Jarka, what new lie will I have to invent? Sometimes I think Jarka doesn't believe all those lies I tell him about all these dressmakers, girlfriends, and trips to visit relatives. It's all such a cliché—you'll find it in any novel. Maybe Jarka is only pretending to believe me, is forcing himself to believe me; otherwise he would have to come to some sort of decision, and I don't think he wants to do that."

"Ruzena," I said, "what does it all matter when there is snow around us?" But this snow in front of my house was stubborn. I had to fight it. My hands were freezing but I was sweating from the effort. It was blackish, dirty, packed snow. I had to struggle to get it off the sidewalk. Hunger began to yell and I began to wish that a thaw would set in and the snow would change to slush, but it was getting colder and colder and I had to scrape it hard.

"That path is too narrow," said the policeman. "It has to be as wide as your neighbor's." He touched his pocket meaningfully; I knew that was where he kept his little notebook. "And look, there's still lots of snow left. The sidewalk has to be cleaner. This is no way to work."

I didn't answer. There was no sense arguing with a policeman—I had no rights. I knew it and the policeman knew it too. He pressed the dirty snow down with his heavy boots so that I had to scrape it off with the shovel. Plop, plop, tink, tink!

That time Ruzena and I danced in the hotel in our heavy ski boots. We weren't at all tired even when we had to climb up the hill in the dark. We kept slipping on the well-traveled path. We held on to overhanging branches and looked forward to our dinner. We ordered cognac and black coffee, then we danced for a while to music from the radio. We were happy and forgot about everything. And outside white snow lay everywhere; the windows in the hallway were frosted over when we went upstairs to the nicely heated room. We lay awake for a long time. When the wind rattled the shutters we lay in the warmth and smiled into our blankets.

"Ruzena," I said, "this is our night, the most beautiful of all. The wind is rattling the shutters but it can't reach us; the snow is swirling around, the roof is full of it, but we are safe, in a warm bed, lying next to each other." "Yes," said Ruzena, half asleep.

And then we fell asleep. We didn't mind the wind or the snow. We slept pressed against each other and woke up when it was already light outside and there were snowdrifts all around the cabin. Plop, plop, tink—and that's enough for today!

I was tired but I couldn't fall asleep that night after work. I had to think of Stresovice. When I did fall asleep I soon woke up and began to think about what I had signed and the significance of the long questions and the mark that the man in uniform had put on my documents. I couldn't imagine such waiting, writing, and questioning having no significance, but I couldn't guess what it could be. I racked my brains to no avail. The people in that villa had devoted too much work to Josef Roubicek; it was impossible for him to come out of it all unscathed when so much paper had been covered with writing. I must pay in some way for all that paper and work, but I didn't have what they wanted from me—certificates, deposits, gold. How would I be able to cover their costs? Perhaps only with this scrawny neck of mine.

Then I couldn't sleep at all and I couldn't read. I was afraid that it would start to snow again and that in the morning I would have to clear it away once more. And because I would keep tossing on the mattress without sleeping, because I would fall asleep sometime toward morning, I would probably wake up late, when the snow would all be trampled on, when it would be dirty, packed, and I would have to scrape it with a shovel that would keep falling off its handle.

5

That week snow fell incessantly. Sometimes it melted and froze again. My hands became callused and I was stuck at home; I couldn't leave, because snow kept falling and I could hardly keep up with clearing it.

Slowly I began to forget Stresovice and the questionnaires. I received no new notices, but a messenger came from the Community with orders that I hand over any musical instruments or typewriters.

I had no musical instrument and I didn't know how to play any; I used a pencil to write with because I had long ago sold my fountain pen. It had been a very good one, a Waterman.

Then another messenger came and asked for clothes and fabric; another wanted furs and microscopes. They continued to want things of me and I didn't have anything.

Then a messenger came with orders forbidding me to sell anything or make any gifts. I was to understand that my property no longer belonged to me, that I was only the caretaker of the clothes I was wearing and of my run-down shoes. I was caretaker of these things and I was rewarded by being able to use them. There, you see! I was mistaken when I thought no notice would be taken of me, as I hid between cracking walls and protected myself against the cold with a sleeping bag. I only wanted to sleep, to know nothing and hear nothing. But they continued to want something from me. I was forbidden to walk certain streets on certain days. I couldn't walk some on Fridays, others on Sundays; on some I was ordered to walk quickly and not stop anywhere. I had the names of the streets and the days all mixed up, and some of the streets I didn't even know. I imagined entering some street by chance, perhaps one called Ermine, and suddenly a policeman would appear and arrest me because Ermine Street was mentioned in the latest list of forbidden streets, which I hadn't read yet. I learned that I was forbidden to enter parks, but I knew I couldn't distinguish them: I wasn't sure what was a park and what wasn't. There were tree-lined avenues that could be considered parks, but then again they might not.

I longed to be an animal. From the windows of the garret I saw dogs playing in the snow, I saw a cat creep slowly across the neighbor's garden, I saw horses drinking freely from buckets, I saw sparrows flying about whenever they felt like it. Animals don't have to rack their brains about which streets they are allowed to enter.

That year I wanted it to be spring. I was worn out by the constant clearing away of snow and by cutting wood. I kept receiving circulars, lists of newly prohibited places. I learned that I was not allowed to attend auctions of works of art or travel by steamer; I was not allowed to hunt anything or to eat pork. I tried to understand the new orders and to keep them in mind at all times. I didn't know how to stick to them, and as far as some were concerned, I didn't know how I could possibly disobey them. I had no intention of going partridge shooting and I couldn't eat pork, because I didn't have any ration cards for meat. But what if I went to the butcher's, and Mr. Halaburda said to me, "Here is some pork, Mr. Roubicek.

What cut would you like? Some cutlets or shoulder or loin?"

"I'm not allowed to eat pork," I would answer reluctantly.

"Oh, I see, you're on a diet," Mr. Halaburda might say. "Well, how about some nice liver, or perhaps some veal?"

No. Mr. Halaburda would never speak to me this way, but perhaps he would sell me some bones again. Bones had not yet been forbidden. No, bones were not forbidden.

I thought a lot about the circular concerning travel by streetcar. I had taken the streetcar whenever I needed to go downtown. It was quite an ordinary thing to do. I got on at the station and paid the conductor for my ticket. Sometimes an inspector came and checked tickets. I always had one and never had to pay a fine. But sometimes I jumped from a streetcar that was moving, and once I fell and broke my glasses. Inside the streetcar there were advertisements, and there were travel regulations too, but I had never read them.

Now I had to walk. Sometimes it was pretty bad because I lived way on the outskirts. The worst part of it was going home. Sometimes snow would be falling and my threadbare winter coat would be soaked; sometimes I slipped on the ice. It was always bad going home because I had to climb a long hill as a shortcut. The road was full of holes and sometimes I fell into snowdrifts. My shoes and socks would get soaked, and I would have a hard time pulling my feet out of the snow. I was very tired and I was also hungry. It seemed to me I would never reach the gate of the house. I couldn't stretch out and rest right away; I had to cut wood and start a fire.

Once Ruzena and I climbed a winding street where open spaces separated construction sites surrounded by high fences. The street was poorly lit. It was the first time we had seen each other since New Year's Eve. We just walked along the streets for a long time, but we were happy. I held Ruzena close and didn't know what to say.

"I am quite an ordinary person, Ruzena. I work in a bank."

It was silly, but I couldn't think of anything better. I walked next to her and touched her short fur coat. The street was cold and dark. I grabbed hold of Ruzena and lifted her toward me; she was now as tall as I was. We kissed for a long time, until she, first, came down to earth.

"It's late. I have to go home."

And so we went on, my arm under hers, not too quickly, because we stopped every so often. We couldn't stand for long, however, because Jarka was probably not asleep yet and was waiting for Ruzena.

I walked Ruzena to her house. It was a new apartment building set among small cottages and construction sites that looked threatening and huge in the black night, when only their silhouettes could be seen.

"I feel bad for you, Josef. You'll probably have to walk home, but I told you not to walk me all the way here."

We held hands but didn't kiss, because Ruzena was afraid someone from the house might see us. We said goodbye very late.

"It doesn't matter. I'll get home all right."

We lived at opposite ends of the city. I set off at a fast pace. I was happy, I was warm. As I walked along quickly, the houses rushed by in the darkness like shadows. I didn't notice if I met any people, even though here and there I heard voices. I laughed quietly to myself, and I didn't even have to order my feet to march; they walked rapidly along the hard sidewalk and slid along the ice without slipping. I thought of Ruzena, of how we had kissed under the bare trees along the snow-covered paths. Ruzena always accompanied me on these long trips, my hand pressed against her arm; we climbed steep streets and went down into quiet city valleys. She left me only when I came to the downtown area, where all the windows were still ablaze with lights. Newsboys called out the names of newspapers in what seemed to me despairing and shrill voices: it was so late and they had little hope of selling their papers to late passersby or drunks. I didn't buy a newspaper. I didn't want to know the news. I would wait until Ruzena took my arm again after I had left the downtown area for the quiet, dark streets. And so I walked with Ruzena as far as my house and there I finally said goodbye to her. I knew it was almost morning.

It was late and I was in a hurry to get home. I had been to visit my aunt and uncle. I didn't like going there, but once in a while I went anyway because I could warm up there and they gave me herb tea and bread with a spread on it. But I had to listen to their complaints.

"We've already lost this war," my uncle would repeat. "They'll kill us, that's for sure."

"They took everything away from us," my aunt lamented, "everything that we saved all those years for our old age. We're beggars," she cried, "beggars!"

"Why don't your English and Americans help us?" my uncle reproached me. I didn't know why I should be responsible for the English and Americans. I didn't even know English.

"You're not so badly off," my aunt would say with envy. "You didn't have anything, so they couldn't take anything away from you. But we're beggars. Beggars!"

I drank the hot tea and ate the bread. My uncle kept reproaching me. They probably wanted me to defend the English and Americans or to say that I was worse off than they were; then they could become even angrier and lament even more. I became numb. I stopped hearing their words; I only heard sounds, shaky, grieving. I knew that my aunt and uncle were always lamenting, blaming, accusing. Perhaps it was my fault that Denmark would not fight.

I was rocked to a half sleep by the droning, irritable voices. My eyes became heavy in the warmth. I began to nod and only woke up when my uncle yelled, "And Russia, your Russia, why don't they send their tanks against them?"

"I had to give them the ring I had from Uncle Poldi and the copper kettle from Aunt Rosa. They took everything. We're beggars. Even the cake tins," my aunt cried.

I said, half asleep, "You shouldn't have given up the kettle. You should have buried it."

I remembered the kettle, I knew something about the kettle, but I shouldn't have spoken. My aunt and uncle got excited.

"Do you want our death? They would kill us for that kettle of yours. You know they need copper for their war."

"We always knew you had no family feeling. You would like that, wouldn't you, for us to be tortured to death for a kettle."

I fell into my half sleep again; perhaps I even fell fast asleep because I flew out of the chair when my uncle pushed me and yelled in my ear, "Don't sit there like an oaf. You have to go home. Look, it's six o'clock and you have to be home by eight."

"I don't have a watch," I said. "I sold my steel watch the week before last. I just have an old alarm clock at home. It only runs when you lay it on its side. If someone doesn't know that, it won't go at all."

"Don't babble about your alarm clock, run along home. You can't sleep here. Don't you know there are searches all the time? Do you want to have our death on your conscience?"

"Go on, Josef," my aunt said in a strangely mild tone. "Here's a piece of cake for the trip home. You have a long way to go. You'll just about make it if you go quickly."

I left the house and the frost grabbed hold of me. I began to shake and shiver, probably because I was sleepy and the warmth had overwhelmed me. I forced myself to walk quickly, but my legs didn't want to pay attention to me. They were numb from the long rest. Though it wasn't late, people were rushing home in darkness. I had to get used to the commotion. I slipped on the sidewalk and almost fell into the street. I bumped into someone who then bumped into me to make things even. I scrambled toward the wall of the nearest building and tried to run. I was afraid he would call a guard.

"You idiot," I said to myself. "It's totally dark—the houses and streets are blacked out and nobody knows who you are. You could be a clerk, a good, diligent clerk coming home from the bank where he added up columns, going home to his family. He is quite close to his house—only a few more steps and he will climb the warm staircase, will wipe his shoes on the doormat for a long time; he'll take off his coat in the hall and put on his slippers. His wife is waiting for him with a hot dinner."

I wished Ruzena would accompany me. She had quick eyes; she was always able to find a four-leaf clover, and I never found one. She gave it to me each time so that I didn't feel bad. But I didn't want to drag Ruzena into the darkness and frost. She would have to catch me if I stumbled. I would be much too heavy a load for her. I wanted to whistle, to conquer the darkness and fear, but I was afraid to. Slowly, I grew used to the darkness and I was walking quite rapidly now; my ears no longer burned and my feet were no longer numb.

There was a law that I wasn't allowed to be on the streets after eight o'clock in the evening. It wasn't written in any police regulation; I wasn't notified of it in any way. It got around by word of mouth, it was demonstrated by example. For a long time I didn't know about this law, but then I had heard it whispered about.

My ears were freezing again when I got to the river. There was an icy wind blowing over the water, but I liked walking along the embankment because I was guided by the icebound river. I saw its whiteness in the dark. I saw the extinguished street lamps. I could make my way by them. I would pick one out and make a date with it. I said, "I'll be with you in a little while," and then when I passed it I apologized, "No, you're not the one. My lamp is different. It's at the end. You must forgive me, you're all so alike." As long as I was playing a game with the lamps everything was fine. I always got the better of them, but the last one I deceived the worst of all and that was my big mistake. I was already walking across the bridge. It was the last lamp on the bridge but it wasn't mine, because I had to climb a long, long hill to get home. And as I walked past this last lamp and mocked it for standing there on the bridge—dumb, just waiting there while I whistled—I slipped on the bank and slid down. The bank wasn't high, but

I fell into snow and got soaked. I had to make my way up through the snow again and was wet with sweat by the time I got out of it.

I finally climbed up the hill, and then I walked very quickly. My house was quite near now. I came to a main road just as a streetcar arrived at the end of the line and people got out.

"You see," I said to myself, "I have just gotten out of the streetcar too. Yes, I was on it with you, but you didn't see me, because I stood on the back platform. Now I'm returning home, and because of the blackout you can't see that I am all disheveled and that there are icicles on my winter coat."

6

Things were going badly for me when spring came. The walls of the house were leaking, and a large puddle formed on the floor that I had to wipe up with a rag. Everything was damp, even my hands and the sleeping bag. I received notices of various prohibitions. Once they even came to look at the house. They arrived by car and hurried into the house without saying a word to me. I didn't have to show them anything: they saw the crack that split the house in two; they noticed the roof tiles, which were strewn across the floor, the broken windows, and the warped window frames. They didn't look at me. One of them cursed in their language. They jumped back into their car and left. I saw the faces of people in neighboring houses hidden behind curtains. They were peeking out and probably waiting for something quite different. They were surely thinking that I would be taken away. It was raining and the car splashed mud on the sidewalk; in the house there were muddy footprints of military boots. I went out to the front of the house and saw the street coming to life, saw people leaving their houses and their lookouts behind curtains again. I breathed the fresh spring air. I knew they weren't interested in my house, that I would live there until they showed up for the last time to take me away. I took a can and went to get water from the pump. It felt good to lift the handle; it felt good to still have an arm and to be able to pump it up and down. A neighbor quickly came out to the pump. She put her can on the ground and looked about her. There was no one on the street. She leaned toward me and blurted out, "What did they want? Did they come to get you? When will they come again?" "I don't know," I said. I already had the can full and water was running over its rim. "They'll come for you again," she said. "They'll put all of you on ships, and when the ships are out at sea they'll drill holes in them and you'll all drown. That's their plan. I'm sure of it. Franclova told me all about it. Her cousin works as a chauffeur for them, so he would know. So I thought we could use that house of yours. My old man could patch it up, cement that crack, and put new tiles on the roof. He loves to do that kind of thing when he gets home from work." "It's not my house," I said. "Ask that chauffeur of theirs about it." I dragged the can toward home.

I made some herb tea and climbed into my sleeping bag again. I looked at the damp circle on the ceiling. It seemed to me it was taking on the shape of a ship. I thought of the ship my neighbor had spoken about. I saw full sails and breathed the fresh sea air. High waves washed over the deck. I sat huddled there, with no land in sight. I heard a drill at work in the hold. In a little while the hole would be large and the ship would slowly sink. First the stern would go—the bow would stay up for some time before the water swallowed it. But I would hold on to a plank, the sea would grow calm, and I would drift alone on the ocean. I would last a long time on the plank because I am used to hunger. Then a large steamer would find me. They would lift me on deck and place me on a stretcher and put me in a white cabin and give me condensed milk. I would fall asleep listening to the quiet hum of the engine. I would fall asleep thinking of how the next day I would go up on deck and shake everyone's hand. But before I set off I must think of Ruzena. I went up to the third floor and rang the bell. It seemed there was no one home, because no one came to open the door. The house was full of lunchtime activity. You could hear doors being opened and shut and smell the cooking. I thought perhaps Ruzena was not at home. For a while I was glad—I would have a reason to leave. I wanted to ring again when the door opened.

"Come in, Josef," she said. She had on an apron and slippers. "I'm cooking lunch. You can keep me company. Sit down on the stool and watch." She was slicing onions on a board and putting them in a pan. "They should be fried golden, Josef." She laughed. Her cheeks were red as she stood over the gas range and the smell of frying onions rose to her face.

"I would like to kiss you," I said.

"You can't now. Wait until I finish cooking. You had better talk to me about something so the time goes by faster."

"I love you," I said. I sat on the kitchen stool and looked at Ruzena. I watched her hands and looked at her mouth and her eyes. Then I jumped up and began to kiss her.

"You must go home," said Ruzena. "Jarka could come at any moment."

I left the house. I didn't feel like taking the streetcar. I wanted to be alone and think about Ruzena. There were very few people in the streets at midday. I walked the quiet streets. It would be wonderful to sit down at a set table and eat the food prepared by her hands. At times like this I didn't feel like eating in a restaurant even though I was hungry.

I slowly climbed out of my sleeping bag because I had to cook something. My hunger had raised its head even though I had lain still, without so much as making a sound. I had nothing but water, salt, pieces of stale bread, and a little margarine. I made soup out of the bread crusts and ate it directly from the pot. Then I went out into the rain to shop. As I walked toward the garden gate, I saw blades of grass shine on the wet, muddy ground. I wanted to buy some lean cheese and some imitation blood sausage, but I decided to buy some vegetable seeds instead. I had a shovel, a rake, and a spade—no matter that I had never in my life done any gardening, that my plants would probably be feeble and sickly. They would be my plants, tended by my own hands.

I spent days digging up a part of the courtyard and throwing away stones. I was making garden beds. I looked at the neighbors' plots and saw that my beds were all crooked and messy, but I didn't have a piece of string or anyone to give me advice. I made furrows with a small stick and planted the seeds. I bent over the clammy soil and breathed the dampness of the earth. At moments like this I felt wonderful. Every day I went to see how the plants were breaking through the soil, how they were slowly forcing their way up. I bent over the soil, tore out weeds, and took out pebbles. I brought water and was happy when it rained.

It was during that time that Tomas the cat came to me. I had seen him often when he crept through the garden. Now when I sat in the courtyard and bent over my plants, he would always sit by me. He would sit by me as long as I was there—when I got up he would leave. He was very thin and skittish. He didn't seem to belong to anybody, and people must have chased him away and thrown whatever was close at hand at him, because whenever I got up suddenly he would run away into the bushes. I called him Tomas because he was so doubting and untrusting.

We would sit together and when we had rested I would tell him about Ruzena. I went to visit her when she was on vacation in a small village in the mountains. We went to bathe in a stream and then we lay for a long time on a slope in the sun. We were all alone and we climbed up into the mountains. We cooked soup over a small burner. We walked in the forest and sometimes we would lie for a long time on the railroad embankment waiting for the trains full of people to pass by so we could look into the shining windows. I told Tomas about meadows where we seemed to wade through the grass, about wooden cabins where we would sit on the front steps when we were tired.

"You doubt me, Tomas," I said. "They thrashed the soul out of you. How could you understand happiness? But happiness does exist, Tomas. It's only now that they're trying to convince us that it doesn't and that it never did. Just try to remember, Tomas—you probably also used to wade through high grass; maybe you once had silky fur and didn't live off garbage."

I turned to him abruptly. Tomas started but didn't jump away.

"You see, Tomas, I mean you no harm. You're beginning to believe me a little. But only a little. Wait, how can I explain what happiness is? Large bowls of milk for you, Tomas, with lots of cream floating on top and a roll spread with butter, raw liver, and then to lie down in the sun and be warm and safe. All that exists. You must believe me."

I got up from the ground when it began to get dark. I was cold and hungry. I didn't look for Tomas. I thought he would creep away to a neighboring garden. He probably had a place to sleep in some shed nearby. But as I opened the door to the garret I noticed something black in my way.

"Tomas," I said, "why have you chosen my garret of all places? I don't think you quite understood me. I spoke about happiness and pleasure, but not in this room. You can't even find mice here, and dampness seeps from the walls. There's no warm spot above the stove; it's just a broken-down stove that gives no warmth at all. You won't find any food here, and I could only share all kinds of imitation food with you and black coffee made of roasted acorns."

But Tomas was already in the middle of the room and did not seem willing to go away. He lay down in the recess of the wall on the floor mat that used to be a curtain. I made the fire, cooked some potatoes, and offered a few of them to Tomas. He accepted them as if it were a matter of course.

Sometimes I had to go downtown to get a little money. I sold books—I didn't have anything else left to sell. I knew I couldn't sell them all. Some were too torn and I was glad that I would have to keep them. When I returned home, Tomas would be waiting for me at the door. He never let me stroke him, and I didn't even try; he didn't trust human hands.

I climbed up the muddy slope of the hill and spoke to Ruzena.

"Ruzena," I said. "I just sold a book that we read together, so that I could buy fake blood sausage that I will share with Tomas the cat, whom you don't know. We won't share it fairly, because Tomas will only get the skin, but you must admit that Tomas can climb up a tree to catch a bird or can sniff out a mouse in a hole. Forgive me, Ruzena, for selling that book. It had words in it that had made us happy; it had a sentence that you liked. We turned the pages impatiently, afraid it would end too soon but eager to know what would happen. We were at the summer cabin and couldn't go out because there was a steady rain. We had only one book, so we read it together. I was always a few lines ahead, but I waited for you so that we could turn the pages together. We were cooped up all day in the cabin and lay on the bunk. The rain drummed on the roof. We were happy under one blanket, reading the book I have just sold."

I didn't say anything about it to Tomas the cat. He didn't like books. When I lay in my sleeping bag and read he would creep up to me and poke his nose into the book. He often knocked it out of my hands. He preferred sitting by the garden beds with me. He would sit quietly, never disturbing me. I felt better when the sun began to shine brightly. I lay down in the grass and looked at the bushes. I saw a pine tree and I was in the forest. I had my own forest since I was not allowed to enter even an ordinary wood. Now even the hill was beautiful. I would rest on it. Its grass was grazed to the ground by goats and it was littered with rusty tin cans and old junk. I would stop and lie on the hill when I was close to the house on my way home from a trip downtown. I would lie quietly and look down at the city, at chimneys, the river harbor, and the white bridge. I saw birds flying across the city. I followed their course and sometimes, when the windows of the villas on the slope were open, I could hear music.

I lay in the grass and a man lay down close to me. I wanted to get up and leave. I wanted to be alone, to think about Ruzena. I wanted to be alone because I didn't know if I was allowed to lie in the grass on the hill, which actually had almost the look of a garbage dump. But I was too tired to leave.

"Nice weather," the man said. I looked at him. He looked like a worker from the outskirts of the city. He had a blue soup pail next to him; he was probably on his way home from work. He had climbed the hill and was resting now.

I was no longer afraid of him, but I didn't feel like talking. I would not even have known what to say to him. Perhaps I was only able to speak to those who could not answer me, to Ruzena and to Tomas the cat.

"In weather like this it's nice to lie in the sun after a day's work."

"I have no work," I said. I wished he would hit the soup pail next to him with his hand, accidentally push it so that it would roll down the hill, jump wildly over ruts, and only stop somewhere on the road leading to the villas. I wanted to be alone because I didn't want to talk to anybody. I only had these few moments on the hill, while the sun was still shining, when I could lie and look out at the city. This was my time and I wanted to be alone. But the blue soup pail did not even budge.

"Are you sick?" asked the worker.

"No," I said, "they're hunting us like rabbits."

"Then what is it?"

We were both still. It was quiet. In the distance I heard the creaking of a crane unloading a ship. The wind brought the distant sound of music.

"But you're alive," said the worker.

"I'm all alone," I said. "I'm not allowed to go to taverns, theaters, the movies, parks, streets."

I was quiet again. Finally the worker said, "That's nothing. When I was unemployed it was no better."

"That isn't it," I almost shouted. "This is different. I'm alone, completely alone. I have no one. I don't speak to anyone. I sleep on the floor on a mattress and I'm hungry. But that's nothing; I wouldn't mind that. There are probably even poorer people than me, who have to sleep in haystacks or under the bridge. It's those laws of theirs."

"Well, tell them to go to hell with their laws!"

"I can't," I said. "I'm afraid of death."

"You have to die sometime."

"You don't understand. You can't understand. I don't want to die this way, like a rabbit pulled out of its cage. If I have to die, I want to know why—if it's from some disease or if I get run over by a car or if I drown when I'm swimming."

"No, that I don't understand. But I have to go now. If you're so alone, you could come and see me sometime. I live up on the hill, in that little house over there. All kinds of people come to see me. We meet to talk things over."

"Thank you. I'll come sometime."

The worker got up, took his soup pail, and walked on the narrow path to the group of houses. I stayed where I was and watched him as he disappeared into one of the little houses. I was glad he had invited me. He was the only person in a long time who had invited me, but I didn't think I would go to see him.

"No, he can't understand me," I said to myself. "He leaves for work in the morning with his soup pail; he sits in the streetcar, arrives at the factory, punches the time clock, stands by a machine. It's not too happy a life, but it's a good life, with his blue soup pail, his time clock, and his pay envelope. He's not creeping along by day and tossing in a sleeping bag by night. He doesn't go to an office with a garage and a policeman standing with his feet apart in the courtyard."

The sun was setting. Cool air was rising from the river below. There was a steamer tugging loaded barges behind it; it whistled shrilly when it approached the bridge. I got up slowly and went home. I passed the house the worker had entered. It was a small ground-floor cottage with a garden of green beds. In the middle of the courtyard there was an old well with a crank.

7

"Take off your shirt," said the doctor. "No, you don't have to take it all the way off—just push it up over your head."

I was being examined again. For a long time I stood in the dirty corridor at the Community, then I sat on a wooden bench when I could grab a place. There were doors leading to various offices in the corridor, but I had been ordered to report to a door at the very end that had a sign, FIRST AID, on it. I had learned not to believe anything I heard or read these days. I knew that behind the door was a recruitment office that sent people to quarries, farms, mines, and clay pits. I didn't think there was any aid coming to me from this office, but I was quite calm because I knew that with a body like mine I couldn't quarry stone or shovel clay. But I was still a little scared: perhaps everyone was already working or sitting in an office; perhaps there were nothing but a few skinny people left. And so perhaps they would send us somewhere to shovel clay.

"I'll give you a classification four," said the doctor when he had examined me. "You are not suited for hard labor."

"Thank you," I said.

"But I don't know if it will help you any." The doctor was fat; the buttons of his white coat were not all closed. He moved slowly and spoke in a hoarse voice. "I'm ashamed to be doing this. It's a disgrace. I should be treating people."

"I can't help you," I said. "I can't help anyone. I'm all alone."

I went out onto the street. I had to force myself not to throw up from hunger. I had no money even for a loaf of bread. These last few days I had eaten nothing except the vegetables from my garden. It was a good thing I had the vegetables, but I couldn't satisfy my hunger with them, and when I ate a lot of them they made my stomach hurt. Tomas the cat refused to eat vegetables. I had nothing left to sell. I had to get a little money somewhere. I went to borrow some from my uncle. I went slowly and reluctantly. I knew it would be no simple matter.

But I had the four written on a sheet of paper that also included all kinds of information about me. It was a good thing to have a four. It meant that they wouldn't send me to hard labor, that I would have the right to be sick. And in my pocket I had a permit for one trip by streetcar that they had given me at the Community. I could go all the way home to the outskirts of the city by streetcar if I got a little money from my uncle. The permit was valid all day, and that day I was allowed to ride the streetcar within the city. It was a big thing to have such a permit.

I dragged myself through the streets, stopping every now and then to overcome my nausea. It was a warm summer day. I saw people boarding the streetcar to travel to the edge of the city, to riverside beaches. I saw sunburned faces with satisfied smiles. I saw girls in close-fitting summer dresses, with colorful handbags. I passed a park and saw people sitting on the benches feeding birds. I walked close to the park and let myself be caressed by a tree branch. It wasn't a tender caress, but the leaves touched my face and I suddenly smelled the greenery. I would rather have lain down at home, next to the garden beds. I no longer went to sit on the hill, because there were so many people there now; they would squat on the flattened grass and play cards. I had a headache. I was very weak and I staggered, but I had to reach my uncle's. Perhaps he would at least give me money for the streetcar.

I had to wait a long time before they came to open the door. I knew that my aunt and uncle were at home—they were afraid to go out on the street and sat in the house all day. I heard someone tiptoe in the hall and then slowly and carefully open the peephole in the door.

"Who is it?" I heard a choked voice behind the door. I knew it belonged to my uncle.

"Open the door. It's me, Josef," I said loudly.

The door opened slowly. I found myself in the dark hall. At first I couldn't see anything because my uncle quickly slammed the door shut. I saw the outline of his figure. They both seemed terribly ancient to me. My uncle was hunched over as if he were carrying a heavy burden.

I entered the room. The table hadn't been cleared, and various objects lay on the chairs. The air was close. The windows were shut, and it was almost dark because the blackout blinds were down. But even in the dimness I couldn't help noticing that my uncle's face was pale, his eyes sunken, and his hair disheveled.

"Your aunt is sick. She's in bed," my uncle said. "We can't offer you anything." He didn't even ask me to sit down. I was tired. I pushed away the mess on the chair—some balls of yarn and scraps for mending—and sat down. My uncle remained standing. He seemed impatient; he couldn't wait to see me go.

"They were here," he cried out suddenly. "They were here yesterday evening. Just look at this mess. They took everything from our larder and they said terrible things to us."

"They took the last of the shortening." My aunt's screeching voice came from the bedroom. "I had three kilos of lard. They took everything—jams and the can of goulash we've had hidden since the beginning of the war. We have nothing left. We'll die of hunger. They took our flour and baking powder."

"Isn't there any justice in the world? You'll see, they'll win

this war. They already have all of France, and the English have
run away, the cowards. Those French and English of yours
don't want to fight, and we'll all die here like dogs. Why don't
you say anything?"

"You've always been an ungrateful one," my aunt screamed
from the bedroom. "This is what we get in return for taking
you in, for letting you graduate from school off of our hard-
earned money. It's a good thing Klara didn't live to see this.
She must be spinning in her grave."

"Yes," said my uncle in a tone that was now flat, depressed,
"you've turned out to be a fine one."

I sat on the edge of the chair in the half-dark room. Rays
of light were making their way through a crack in the blinds.
I lowered my head all the way to my knees. I had to fight the
pain in my stomach. I would have liked to lie down on the
floor and cover my face with my hands. I had only come to
get a little money. Five crowns would have been enough—
that was no money at all. I would have bought some bread
and gone home on the streetcar. I didn't want anything else.
But I couldn't speak; I was afraid to make the slightest movement with my body. The room was very close. I sweated and
looked down at the dusty carpet.

"What happened?" I said finally.

"Don't you know anything? Well, that's clear enough. They
didn't come to you. You live far away, too far for them. You
always have to be lucky," called my aunt from the bedroom
in a voice full of recrimination. "Yesterday evening they were
all over the city. They looked through all the larders, and
whatever they found they took. They took my farina and oat-
meal too. I had a few onions—they didn't even leave those.
And there you were, sitting nicely at home, as if nothing were
happening. And we can be glad they didn't beat us up. Young
Frischman, who lives on the third floor of the house, had two
teeth knocked out when he wasn't quick enough getting them
a jar of marmalade hidden in the closet."

"I have nothing," I said. "I don't even have a single crust

of bread, only Tomas the cat and he isn't mine. They couldn't have taken anything from me."

"So you have a cat," my uncle began to yell again. "Yes, that's just like you, to put on airs and throw money around. You didn't save a penny even though you had a nice income when you were at the bank. You spent it all, and now you even get yourself a cat in times like this, when we don't even have a piece of bread. You should stop coming to see us. As if we didn't have enough trouble, with that cat of yours you could bring ruin on us."

"What do you mean? How could Tomas harm you? You don't even know him!"

"Don't you know we're not allowed to have domestic animals?"

"I haven't read any circulars for a long time. Or maybe I've read them but forgotten. There are so many I don't remember them all. Besides, Tomas isn't really my cat. He went begging and they hit him wherever he went, so now he sleeps with me. I can't give him anything either, because I don't have anything. If he wants to sleep with me I can't very well stop him."

"You think they'll believe you, that you'll be able to explain anything? They'll arrest you and they'll look in their files and see that we are your relatives, and they'll kill us too, all because the gentleman allows a cat to sleep with him. Either you throw that cat out or you don't set foot on our doorstep ever again."

I didn't answer. I had to force myself to get up. I would have liked to have rested a while and to have waited until the twisting pain had stopped, but I had to get up if they were throwing me out. I didn't have the courage to ask for money for the streetcar. It would have been a small amount—perhaps they would have lent it to me—but I would have had to listen to more crying, complaints, and reproaches.

I shook hands with my uncle and staggered toward the door. I called out a few words of parting to my aunt in the bedroom. My uncle remained standing in the middle of the room. He looked at me listlessly. He was depressed again, but I knew that in a while he would recover and begin to yell some more.

I walked down the stairs slowly and thought about how to get home. I would have to rest every fifteen minutes to fight back pain and nausea. Perhaps I could make it to my garden gate, but downtown it would be terrible. I wasn't allowed to enter the park and I couldn't sit on the curbs. I had to force myself to walk to the foot of the hill in one stretch, without pausing, and only there could I sit down and rest.

I dragged myself through the sunny streets in the afternoon heat. I had to walk close to the houses. I was afraid I would fall at any moment. I had a long walk ahead of me and I didn't think I could make it.

I would fall on the sidewalk, I thought. People would walk around me indifferently. They would think I was drunk. Then someone would stop anyway, out of curiosity, and call an ambulance. And I didn't know what would happen after that because we weren't allowed to use ambulances. I had read that in some circular. And no hospital was allowed to accept us.

I leaned against the walls of the houses and tried to remember if someone I knew lived in the area, someone who would let me rest a while and from whom I could borrow some money for the streetcar. I didn't think I would meet anyone on a summer day like this, when everyone was either at the beach or at home with the windows open, waiting for the coolness of evening. But then I remembered that a classmate of mine from high school lived in one of the neighborhoods I had to go through. I hadn't seen him since graduation until I had recently run into him on the street. He recognized me and spoke to me and invited me to visit him. He used to be a rich lawyer and owned real estate and stocks. I'm sure that earlier he wouldn't have spoken to me and I wouldn't have known what to talk to him about if I had paid him a visit. I had forgotten the address he gave me when we met. I only remembered the district. I concentrated on trying to remember the name of the street and I finally succeeded. In the end I even remembered the approximate house number—it was either 7 or 8—but that wasn't important. I would be able to find him. I still had some way to go, but I made up my mind to make it. I had to make it.

I found the house and rang the bell. I didn't know how long the trip had taken me. I only knew that twice I had to jump away from moving cars when I crossed a street. Perhaps I also ran into pedestrians. I didn't even remember the path I took. All I knew was that I had to reach the bridge that crossed to the district I was heading for. It was a well-to-do neighborhood, with new houses. I usually avoided it when I went downtown because *they* lived there. But this time I had no choice.

I waited in front of the door for a long time, but now I expected to have to wait. They had probably been here too yesterday and taken everything from the larder. The people inside would probably take a long time making up their minds and whispering to one another before they opened the door.

"It's you," said my classmate Pavel. He seemed relieved to see my face through the peephole. "Come in. I'll introduce you to my wife, Heda, and my daughter, André." I entered the hall. There was a carpet on the floor and a table with comfortable armchairs. I opened the door to a room. It felt strange to find myself in comfort and luxury again. I had forgotten what a well-furnished home was like, a place where it was possible to sit in an armchair with your legs crossed. I had visited a dark slum, full of the musty smell of old age, where my uncle lived. I had walked the streets in the afternoon heat among smells and dust, and now I was in the midst of cleanliness, light, and coolness.

We all sat in easy chairs, drinking tea from glass teacups. I looked at the paintings on the walls; my eyes ran over the Meissen figurines. I stirred my tea with a silver spoon and ate cookies. I took whole fistfuls of them out of the bowl because I was hungry and because I didn't care about anything except this moment, which was so like moments I had lived long ago.

"We should have left," said Pavel. "It was a great mistake. But I didn't want to go. You know, a person becomes lazy, then is unable to act." He looked about the room. "A person becomes the slave of things." He spoke quietly and calmly, as if he were prepared for anything, as if nothing could surprise him anymore. "The worst part of it is this inactivity. You just sit and do nothing. I believed in money. I used to make a lot of money. Now I just sit and wait."

"What are you waiting for?"

"Until they finish us off."

"Do you believe that?"

"Believe it? I know it. It's hopeless. We're all doomed. We can only sit and wait. It's so easy and there's no need to rack your brains to think up ways to escape. Everything has already been determined. That will be the end. Do you understand? The real end." He spoke softly, resigned, as was appropriate in this house with its deep carpets and its polished furniture, its pretty china dancers and antique goblets. A grandfather clock accompanied his voice with the silvery sound of chimes.

"You're lucky." His wife spoke for the first time. "Pavel tells me you're single."

Everyone was telling me that I was lucky today, even my aunt and uncle. I couldn't quite understand what my luck was.

"Yes, I am lucky," I said. I had to talk about luck in this house. What else was there to talk about? "Only I don't want to die."

"Let's talk about something else." Heda frowned. "Tell us what you do. Pavel often talked about you when he spoke about his school years."

I told them about Tomas the cat, how I worked in the garden. I spoke about pleasant and happy things, as was fitting since I was sitting in a comfortable armchair, picking up fistfuls of cookies. I wanted to thank them for their hospitality in this house full of light, where the tables had vases with roses in them. Here I could laugh gaily at my burned furniture and damaged roof, the torn-out water pipes and broken-down stove. I could overcome things. Perhaps that was the luck they were all talking about, and yes, only in this house did I realize my victory. Everyone laughed at my adventures; even André laughed when I told how they came away from my house with nothing to add to their list, how they spat in scorn as they got into their cars.

"They won't get anything," I boasted. "Only the coffee table will be standing in the middle of the room."

The doorbell gave a shrill, commanding ring. Pavel reluctantly went to open the door. We sat quietly at the table, waiting for another guest to appear. The only thing that seemed strange to me was that I could hear the sound of the door opening and of steps in the hall but no human voice. Pavel entered the room, followed by a man and a woman. They didn't say a word. They didn't look at us; they pretended not to see us at all. I remained sitting at the table, and in my embarrassment I began to stir the tea I had drunk long before. They only looked at the objects in the room. They caressed the furniture, took the pewter mugs in their hands, felt the upholstery on the sofas. They calculated loudly between them the quality and sturdiness of various objects; they discussed how they would move the furniture around. We were already dead. They had come to claim their inheritance. Pavel accompanied them silently into the other rooms and into the kitchen. We could hear their happy voices. They returned to the living room again and went by us. They looked about once more, as if counting all the objects in the room so that not a single one could escape them. We kept sitting with our empty cups. Only when they left did they look at us, but I noticed that they were actually looking at the teacups, spoons, and sugar bowl. Pavel showed them back to the hall. He was there for quite some time. They were probably inspecting the carpet and the armchairs. Then we heard the loud slamming of the door.

Pavel came back to the living room and sat down in an armchair.

"Will you pour some tea, Heda?" he said. "Will you have some more tea, Josef?"

We drank our tea without speaking. Pavel said, "If it weren't for the child, everything would be simpler. You're lucky not to have a family, Josef."

I couldn't answer. I knew I should be leaving. But I had no money for the streetcar and I didn't like asking for it. It was late already and I couldn't make it home on foot by eight o'clock, even if I now felt rested and could walk faster.

"Pavel, you'll have to lend me something for the streetcar," I managed to stammer.

"You don't have any money, do you?" Pavel smiled. He seemed to wake up suddenly; his face relaxed. "Take this." He pulled five large bills out of his wallet and gave them to me.

"But that's five thousand crowns, Pavel, and I only need some change for the streetcar."

"Here's some change," and he took five crowns out of a small purse.

"But . . ." I stammered.

"Take it and don't say another word. Do you want them to get it, silly? This is the thing to do, right, Heda?"

"Yes," said Heda.

I said goodbye, and Pavel walked me to the door. I stood on the street with my head going around in circles. I had money. I would have no worries in this respect for some time. So this was the way this particular day was to end. At home I would open the window and breathe in the summer air. Tomas the cat would come to ask me to stroke him. I would look out for a long time, until it grew dark, and then I would continue to look into the night. I would think of Ruzena, and in the small pocket of my trousers, carefully folded and hidden, I would have the money to keep me warm.

8

Tomas and I sat in the garden, crouched down so that we couldn't be seen from the street. People might say we were just lazing about while they had to work.

"You see, Tomas," I said, "it's clear you were born under an unlucky star. First they were always chasing you away and beating you; you had to dodge stones, tin cans, and sticks, and then you thought you'd improve your lot by moving in with me. But nothing doing. Today I found out that you've been proclaimed an enemy animal, and now you'll have to share my fate, unless of course you run away from them. You don't need any documents. You don't have an identification card. But don't be too sure of yourself. They have guns and rifles and that could be pretty tough."

We sat by the flower bed, at the end of which a flower called a marigold grew. I liked sitting by this flower although I didn't like its yellow color, which reminded me of the armbands the officials in Stresovice wore. Tomas lay by me in the grass. He looked better now, even though he was bald in spots. He had become lazy and had learned to lie about for hours, only rarely setting off.

"I have money, Tomas. Where did you think today's potatoes and imitation blood sausage came from? And I promise you, you'll eat real meat with me because I have lots of money and I must make up to you for the fact that you've been proclaimed an enemy animal, without even having been asked for your opinion. But I must ask somewhere about buying black-market meat. It's very dangerous and I don't know anyone. I used to know lots of people, but now I don't know if I should visit them. Maybe they'd throw me out. Here we are, lying in the grass. All we can see are people's feet. We can't even guess what they're like by their feet. I'd rather tell you about my last date with Ruzena. It's a sad story and I must tell it to you now and not in the evening, because now the sun is shining and people are walking on the sidewalk, because we're crouched here and no one can see us."

"This is the last time," Ruzena said. It was winter. We were walking along the embankment. The river was frozen over. We couldn't walk hand in hand because Ruzena had her hands in a muff. "It's too late now to go away, and anyway, in times like this I couldn't leave Jarka."

"I lost because I was a coward," I said, "because there always comes a moment when one must make a decision. And all I did was close my eyes and put my fingers in my ears. All I did was wait, pointlessly. And the moment passed."

"I love you, but that won't help you . . ."

"Nothing will help me, even if I keep telling myself endlessly that people are always coming together and parting again."

"Even when they love each other," Ruzena said. "Anyway, there's going to be a war."

"I don't care about war. I don't know anything about war. Everything will end if we never see each other again."

"I will always love you."

We walked quietly along the embankment. Ruzena began to walk more quickly.

"I'll take a streetcar at the station here. Goodbye, Josef."

That's the whole story, Tomas, but you don't understand it anyway. If you could tell me stories, they would be about simple things, about fights on rooftops, climbing trees, and hunting in the grass.

I lay and thought where to get some meat. I made plans to go to the tavern Wiener had taken me to, but then I reminded myself that I didn't know anyone there and that nobody would trust me. The only person I knew was Wiener, and he had left for Lipa. And then I thought of the worker with the blue soup pail whom I had met on the hill. His name was Materna, and he had the same first name as I did, Josef. I knew where he lived. I had walked past his little cottage. There was a well with a crank in the courtyard. I could trust him because he had spoken to me openly. I knew that the city was full of informers with strange, secretive faces, who listened to what people were saying to one another in tobacco shops, who looked at the covers of books that girls carried to read in the streetcar. I also knew they accosted people walking in the streets and asked them if they had any news, fishing for any hint that the people listened to foreign newscasts. I had never met one. I never spoke to anyone I didn't know and I never answered if a stranger happened to speak to me. What could my neighbors say about me? That I lived in a decrepit little house, that I went to the nearest shop to pick up my very small rations, that I carried a soup pail full of blood from Halaburda the butcher, and that I pumped water into a pail at the well. Of course, they might have informed on me for keeping Tomas the cat, but everyone knew that Tomas was a stray, that he trespassed into gardens like a robber, and everyone was probably glad that he had finally found a steady place to stay. No, I didn't think anyone would hold Tomas against me. Once an informer came to see me. He wanted to find out if I had a radio. I showed him my garret. He looked through the whole house from the attic to the basement and didn't find anything anywhere.

"The best thing would be to poison you all like rats," he had said. "By next Christmas you won't be here."

I was quiet. I had to be quiet. I knew this person was after blood, just as I was when I went to Halaburda the butcher, except that he was paid for it. I had no wish to help him make up for his loss of time. The worker with the soup pail was certainly not this type of person. He carried a very ordinary kind of pail, the kind one carries ordinary soup or coffee in. Then one drinks from it at lunch break in the factory, among the heaps of rusty metal rods and slag.

I entered the courtyard, walked through the garden, and knocked on the low door. An old woman came to open it. I asked, "Does Josef Materna live here?"

"Yes, that's my son. What do you want? Because if you think that he'll take on some work for you, you can go right back home. He has enough backbreaking work in the factory."

"No, I only came to visit. He once asked me to come. Is he home?"

"Yes, in that room over there. He has some friends."

I knocked on the door and entered a small room. It had a large bed, on which two people sat, a table with a small vise attached to it, covered with various metal parts, and a chair, where Josef Materna was sitting.

"Hello," I said.

"What do you want?" he said in a somewhat sharp voice. He was clearly puzzled and considered me an intruder. His friends gave me hostile looks. "Oh, it's you," he remembered. "Of course. We talked together on the hill the other day. It's all right," he said to the men on the bed. "Everything's all right. Sit down on the bed too. We don't have any chairs."

I sat on the edge of the bed and was quiet. I didn't know how to ask him to get me some meat when there were strangers present, and I didn't want to ask him to come out into the garden with me for fear that we might be seen from the street.

"I don't know if I came at the right time," I said. "Maybe I should come back some other time."

"No, stay where you are. These are friends from the factory; this is Franta and this is Olda. And your name is Josef, like mine, isn't it?"

We were all quiet. Then Olda said, "So, Josef, you say that they're already beginning to lose. But have you heard their boasts? And have you seen the way that engineer Johann struts about and smiles?"

"We'll win this war. It's their war, but we'll win it. A lot of people will be killed, but in the end we'll win it."

They all talked at once, constantly interrupting one another. They mentioned names of people, of towns and regions that were foreign to me; they mentioned books I had never heard of. I felt out of place listening to feverish words whose meaning I didn't know. I looked around the room and discovered a radio on the chest. It seemed to be the work of an amateur.

"Why don't you say anything," Materna said. "You needn't be afraid; you're among your own here."

"I don't know what to say. I don't get together with any people, I don't read the newspapers, and I don't have a radio." And then finally I found the courage. "You know, I came to ask if you could get some meat for me."

"Meat? I'm not a black-market dealer. I'm a locksmith."

I began to stammer that I hadn't eaten any proper food in a long time, that I was very hungry, that I received ration cards only for potatoes and bread and imitation coffee made of roasted chicory, that I had happened by chance to get hold of some money, and that I didn't know anyone who could get me food.

"Well, all right, I'll give you some ration cards for meat, and my friend here will also add a bit."

"But ration cards won't help me. I am not allowed to buy meat at the butcher's."

"Well, then, give me the money, and Mother will shop for you. But of course at official prices."

"No, in that case you would be losing on me."

He looked at me, puzzled, for a moment. Then he began to laugh.

"But that's silly. I know how it is. We must help each other. I'll get you some lard too, but that will have to be at black-market prices. There's a man who comes to the factory often. I'll ask him to get it. Let's not talk about it anymore."

They began to discuss the factory and various people I didn't know. They talked a kind of slang that I had never heard before. I didn't understand anything and began to look around the room again, but I was satisfied. I would get meat and lard. For once I would be able to eat my fill.

"I must be getting home." I got up from the bed. "I have orders to be at home by eight o'clock."

"Well, if you're concerned about these stupid orders. But wait, I'll tell Mother to give you something to take with you. She baked some filled buns today."

I went home while it was still light out. I walked along the narrow path around the back yards of the houses. Tomas was there to welcome me at the gate. We went up to my room together, and I gave him a piece of the bun.

"Tomas," I said to him, "it seems I have forgotten how to talk to people. I know how to answer questionnaires, but that is not the spoken language. But I used to talk for hours with Ruzena. I told her all about what went on at the bank and what I saw on the street. We talked about films or about how we would run away together and settle abroad, how Ruzena would cook for us. We repeated foreign words that we remembered from school, and sometimes we recited poems to each other. We never lacked for words, even if we were silent for long periods of time, but that silence was better than the words we spoke. I was with people just now, Tomas, and I couldn't say a word, and in the end I could only stammer about not having any meat and being hungry."

I found a dog-eared folder full of snapshots of Ruzena and letters from her, as well as my own illegible notes, written when I was lonely and couldn't see Ruzena or write letters to her. I read the words I had written but I didn't understand them. They seemed empty. They were dumb words, not like the words I had heard exchanged at Josef Materna's place.

"I'm probably already dead," I said to myself. "My body is probably floating down the river. The current has driven it into the rushes, and floods will take it back into the river. Along the way it will probably be cast up on the riverbanks of big cities, and people will turn away from it in disgust because it is all purple and bloated. They'll use hooks to push it back into the river again, and so it will keep floating along, unable to come to rest on land. Maybe I can only speak to the dead, because they have a different language from others', and to informers, who have learned this language so that they can rob dead bodies. Maybe I can only speak to Tomas, because he too is a carcass that people throw sticks and tin cans at to chase him away. And I can speak to Ruzena too, who is only a shadow, who maybe never lived in this world. I probably made her up, out of smoke and smells, as I tossed and turned in my sleeping bag all night, so that she would become a ray of light to penetrate a crack in the blackout blinds."

9

It was warm that fall. Tomas and I were well off. I had learned to be frugal, and I knew that with the money from Pavel I could last a long time. Josef Materna got some meat and lard for me, as well as cigarettes. Nobody troubled me much. Sometimes messengers from the Community would come with new regulations, and various inspectors came too. I was no longer so afraid of them. I was certified as unfit and I had a document to prove it. I didn't go downtown; I didn't even know where Pavel had been moved to from his apartment, and I was no longer allowed to visit my uncle. Tomas the cat now lived with me. He no longer strayed at all; he became a domesticated cat who never left home. That was bad. I had hoped that he would be regarded as a stray, so that the authorities would continue not to be interested in him.

I sat at home and repeated the vocabulary words from an English textbook I had bought long ago, when I was still planning to go abroad with Ruzena. I only turned to it now, to kill time. It was a textbook for a course. It didn't have a guide to pronunciation, but I didn't mind; I pronounced the words my own way. I wasn't interested in how they were really pronounced, because I would never run away to England now. I learned the words only because they were foreign, because they came from a different world. It was raining outside and the damp circle on the ceiling was taking on the shape of a ship again. I was sailing on a British ship now, walking the deck with Ruzena. We would sit on deck chairs and look at the seagulls flying around the ship.

"We'll be landing soon," I said. "We're near land."

"How do you know?" Ruzena asked.

"Gulls never fly too far from land."

"I think we'll do quite well in that country with you knowing so much, Josef. I would never have thought of that."

"Can't you get yourself a doorbell? I've been standing in the rain for half an hour, banging at your door," yelled a man when I opened the door. I recognized him. He was a messenger from the Community. I didn't ask him to come up to the garret; I didn't want him to see Tomas. We stood by the door, the damp air all around us. I didn't understand why he was so angry, since he was bringing me a circular advising me that I was allowed to travel only in the last car of a train, a circular I didn't understand at all, as an earlier one had strictly forbidden me to leave the city.

"I don't have money for a doorbell, and nobody is allowed to sell me electric wiring anyway—I read about it in one of your circulars. Let's have the new regulation."

"This is a summons," said the messenger self-importantly. "You're supposed to come to the Community."

I didn't ask what they wanted. I had become used to the fact that messengers always put on a mask of secrecy. Perhaps it made them happy and gave them a feeling of satisfaction when they visited homes as the heralds of unhappiness and destruction.

Upstairs in the garret I looked at the summons. It said I should come to a certain office, and in parentheses it said "auxiliary service." I became alarmed at those words. I knew I wouldn't sleep all night and that I would try in vain to guess their significance. I knew words had a different, more threatening meaning now. I had been afraid of the word "service" ever since I had seen it on the door of the district office.

"The time will come when we'll have to part," I told Tomas. "You must be prepared for that moment. I would leave you this house, so that you would have some shelter and not have to stray to strange gardens, but it doesn't belong to me. I'll put in a word for you with Josef Materna. He's a good man. Maybe he'll take you in, but I can't promise anything."

I took up my English textbook again and tried to repeat the foreign words, but they eluded me. They seemed threatening; they didn't invite me to cruise on any ship. I took my old raincoat and went out into the rain. I passed back yards and Materna's little cottage too, but I didn't go in. I didn't have a reason for going to Materna's. I walked in the rain in order to get tired, so that I wouldn't have to think of the word "service." I walked in the semidusk, around blind, blacked-out windows. When I came to the villa of an informer, I picked up my pace. His window was open and I could hear his radio blasting out the voice of a comedian: "Oy, oy, oy, oy, oy, oy, we're not allowed to use the streetcar." Even when I was far from the villa I could still hear his voice. I knew it well. I had sometimes gone with Ruzena to laugh at his theater performances. I knew that he was rich, that he had a car. Why then did he think it so funny that I had to walk in worn-out shoes with loose soles?

I returned to Tomas all wet. I made a fire in the stove to warm up my supper.

"It's their war, but we'll win it," Josef Materna had said. I remembered those words exactly. Their war was none of my business. I didn't want to win it. I only wanted to live. I avoided the posts where they hung their regulations; I lay in the courtyard and touched the blades of grass. Even the rich comedian could have his fun about my not being allowed to use the streetcar. He was welcome to his jokes because I could live even without streetcars.

"Savages," I said to myself. "This isn't for me. I don't understand. The thing for me is to walk in the park with Ruzena and look at the little ducklings, led by their mother, swimming in single file on the lake and at the way their mother teaches them to dive. The thing for me is to lie on the riverbank with Ruzena, to entwine my fingers with hers and dream about a steamship that will take us abroad."

I went to various offices at the Community and asked for the office I had been summoned to. I asked for "auxiliary service" but everyone looked at me bewildered. No one knew what "auxiliary service" meant; the office surely had a different name. I entered a number of offices but stopped at the doors. There were people everywhere and all of them were working feverishly. They answered my questions irritably, annoyed that someone was disturbing them at their work. At last, in an office on the fourth floor, they told me that "auxiliary service" might belong to the labor department and that I should look for it under the heading "social welfare."

"So they'll finally give me some work," I told myself. "Now I understand what's meant by 'service.' "

"We have an easy job for you," the official began immediately when I presented my summons at his desk. "You'll come to this building two or three times a week, for the night, for standby duty. You'll come at eight in the evening and you can leave at seven in the morning. Naturally this is an unpaid job. But I see you live far away, so for the days you come here you'll receive permits to use the streetcar."

"I have a request," I told him. "Does this mean I'm assigned in some way?"

"Yes."

"Could I get a haircut in your barbershop?"

According to a regulation that had been delivered to me by a messenger from the Community, I was not allowed to go to a barbershop. But when I was searching the offices for "auxiliary service," I had discovered a closed-off corridor with a sign, WASHROOM, and behind the half-closed door I could see people sitting on chairs being attended by barbers in white coats.

I was in a good mood as I left the Community building. My hair was cut and I had a permit to use the streetcar.

"I'm not a barber," the man who cut my hair told me. "I had a phonograph record shop. The most popular record was 'Ramona.' It sold like hotcakes."

"What about 'Always'?"

"Yes, people would ask for that a lot too. Cutting people's hair is stupid work. They should think up an ointment."

Just before dusk I climbed to the fourth floor of the Community building. I had walked through a district that was all crouched, hunched, as if blows were showering down on it and the black town hall were writhing in pain. People kept close to the walls to escape the blows that fell on the houses. I found myself among sickly old men. The room was full of camp beds covered with dirty, torn blankets, the walls were cracked, and pails and brooms were scattered in the corners.

"Are we supposed to put out fires with these?" I asked the people in the room.

"No," said a barrel-shaped man. He was bald and looked like a circus clown. "Those pails are full of white paint that we're supposed to use to paint over signs that people paint during the night. But only in case the police can't cope with them all. Then the telephone rings and we go out with brooms and pails. Don't worry, it doesn't happen often."

"We lack willpower, but we have enough will to succumb to the will of others. And if Kant . . ." said a man with glasses who sat at the head of a bed.

"Leave Kant out of it. I don't know who he is. I'm quite happy to be here. I'm always happy when I don't have to be at home listening to my wife's constant nagging. Mister, do you know what it's like to sit at home? I used to be a traveling salesman, and I only came home on Sundays."

"When the time comes, there won't be any traveling salesmen. Show me in the Bible where traveling salesmen are mentioned. They're all impure, because when they travel they can't observe the laws. How can they fasten their phylacteries on a train? The Lord will never call them to His tabernacle," said a man bent over a thick book of Hebrew writing.

"Everyone will be delivered, everyone who truly repents. That's what our church teaches. It's the only true church. You should have converted to Unitarianism while there was still time."

"What's that? It sounds like a good name for a drink. It's a pity I don't work in that line anymore. Old Lobosicky would certainly have liked that for a name. We always had the toughest time thinking up new names for drinks."

"My house is falling down," I said. "And I have a cat named Tomas. We never sit together in the garden in the evenings. It's dangerous."

"I lived in Bahia Blanca. The jungle was full of Indians with poisoned arrows. People were dropping like flies from marsh fever. That was really dangerous."

I went out onto the balcony to get a breath of fresh air. My head was spinning from so much talk that I didn't understand and that I couldn't contribute to. Below me I saw the district as if it were in a deep black chasm, calling out to the Lord in vain. Now it seemed even smaller and more huddled, a dark junkyard. It no longer belonged in the world. It was simply suffered to exist. It seemed that only the shadows of the damned lived there. It was really a district of shadows that had nothing in common with the rest of the city. I looked at the rooftops so as not to have to look into an even deeper chasm, but they too seemed to writhe with pain. "My fear is not that big," I said to myself. "My fear oozes between bare cracking walls and trembles beside a broken-down stove. Here, inside the city, fear has long had a home. Here, it has knocked at every door, on houses that have been torn down and rebuilt ten times over." I turned away from the black chasm and looked at the sky. I saw stars. They were shining brightly in the autumn night. They were cold, indifferent, but they shone over the whole city, including this district, crouched under blows. "I must look only at them," I told myself. "It's a pity I didn't think of them earlier. I won't be alone anymore when I think of them. They belong to me and have always belonged to me. Nobody can take them away from me."

I went back into the room. The men were already lying down on the bunks and covering themselves with the torn blankets. I too lay down on a bed. It was a camp bed with a worn straw mattress that I had to turn about on for a long time before I found a position in which the twisted springs didn't hurt. I soon fell asleep, while the others talked to themselves and to one another or mumbled prayers. I slept high above the district, all twisted with fear, but I slept in safety and certainty, and before I fell asleep I thought of the stars.

10

"Do you have ration cards for sugar?" the official asked. "You have to have ration cards for sugar or you can't get a star."

I didn't particularly care for the star. It was yellow and had a word in a foreign language written in black scraggly letters. It was a poor trade for sugar rations. I needed the sugar to sweeten my fake coffee.

"You needn't worry about your ration card. You only have to show it to me. And from now on you mustn't appear outdoors without the star, I hope I don't have to tell you what would happen to you.

"You have to stitch down the corners of the star and wear it on the left side, directly on your heart, not any higher or lower. There are very strict regulations about this. You must be wearing the star by tomorrow."

He handed me a piece of rayon material. "You mustn't get it dirty. Come and get another later. Today we're passing out only one."

The official had the expression of a busy man who is happy in his work. He had probably been a shop assistant. He must have been glad there was such a demand for his goods. They were of high quality and cheap, a real bargain. Only one crown for a star made of fine prewar material. In fact, they were practically giving them away.

I went home and stitched down the tips of the star with a

needle and thread. There were six tips and a word on the star, all contorted and twisted, in a foreign language that seemed to make a face at me. I felt for my heart through my coat and marked the place with pins. It beat quite regularly. I looked into the splinter that was my mirror. The black and yellow star looked provocative; it called out for help or screamed in alarm. "I must get used to going about with this emblem," I told myself. "It will probably be difficult. I probably won't be able to slink along the streets as well. People will point their fingers at me."

I went out the next day. After all, I had to go shopping. I saw people looking at me. At first it seemed as though my shoelaces must be untied or that there was something wrong with my clothes. In some way I had upset the everyday, accepted order of things. I was a sort of blot that didn't belong in the picture of the street and everyone seemed to be aware of this. And I was alone among other people, completely alone, because people would make way for me. They would stop and look at me. I was no longer one of them.

And then I raised my head and became dizzy with a strange feeling. It seemed to me I was no longer even Josef Roubicek, an ordinary bank clerk, one of the many walking about the city. I had become a special person whom everyone looked at and made way for. I was now proud that people were looking at me. Yes, it's me; take a good look. I have the same hands and feet that you do, I'm dressed the way you are, yet I'm different.

"Hello, sheriff!" a boy called to me. And everyone laughed, but I knew they weren't laughing at me. I laughed too. It was a funny thing to be going about with this emblem. It was a masquerade that was alien to a world where people worked. It belonged to a fair, to a Punch and Judy show, to somersaults, powdered faces, and kicks in the behind.

And at night I had a dream. I was on board a ship at sea. I was with Ruzena. We looked out across the water, and in the distance the outlines of an island could be seen. I knew it was an island that lepers were taken to. I knew that Ruzena was only accompanying me and that we would be saying good-bye as soon as we landed.

"I will never see you again, Josef, and I love you so much. Please don't cry. Look, I'm not crying either. I'm laughing, see?" She pushed the corners of her mouth upward with her fingers, but I saw she had tears in her eyes.

"It's nothing, Ruzena," I said. "I like islands. We were always arguing when you claimed that Kampa was a peninsula and I said it was an island. And you know that I don't have leprosy, that I'm healthy, that I'm here by mistake. They'll find out on the island and send me home by the next ship, or maybe you can come to get me."

We landed, and the ship immediately set sail again. I looked at Ruzena. She stood on the deck and waved to me with a handkerchief. I took a handkerchief out too and waved to her from the pier. And then the ship rapidly disappeared, as if it had dissolved. Suddenly I was surrounded by the inhabitants of the island, all of them cripples. One was missing a hand, another a leg. I didn't even want to look at the third. Somehow I knew he didn't have a nose.

A girl came up to me. I didn't quite know what she looked like, because I didn't look anyone in the face.

"Take me for a wife. Everyone must get married here. You'll do well with me. I'm rich. In the cliffs I have a hidden jar of lard."

"Don't be foolish. Don't promise her anything," a voice behind me said. I saw that it belonged to Wiener. "Other girls, richer and more beautiful than this one, are waiting for you on the island."

"I don't want to get married," I cried. "I love Ruzena. I'll go back to her, because I don't have leprosy. I am healthy. I'm here by mistake."

"Nobody returns from here. You must stay for the rest of your life and you must get married. That's the law here."

"Help me, Ruzena, help me," I cried, but the cripples all

laughed at me and pulled me into the interior of the island. I resisted and yelled. I was still yelling as I awoke and as Tomas reminded me with loud mewing that he wanted something for breakfast.

"I don't have anything," I told him. "I can only give you a piece of dry bread, and you won't drink my fake coffee anyway. I'll open the window for you. Go outside for a mouse or a bird. If you're not successful hunting you'll have to eat the dry bread."

Tomas went up to the roof slowly and without enthusiasm. I washed, drank my coffee, went down to the garden, and dug up a few radishes. I chewed the radishes and waited for Tomas. He was away a long time. Finally he came back, his fur all wet.

"You had no luck, did you? I knew as much, but I still thought you should have a go at it. Here's your piece of bread. I saved it for you."

This wasn't true. I had been eating the bread with the radishes, but I wanted Tomas to be pleased.

"Tomas," I said, "I should be telling you a story, to make up for the meager breakfast, but my stories aren't amusing. I was never really happy with my aunt and uncle. They were disagreeable people who tolerated me only out of pity. They wouldn't allow me to read in bed, because electricity was too expensive. I had to spend the summers with them at a small spa where they took the waters. Everything was terribly boring. I had to stay close to the main building and wasn't even allowed to the edge of the woods. And there were no boys there to play with, only old, boring people. The janitor had a little girl whom I played with, but that was forbidden too and my uncle beat me for it. But one summer they sent me to distant relatives who had a farm where I had a great time. There was a large yard with various animals—chickens, geese, ducks, turkeys. And sometimes also rabbits, when they were let out of their pens. I got to know some of them and gave them names. But they were always being slaughtered, and I wasn't able to beg mercy for any of them. There were two ducks who were together constantly, apart from the others. They put one duck into a pen to fatten her up before slaughtering her, and the other kept hanging around her pen and quacking away with her; even that last day, when her throat was cut. But believe me, Tomas, I didn't take it too much to heart. I was happy. I could go where I liked. I went fishing with the village boys and swimming in the fish pond. I ran about the woods and came home in the evening. I collected stones in the stream and made pictures with them. They were various colors but most were gray. Sometimes there were pieces of glass washed smooth by the water, shards from green bottles that were tossed about in the stream until they looked like pigeon eggs and shone like gems. I would go to the stream early in the morning, wade through the early-morning dew in the meadow, past ditches where forget-me-nots grew. I would sit by the stream and look for stones and pieces of glass. I brought a whole bagful of them back to the city, but my uncle threw them away."

Tomas was lolling about lazily and didn't seem to be listening to me.

"Well, I'll tell you something you don't know. If you were more attentive you would have noticed it yourself, and I wouldn't have to tell you. They gave me a star. It's not at all nice and there's something special about it. It doesn't shine at night, only in the daytime. No helmsman could steer a ship by it, because he'd lose his way. And it must be worn precisely over the heart."

In the evening I sat and looked out the window. I idled about, waiting for the stars to appear. The street was empty. Nobody walked near the small houses on the outskirts at this late hour. Windows were open, and one could hear music from radios. Marches full of pipes and drums announced special news reports about ships sunk in some distant sea. It was bad music, and the news was bad too. I didn't like listening. I didn't want ships to sink. Among them might be the ship going to America that would someday save me when I was sinking in a ship full of the dead. Perhaps they had already sunk that proud ocean liner called *Esperanza* that glided softly over the waves, and a whaling boat would be sent to get me. No, it wasn't true. They didn't sink any ships. They made up those news items so they could play the drums.

I saw someone stopping by the garden gate. It was open, and a man was walking to the door of the house. I couldn't make out his face. I didn't care for evening visits, and it couldn't be anybody from the Community, because they didn't walk about the streets so late. Perhaps someone had the wrong address. I ran down the stairs and opened the door. Josef Materna stood before me.

"I was passing by, so I thought I would look in on you. You haven't been to see us for a long time."

"I can't visit you, I wear a star."

"That's silly. So don't wear it."

I took Materna up to my room.

"You don't have much here," he said.

"The main thing is that I'm here alone."

"I couldn't stand not talking to anyone. I think I would rather let myself be locked up in prison."

"I wouldn't care for prison. What I want is for them to leave me alone. I'd like to sleep through it all and only wake up when it's all over. But that isn't possible. The radio yells their news into my window. And messengers come with orders and circulars."

"Prison isn't so bad. They lock you up and then they let you out again. I've been there."

"But they wouldn't let me out."

"Let's change the subject. I came because of something else. I have some scribblings here that we want to put up on walls. I came to ask you to correct it for us."

I read words written in clumsy handwriting, ordinary words, but I had never heard the words used before.

"We wrote it as best we knew how. You know how it is."

"You want to put it up."

"That's right. We will."

I corrected the spelling mistakes and changed the order of the words to make their meaning clearer. I would have liked to speak this kind of language, but I didn't know how. I could only play with the words.

Materna took the paper. "You should come see us again. You must talk to people."

I watched him from the window as he closed the garden gate. It was a pity he had left so soon. I probably would have spoken more to him today. I was dying to talk because I was happy to have been able to help in some work.

Ships are sinking and people are drowning in stormy seas. Only a flag remains above the surface, and then the waves close over it. The sea is quiet and people walk through the streets of the city putting up posters that have my words on them.

The barrel-shaped man with the clown face told me, "I always played comic parts. I was an actor, you know. They never allowed me to play a tragic part. Who ever heard of a bald Hamlet with a beer belly, they would say, or a King Lear who looks like a great big drunk? And now I have a tragic part to play and I don't like it one bit. I'd like to play Falstaff again, stuff myself with goodies, even if they're made of papier-mâché."

We were sitting on our beds in the standby-duty room, getting ready to go to sleep. The barrel-shaped man was my neighbor.

"I rarely went to the theater. I was a bank clerk. And I never went to see a tragedy. I only went to see comedies or operettas."

"I'd like to play in an operetta if I could. They kept asking me, offered me lots of money, but I refused. I thought I might get a tragic part to play if I stuck to the theater. The worst of it is that now I must play my tragic part under my own name. And nobody knows about it."

"How is that?"

"When I went to the theater and told them my name, they told me to get rid of it quickly. They said, how can an actor have a name like Ludvik Porges? I chose an ordinary, quite nice name and it served me for thirty years. And now that I am suffering as Porges I swear to take revenge on them as Porges. Isn't that terrible?"

"I don't know," I said. "My name is Roubicek. Good night!"

We turned out the light and fell asleep, but during the night the telephone woke us up. I thought it was a wrong number. Our emergency service was supposed to be make-believe. We only slept here above the cringing city so that someone somewhere could check off names and fill in forms.

It was police headquarters. We were told to report to the nearest station.

We went out with brooms and pails and crept along the blacked-out streets. Our stars were invisible. It was a parade of hunched old men. The bald head of my neighbor, Ludvik Porges, shone in the starlight as he played the tragic role of squad leader.

We stood in front of the police station. The city was very quiet. Porges came out after a little while with a policeman. In the blue beam of a flashlight we walked from corner to corner, dipping our brooms into white paint and painting over the white pieces of paper, full of writing, posted on fences and billboards. There was too little light for us to make out what was written on them. But in the faint gleam of the policeman's flashlight I made out a single word. It was my word; I remembered it well. It soon disappeared under the white paint.

We returned in the morning, exhausted and sleepy, dragging our brooms and pails. Our group was even more hunched now, and it clung close to the walls of the buildings, because it was light by now and our stars shone in the dawn. We met the carts of vegetable vendors and people hurrying to work.

It was too late to lie down and go to sleep. We sat on the rickety beds and waited for the hour when our service was over.

"Where is Solveig?" asked Porges. "I'm sure Peer Gynt returned bald and with a big belly. But did he return with a broom and pail? That is the question."

"I wonder what was on those posters," I said.

"Silly things. It's all a comedy that we're not playing in. We're only the stagehands."

I was quiet. My eyelids were drooping from fatigue. In a half sleep I was thinking of that word, my word, which appeared before me for a moment in the rays of the flashlight.

11

I was raking leaves. They rustled in the stillness. I raked them all into one pile. We didn't hurry. We walked around the cemetery slowly. We passed marble monuments; there were many such gravestones, with proud names and titles. They were made of black marble with gilded inscriptions. They stood in the main lanes.

They had sent me to the cemetery for gardening work, but there was nothing to do but rake leaves and look at the monuments. Their glory extended only to the end of the field. There were new graves there, freshly dug. The mounded earth had been washed away by the rain. I couldn't read the names, written on small tablets in foreign letters. I only saw the dates; they were recent dates.

It was good work being among the dead at the cemetery all day. It was highly prized work for which one had to have pull somewhere; I got it by chance because it wasn't possible to assign me to heavy labor and clerical work was in too great demand.

I had to travel all the way across the city and stand on the platform of the streetcar the whole trip. It wasn't too bad.

What was worse was that when a full car came along I had to wait for a half-empty one; worse still was having to get off somewhere in the middle of my trip when the streetcar filled up and someone demanded I leave. There were people who enjoyed throwing others out of moving streetcars, kicking them, and saying nasty words. They were on the lookout for stars so that they could demonstrate their power. I never knew if I would make it to work or back home, but at the cemetery all was peaceful. It wasn't possible to order the dead to spring from their graves and make room for someone else. It might have been possible to knock down the monuments, dig up the bones, and plow up the field, but that would have required a lot of people and a lot of time, because the cemetery was large.

I didn't talk much to the people I worked with at the cemetery. They weren't interesting. They only talked about the businesses they used to have, about families I didn't know. They would point to the monuments and brag about their relatives or their dead and call on them to testify to their claims. They didn't want to talk about the insults they suffered on the streetcar, about the effort it took to get some food. They loved their dead and their proud gilt titles.

I now knew where I would take Tomas if something happened to me. I knew I could bring him here to the cemetery because other cats lived here who had been designated enemy cats. They lived in the tombs, and the dead didn't mind their presence. They wandered about the cemetery freely, and no regulations could touch them. Tomas would be sure to get on well with them.

I walked slowly, raked leaves, and thought about Ruzena. I was telling her a fairy tale about a magic rake. First the rake was leaning against the wall of the cemetery chapel. It stared dully at the windows. And from the windows prayers for the dead could be heard. There were thousands of dead and many of them would never be laid to rest in the earth. Vultures would fight over their bodies and crows would peck at their eyes. The prayer was for all the dead, even those who had died a thousand years ago, but above all it was for martyrs—men who welcomed death as one welcomes a bride and whose blood had been splattered on the walls of the temples and had stayed there, always fresh, in memory of them. And the prayer rose upward, to the gates of heaven, where the angel of death writes down the names of the just. Then the prayer dropped downward and, in the form of pebbles, rained upon their graves. The eyes of the Lord of Life and Death were full of tears, and one of them fell on the leaning rake. And a miracle happened. The soul of a just man entered the rake. Then it went through the fields of the dead, turning over leaves and changing them into words. The fall wind lifted the leaves and carried them all through the land—words about silent pain in the hour of submission to death, about the wall splattered with blood that never dries. The rustle of the leaves when they fell to the earth became a song, with the sobbing melody of a prayer as it rises to the heavenly gates and rains down in the form of pebbles. Whenever leaves touch the rake they change into words. And these words live, even after the bones of martyrs are scattered, even after their bodies change to dust and ashes.

" 'So you have an affidavit, you Jewish swine,' he said. 'The only way you'll emigrate is in a horizontal position.' And he tore up all my documents. The trouble my cousin Robert must have gone to, and the number of times I had to go to various authorities and the way they yelled at me everywhere! So now this is my America."

"Why are we raking these leaves?" I asked someone nearby.

"They make good fertilizer. We grow vegetables here. Everything grows well in a cemetery."

"What will we do when snow falls and there are no leaves?"

"We'll shovel snow and then warm up in the office. We'll drink linden tea, because the cemetery is full of linden trees and we have a stock of dried blossoms."

"There won't be any linden tea," said the man raking leaves on the other side. "There won't be any linden tea, just like there isn't any America."

"The cemetery will remain," said his neighbor.

"Not even the cemetery will remain."

"Stop it," cried the man who used to be a coffee salesman. "Don't provoke a panic. The cemetery will remain. What's your opinion, Mr. Roubicek?"

"I don't know," I said. "The monuments are heavy. They're made of marble and crush the grass. Maybe they won't be toppled to the ground. Maybe they'll remain standing. Maybe everything should stay in its place; once everything is moved no one can know what will happen next. Can dried linden blossoms be smoked?"

"Yes, but they're not good. It's better to gather some leaves and boil them in a brew made of cigarette butts."

"It's nice here in the summer. Pity you weren't here then. People come here in the summer—mothers with baby carriages, and on Sundays, people come to lie in the grass. They hide behind the tombstones and play cards. Once there was a police raid on a Sunday and people were throwing away all the cigarettes they had on them. We had some good smokes then, didn't we, Robert?"

"What were they looking for in the cemetery?" I asked.

"A treasure. Someone reported that we had buried something. They chose strong people from the ones they'd caught and made them dig. They stood over them with guns and prodded them. They were out of their minds. Finally they found what they were looking for. Scrolls of old, torn Torahs. They were furious and beat up a number of people."

"Why were they buried?"

"Well, that's our custom. Don't you know it? Torn scrolls must not be burned or destroyed in any other way. They must be buried in consecrated soil, like people. God's word is equal to a human being."

"A human being has no value," said Robert, "especially when they bury him. Words don't have any value either."

"Did you notice those red posters? They have words with death in them."

"What does it matter? Death is everywhere. Death is cheap, too."

"According to you everything is cheap," I said, "and everything is free. I don't see it that way. I think there are also other words, which don't need to be buried in the ground."

"Don't believe in gossip or rumors. We're finished, just like they say. Did you know they shot two high officials from the Community?"

"Why?" asked Robert.

"Because they knew too much. They knew what was going to happen and they gave it away somewhere. Or one of them let it out and then put the blame on those two from the Community."

"I have an uncle," I said. "We quarreled because of my cat. He's afraid the cat will bring about his death."

"Everything is possible. We've come to a point where anything can mean death. Even an apple or a cigarette or an ordinary thing like a broom or a streetcar. Knowing means death and not knowing does, too."

"What did those two really know?" asked Robert.

"I don't know. Maybe it was nothing important. But all sorts of things are being said about it."

It felt good to walk with the rake and make piles of leaves. It felt good to dump them in a cart and push them around the monuments. The wheels left a trail on the sandy path. I followed it. The cart was in a good mood, too. It squeaked and sang. I listened to the talk and I myself talked as well. I knew that all this talking wasn't getting us anywhere, that people were only talking to kill time, arguing pointlessly or scaring or comforting one another. It was all the same on that fall day. There were many leaves, and they kept falling. And it was nice to sit on a pile of dry leaves and eat bread with lean cheese. It was nice to get a little water in the office and make tea.

"Ruzena," I said, "I didn't finish telling you the fairy tale about the rake. At first there were sobbing words in the song, noble words about the blood of martyrs. But then, as the song flew far off with the leaves and the leaves fell into the mud and dirt, they were raised up again by the wind, and they fell on plowed fields and flew about garbage dumps. The song became trite, the kind played on the accordion in dance halls; drunks wept when they heard it. Then it sank even lower—to fairs and traveling-circus wagons, where mangy monkeys and an old skinny lion would listen to it. But someone who was passing by a wagon heard the song and wrote it down. Then it was played in great halls and became grand again. But the tears of the angel of death, falling as pebbles, had always been in it; the rake had always been raking leaves in it; the song had always flown all through the land with the blood of martyrs."

"Did you know Wiener?" Robert asked. "He's in prison. He was arrested in Lipa. He was receiving forbidden packages from home."

"I spoke to him before he left. He said Lipa was a good place."

"It was a good place, but some flunky of theirs got a toothache. They can't stand toothaches, and Wiener didn't know."

"Nobody knows anything. It's all a whispering campaign. Something's up."

"They'll lose this war," I said, "and their cemeteries will be far away. Not even linden trees will grow there and no leaves will drop on their lanes."

"Did you know Ludvik Porges, the actor?" Robert asked. "They caught him after eight o'clock. He had a pass, but for a different street. He'd gone to visit a family where they gave him tea and he played Hamlet."

"Hamlet isn't worth dying for," the former owner of a clothing store said. "I know what I'm talking about. The biggest actresses used to buy their lingerie in my shop. They'd offer me theater tickets, but I never went. If one could have gone there to get meat, that's something I would have understood."

"Old Bondy got some pork. They say it's very expensive, but it's worth it. There's a lot of fat on it."

"I must stop by to see him."

"Did you know Dr. Bloch?" Robert asked. "They caught him with a package of margarine in his briefcase."

"Stop it," I said. "Don't tell us how they catch people for Beethoven or Hamlet or for meat, or because someone has a toothache. Here we are at a cemetery, among the dead, raking leaves—we should at least have some quiet. We would do better to talk about old times, when nobody caught anyone on the streets, when we went to football games, when we had coffee with whipped cream in coffeehouses. What if we said to ourselves that there is nothing but this cemetery, where we take walks with rakes?"

But the others wouldn't listen to me. They wanted to hear where, when, and how some person was caught. Maybe it gave them a greater sense of security because their feet were still walking the ground and their hands still gripped a rake while others were caught and were suffering in prison. Perhaps talk about forebodings of death made their lives, so little valued, more valuable.

"I refuse to take part in this game," I said. "This is blindman's buff—one can't see what's going on. It's a constant race, where the winner doesn't even get a prize."

"What do you think should be done?" retorted Robert. "We didn't think up this game."

"We'll lose," the owner of the clothing store mumbled.

"I hear that all the time. But I'd like to get out of this game. Let them play it without me. First I tried by closing myself off in a broken-down house with cracked walls, in a room with no furniture. But they pulled me out by the ears, like a rabbit from its pen. They pulled me out into the open, so they would have more room for their crazy chase. What if we said we weren't playing anymore?"

"Some will survive," Robert said.

"I know. Hope. But you yourself say there isn't any. You scare each other. You have hope, yet you don't have hope, and so it goes, all the time."

"You have nothing to blame us for. You're in the same mess."

"I'm not blaming you. I'm in the same situation. But I'd like to find a solution. One where a person could use his own will."

"In that case only death remains, but that won't be your will; that will be their will again."

I knew they didn't understand me or didn't want to understand me. I knew that the conversation embarrassed them, that they were irritated because I reminded them of their helplessness. They felt better when they considered themselves victims, who with the passing of each day had escaped danger once more; they felt better when they decided they had no choice. In fact, they liked to think they couldn't make decisions. But I kept talking, because I felt like talking that day. I knew they would all be angry at me and wouldn't even be willing to lend me sugar to put in my linden tea when I forgot to bring some from home.

"That's no solution," I said. "I've thought about it a lot. There must be some other way."

They laughed at me. They probably thought that I was bragging, that I, Roubicek the bank clerk, wanted to put on airs, that I wasn't willing to pull with them. I raked the leaves in silence.

"Ruzena," I said, "I told you about the rake, but there are some problems with the song. Many people didn't even hear it, and others put their hands over their ears when an organ-grinder played it for them. I would rather not be alone anymore, but I didn't want to be slaughtered with the others. I looked at the city crying and kneeling in front of its enemies but still hoping to be saved, to be rescued and to stay alive. Even this city, standing in puddles, could have come to a decision. What kind of song can be sung in the middle of a chase when a person has taken off his suspenders and has to hold up his trousers as he runs? What kind of song can be sung when one's coffin is floating in the air and never touches consecrated ground? We used to lie next to each other with happiness between us. That happiness has been cut down and humiliated. I didn't want to decide, I didn't want to leave, but

I could have chosen. There was always a choice, Ruzena, really, and there always is a choice. Only I didn't want to make a choice, just like these people here."

I put the rake away, leaned against the wall of the chapel, and waited for a streetcar. I left earlier than the others. I had had enough of their company. "What are you complaining about?" I said to myself. "You're alive, and that's the most important thing. You have nice, quiet work among the dead, you have something to eat, and you can sob and cry about the past and talk about the misfortunes of others. They're dead already and you're still alive. Look at your hands, how they obey you when you order them to do something, how they grip the handle obediently when you order them to grasp the rake. You can ride on the streetcar—that's a great thing, to be able to use the streetcar and not have to walk in the heat, the rain, in a snowstorm." And I also remembered that I had books at home, new books—not really new, but books I hadn't read. I found them at the cemetery, nicely wrapped. Somebody had thrown them away there—good books, in hard covers, but forbidden books. The person who threw them away was probably afraid. I took them home and read every evening. I read slowly so that they would last a long time. Every day, from morning on, I looked forward to coming home. I imagined how I would come home and lie down and read a few pages, new pages. I remembered how I used to read late into the night, until my eyes hurt, and how I got conjunctivitis. I remembered how my uncle forbade me to read because I used up too much electricity, how he went to the meter every morning and calculated how much I had spent, how he took my books away, books I had borrowed from the public library, how he locked them up for the night and gave them back to me in the morning, how I was always able to hide one book under the mattress, put the light out, and then turn it on again when my aunt and uncle were asleep in the next room, how I would quietly pull the book out from under the mattress and start to read. I didn't go slowly then; I turned the pages quickly and read until my eyes began to smart.

"Get out, you dirty swine," yelled a man with an emblem in that foreign language on his lapel. He pushed me so hard I almost fell. I looked around the streetcar. It was quite full. People's faces were set; they were looking at the floor, as if they were searching for a coin that had rolled under the wooden slats. Nobody spoke. Only his sharp voice was heard: "Get out, you swine, or . . ."

The streetcar was traveling through empty streets in the neighborhood of the cemetery; the next stop was still fairly far away. He gave me another hard push. When I was on the steps of the car I jumped. I ran along for a few seconds, then I tripped and fell on the pavement. I saw my glasses fly off my nose and land some distance from me. I got up slowly. I was dirty and my hands were scraped, but I didn't think I was seriously hurt. I was groping for my glasses when I saw that someone was handing them to me.

"That's a silly thing to do, to jump from a moving streetcar. Are you out of your mind? You could have killed yourself."

I didn't feel like talking. I pointed to the star. It was dirty, but its yellow color was still shining in the dusk.

"Uhm," said the man, "I see. That's the Order of the Legion of Honor. Are they allowed to do that?"

"I don't know. Why shouldn't they be?" I said. "Goodbye."

"Wait a moment. I'll walk with you to the next stop, and on the way I'll clean you up a bit. I would take you home so that you could wash up, but I live far away. Nobody lives here at all."

"You can't do that," I said. "I'm wearing a star."

"I'm just the one to ask them what I can or can't do. I'm a trainman."

"I don't think that's a good reason to them. They don't make exceptions for trainmen."

"So tear it off."

"Do you have a knife?" I asked. He handed me his pocket-knife, and I cut the stitches around the star. I thought there were still traces of it on my coat, but that was nonsense.

"There's a tavern on the corner," he said. "Come and have

a beer. Let's drink to it. Don't worry, I'm paying. And you can wash in the bathroom so you're not conspicuous on the streetcar. I hope you're not one of those who used to put on airs!"

"Let's drink to it," I said. I didn't care anymore. I was probably still afraid, but I was angry and I was all bruised. I wanted a drink. The door of the tavern had a sign, but all public places had them. They were strips of cardboard with black block letters printed on them.

There were only a few people in the tavern. We ordered beer, potato salad, and pickled herring, the only food they had. The place was dirty and stank of stale beer. It was a tavern gravediggers went to, a place where they came after work and where mourners who had attended a funeral sometimes came to have a meal and to drink a whiskey in memory of the deceased and to his eternal glory.

There was no more whiskey in the tavern. We drank weak beer. I didn't feel relaxed so close to the cemetery. I had to force myself not to turn around. I felt as if I were sitting naked among dressed people. I smoked a cigarette made of home-grown tobacco and kept looking at the door for policemen or people from the labor office who might come in and ask for identity cards. I didn't want to be caught in a gravediggers' tavern drinking a large glass of weak beer at a forbidden hour. Although it was now all the same how many forbidden things I was doing since I had already done one. And I had to think about the trip home without a star, by streetcar, where soldiers might block the exits and demand identity cards from everyone; it was out of the question for me to walk home all the way across town.

"You don't seem to be very talkative," my companion said.

"It's been a long time since I've been among people. I'm not used to talking to people, except those I work with, who wear a star. And they talk only about death."

"That's a subject we can skip. There's time enough for that.

There's no lack of death among us either. With the war, everything's going wrong, but why talk about it."

"You know they're saying that death is our best friend. Maybe it really is their best friend and maybe it's their only one, but it certainly isn't my friend."

At the next table people were playing cards. They hurled the cards down on the table and shouted cardplayers' talk. The bartender was dozing behind the bar. I had to think of the trip home. I wasn't listening to what the trainman was saying. I caught only his last words:

"It tore him in half. His guts were all over the place, and his head was smashed to a pulp. I can tell you, it wasn't a pleasant sight. But that's part of our work. Where did you say you worked?"

"At the cemetery," I said. "I rake leaves."

"That's good work, quiet and safe."

"I can't explain it, but it's not just a question of death. I'd like to be equal to death, but somehow it doesn't work."

"I don't understand that. When your number's up, it's up."

We ordered a second round of beers.

"They travel; they're always traveling. They're a restless people. Are they driven by fear or what?" the trainman spoke slowly. "They travel from one country to another. Everywhere they go they steal and murder. They carry loads of junk with them—various odds and ends, photographs. They sit in trains and cry over pictures of their children. On the platforms they pat other people's children, but the children glare back at them as if they had been bitten by a snake. It's impossible to run trains for such people. They don't even know what trains are for. Trains are for people to visit their aunt or go on a picnic, for children to go to school and for workers to go to work. Tell me, what do they need trains for? Why don't they make do with large freight trains, covered with canvas, where people can write in chalk: STOLEN IN FOREIGN COUNTRIES. You can't write something like that on a railroad car, even if they themselves do put all sorts of silly signs on them."

"I have a public notice that says, first, that I am absolutely forbidden to ride on a train and, second, that if I take a train I must use the last car and only a local train. I never knew before which was the last car. I always got on the one that happened to be empty. I don't know what it is they have with these trains."

"They don't understand railroads, that's it. With a train a person has to be considerate and responsible. The railroad carries people who entrust their lives to it, and that's some responsibility. I'll tell you, you can't have madmen and criminals running the railroads. I'm telling you as a railroad man that it's all the same, the last car or the first. Each car has to have its suspension and brakes in order. They thought up that nonsense because the only thing they know are their own freight cars with canvas tops."

"I don't do any traveling anyway. I only watch the trains leaving the station. I wait at the crossing until the train passes, and I see people at the windows looking out. I can tell by their eyes that they're looking forward to the woods and the river, that in an hour they'll be sitting in a meadow with their mouths full of wild strawberries. Then the train passes, and I wait at the gate until it opens so that I can cross to the other side."

"Soon you'll be traveling by train again. That's what trains were built for, so that all people could use them. Their politics don't carry any weight with trains. The trains wouldn't stand for it."

I got home all right that time without the star. I sat comfortably on a seat in the streetcar and looked at the floor. The streetcar moved rapidly through the blacked-out streets. People were sleeping in the blue glow, and outside a light rain was falling.

12

That night I dreamed that I was standing before a court of justice. A man in riding boots, with a skull on his cap, was presiding. Death came forward as the prosecutor, a woman, as she appears in pictures, with a torn cloak, carrying a scythe over her shoulder. A picture like that used to hang in my grandfather's house. It showed stairs, and at their foot there was a small boy, higher up a young man, at the top of the stairs a big, strong man with his feet apart and a beard; and then the stairs went down again and at the bottom Death stood with a scythe, nodding to a hunched old man who was walking down the stairs with effort. It was that kind of Death.

"He insulted my majesty," Death cried. "He cursed me and laughed at me. He sat in a tavern where he had no right to be, and he bragged that he'd get the best of me. I demand he be severely punished."

All at once my aunt and uncle appeared before the court.

"Your Honor, we're not guilty of anything." They both spoke at the same time. "He doesn't belong to us; he doesn't even live with us. We only brought him up out of pity, but he repaid us with evil. He's a bad person who has no sense of family, and we only learned about that cat when he told us about it. We forbade him to come into our house when he told us."

"This court is not concerned with a cat," the presiding judge admonished them. "This is an action brought by Death. Did he blaspheme about Death in front of you?"

"I don't know, Your Honor. He never spoke about Death to us. We are plain people. What would he say about Death to us?"

"These are no witnesses," shouted the presiding judge. "These are liars and frauds, who only want to confuse the prosecution. Take them away and arrest them for contempt of court."

"Your Honor," my uncle and aunt cried, "have mercy on us. We're innocent. We didn't know a thing about that cat."

"Take them away," said the judge, "and bring in the next witness."

All of a sudden Ruzena stood in front of the court. She was dressed as if they had caught her somewhere on the street. She held a shopping bag in her hand.

"Forgive him, Your Honor," she said in a quiet voice, but it was clear she was not at all afraid. "He's such a good-for-nothing. He was only bragging—he didn't mean it seriously. Probably the beer went to his head. He's not used to it. He never drinks. He was only babbling and didn't mean anything."

"This court does not forgive," the judge shouted at her. "This court only punishes. Take her away."

The attendant was leading Ruzena away. She looked at me sadly, as if she were saying goodbye to me.

"The court will now adjourn for deliberation," said the judge. I was looking at a door, not the door where the court had adjourned, but the door Ruzena had gone through. Perhaps I was hoping she would return for me and set me free. But instead of Ruzena, Death was standing there, as if she was watching to see that no one came through the door.

"Hear the sentence," recited the judge in a slow, drowsy voice. "The accused is sentenced to punishment for his blasphemy. He will be handed over to Death. What she does with him is up to her. He is now her property."

I saw Death stretching out her hand for me.

"But I'm not standing on the last stair!" I cried. "I'm not a hunched old man. I haven't even reached the top of the stairs. Help! Help!" I tried to yell, but my voice was strangled and I couldn't move.

I woke up and found Tomas the cat sitting on my chest. I didn't want to get up. I was shivering with cold even though I was all bundled up in my sleeping bag. Finally I crawled out, but I was dizzy and everything dropped from my hands. It took me a long time before I could cook my breakfast and shave.

"I have a temperature," I told myself. "It would be very inconvenient to be sick. If I stay here on the mattress nobody will help me or bring me anything to eat. I can't very well send Tomas to go buy my bread during the permitted hours."

I forced myself to dress and went out into the street. Everything seemed different to me. I noticed things that had never caught my attention: the signs in two languages, a notice about how to get eggs, and the gratings over the sewers. I didn't notice people. I avoided them on the sidewalk and waited patiently for a streetcar.

It wasn't far from the streetcar station to the clinic, but I took a long time. I walked through various streets and stared dully in front of me. I took the wrong street even though I knew the way very well.

In the hall of the clinic some children were playing, happily calling to one another, oblivious to the smell of disinfectant. There were a lot of people in the doctor's waiting room. I sat on a bench and looked down listlessly. Meaningless words kept running through my head: "kukureke, tucivod." I tried to put them out of my mind. I took out a book, but the letters seemed to run together. I tried to force myself to listen to what people were saying, but their words made no sense.

"Floor wax," one of them said and then went on at length, but those were the only words my mind accepted, and they kept merging in my head with the other nonsense words.

"You're running a temperature," said the doctor when it was finally my turn. "It's influenza. You should have stayed at home. They'll give you some medicine downstairs. Ask someone to telephone your office that you're sick."

"I don't have anyone," I said. "If I died, no one would know for a long time. I have no friends; on the outskirts of the city, where I live, only messengers with notices come to see me."

"I can't help you," said the doctor. "I can't help anybody. And you can telephone from the office here."

The people in the office were unpleasant and angry. They didn't want to let me make a telephone call, but I listened to their loud voices indifferently. I waited meekly until they changed their minds. The young woman who sat in the office had red nail polish on her fingers. I remember looking only at her nails, but she took no notice of me. She didn't take part in the argument. She just stared at her desk, which had a vase of flowers on it. The office workers, in their white coats, looked smug and satisfied even though they were shouting something at the supplicants standing before a partition, waving cards. One of them was the one who had been angry with me when I asked if I could call the cemetery. I was standing in front of the partition, with the other supplicants, while behind it was the office, the powerful and mighty office where officials were writing busily, pretending they were physicians, since they wore white coats.

"I'm sick," I said slowly. I had to work hard to put the words together, because they seemed to be running away from me. I felt like saying "floor wax" and "tucivod."

"We're all sick," said the official, looking annoyed, as if disease was something that polite people didn't talk about.

"Tails," cried the children in the hall. It was some sort of children's game.

I didn't want to argue with the official. I wouldn't even have been capable of it. I preferred looking at the red nails and the flowers on the desk.

I stood in a line leading to a room in the basement and waited to get my medicine. At times I didn't know where I was and what I was waiting for. I kept having to wake myself out of my drowsiness.

Somehow I got home—I don't remember how—and crawled into my sleeping bag.

I lay on my back and looked up at the ceiling. The circle grew and no longer had a regular outline. It had spread out in jagged peaks. I tried to read again, but it was impossible.

In Gaza he lay, bound to a column; Samson tore down the building that was his prison—and I can't even raise myself to touch the large circle to cool my brow. Where did those young men find girls who slept with them in their cottages and cooked their dinners while they lounged about in armchairs? What words did they use to persuade them, make them lie down naked on hard mattresses, and rise up early in the morning to start a fire in the stove? I never met such a girl.

"What about me?" said Ruzena, and sat on the edge of the mattress.

"You're only a dream," I said. "You came out of a book of fairy tales, from beyond seven hills and seven rivers, where you collected leaves in the woods and brought home a bagful of gold coins. You freed a rabbit sitting behind a window and it showed you the way to the castle and taught you what to say to make the silver drawbridge lower for you. You won out over the wicked stepmother and her daughters, and a squirrel brought you some magic water to make your body whole again. Go back to your fairy tale. You have no business here between cracked walls. You belong in a castle, where footsteps are muffled by carpets."

"Go to sleep," said Ruzena. "Sleep and don't think about anything. Nobody can harm you and nobody can scare you. I put a magic animal on guard, a cat in high boots who knows the magic words 'kukureke' and 'floor wax.' He'll watch over you and never abandon you."

"Ruzena, I don't like high boots," I replied.

"Well, then, he won't have high boots. Only silky paws to caress you with. Nobody has caressed you for a long time, have they? Sleep. Do you hear leaves falling?"

"It would be better if you were on watch, Ruzena, even if you are only a dream. I feel good with you. Remember how we once stood for a long time in the rain, the time we were waiting for a bus—how the water ran down our faces and we laughed?"

"I can't stay," said Ruzena. "I have to go shopping and cook lunch. It's been a long time since we parted."

I knew that Ruzena was leaving, because it was fall again. It was rainy and windy outside. Soon there would be snow, and the room would be cold again. I wouldn't have money for coal and wood; I would freeze again by that broken-down stove. There wouldn't be laughter or tears when the time came . . .

"What's the matter with you? I've been shouting and banging. Nobody opened the door but people told me you were home, so I kicked the door open, and here you are, lying, looking at the ceiling."

It took me a long time to return from saying goodbye to Ruzena and to recognize Materna.

"I'm sick," I said. "I lie here and look at the ceiling. That circle is getting bigger and bigger, but that's probably because it's autumn. Leaves are falling and people are whispering that terrible things are being planned. I'm sick. I caught a cold, probably because I walked in the rain."

"What's all this nonsense? Who cooks for you?"

"Nobody," I said. "I'm not hungry. I'm all right."

"Wait a minute. This can't go on. I'll send my mother to clean up a bit here and bring you some soup."

I wanted to say that that was impossible, that someone might inform on him, but I was too sluggish and I didn't feel like talking. I wanted to return to my drowsiness, to talk to Ruzena.

But the soup was very good and rich, made of beef. I didn't notice its taste, but I did know it was hot and it warmed me up.

The next day Materna came again. I was no longer dizzy. Everything was back in its proper place—the small table and the crooked pipes of the stove.

"I think I'm over it," I said, "but that doesn't make me happy. They threw me out of a streetcar when it was going full speed. A trainman took me to a tavern near the cemetery. Then I took a long streetcar ride in the rain. The next day I was dizzy and I went to the clinic. There were children there playing and shouting 'tails.' "

"Stop it. It's no use pretending to be a fool. They'll wring your neck one day anyway."

"I know that too. But you know, I'm not alone in thinking

like this. The others are worse. They say that it's all over and done with for us. They're preparing to put on a shroud and lie down in a coffin. I told them that outside of here there are other people, but it was no use. They don't understand. The worst part of it is that I understand them quite well."

"This isn't my kind of talk. I'll tell you quite frankly, I'm surprised at myself that I keep trying to talk you into something. I don't really like crybabies. I got knocked around a lot when I was an apprentice. So what, for God's sake? A knock on the head here, a knock on the head there. But it's true that nobody has ever thrown me off a streetcar."

"That's not the point," I said. "But look, I'm one of them. Which means I shouldn't be breaking ranks. It's as though a lamb were pretending it had claws. If some of them would follow me, that would be different. But they don't want to. They say this isn't their play; they're just the stagehands. One of them was killed because he played Hamlet in secret. He was the one who said that."

"Look here, Josef, this is getting us nowhere. I know those leaflets aren't important. That's just tickling the beast. But it doesn't matter. The main thing is to show that we're here. You climb the stairs and you meet a chimney sweep. The chimney sweep is coming down from the attic because he was just on the roof. But a chimney sweep brings luck; when you meet him you at least know that he exists. Come join us again sometime. We'll turn your head in the right direction."

"I'll come," I said. "I tore off my star. I've already been in a tavern and drunk lousy beer, and I took a streetcar after eight o'clock."

Materna didn't understand me.

13

The time for raking leaves had passed. They lay deep in mud. I didn't know what we were supposed to do. But we probably did do something, because the clerks in the office filled in forms and sent them to the Community. We came to work on time, then we sat around the stove trying to keep warm. It was cold in the chapel. We drank linden tea to get warm—and sometimes tea made of rose hips or apple peels.

People talked about what was happening in the war. They mentioned the names of unknown regions, but nobody really cared about the war and everything that happened at the front seemed to take place in another world. People talked only about a single subject—themselves. They told one another about arrests, about new persecutions, prohibitions, about being thrown out of streetcars. There was always someone who scared the others, and there was always someone who would argue with him or say even worse things. These roles alternated every day.

Perhaps it had once been good to walk in the rain, to look into lighted store windows; perhaps it had also been good to duck into a movie and see a film in which the sun was shining. Perhaps it had been good to stretch out on the sofa and listen in the dark to some silly comedy on the radio while the rain drummed on the window. I no longer knew. That other world was dissolving for me. I no longer saw it in bright colors; the sun no longer shone in it. It was breaking apart, and my efforts to put it together again were futile.

I looked out the windows of the chapel at the cemetery. Rain was running down the black marble, and there were puddles on the paths. Death, useless and stupid, gaped out from the rows of graves. She was as ordinary and meaningless as those monuments.

I arrived at the cemetery in the morning. It was a bright fall day and still quite warm. I was in a good mood because I had stayed at Materna's place until late, and when I snuck back home I felt the way I had when I played hooky from school and thought about how the others were sitting at their desks, trembling lest the teacher call them to the blackboard. When we played hooky we used to gamble in an abandoned beach house. We would slap the cards on a wooden table as if we owned the world, but we only pretended to be daring young men. We knew that if we were caught or if someone told on us we would be expelled from school.

I lit a cigarette. It was a good cigarette, a French make, full of black tobacco and thick.

I wasn't the first or the last to arrive. Several people were already sitting around the stove, and others drifted in slowly. But none of them spoke. They didn't even answer my greeting. They just sat on their chairs and stared. Some bent their heads low, down to the floor.

I had never seen them sit like this. I didn't think that anybody close to them had died or that they were holding a wake. They were from various families, and people were dying like flies. I knew, because they were being buried at our cemetery. The men I worked with were always depressed, and their talk was full of terrible forebodings. They threw their words against an invisible wall, and they threw them so hard the words rebounded.

I was silent too. But it was difficult to just sit and stare for such a long time. If I had been at home, I could have managed, but I would have had to be alone.

"It's beautiful out," I said finally, without addressing anyone, "as if summer wanted to come back."

The others were silent. Any other day someone would certainly have answered that it wasn't at all nice out, and if the sun did shine a bit, that was only because in the afternoon it would be rainy and windy and that after all it didn't matter if it was beautiful or if it was raining. It wouldn't help us either way, because we were lost in any case. We had lost the war and Honduras wouldn't let us in, not even British Honduras, whose stamps had a British king on them.

Someone else would then have started an argument about

Honduras and would have tried to prove that, even if Honduras let us in, we still wouldn't make it, because soon they would kill us all.

A third would say that the war would end within two months (it was always two months—never more, never less), that his sister-in-law had told him that her neighbor had told her that she had seen them pack in preparation for running away.

And a fourth would argue that that was nonsense, because the whole planet Earth was going to die, including birds and fishes; only insects would survive. The day of the Last Judgment was approaching and no one would be saved.

"That won't help us," a fifth person would wail. "Even if everyone dies, we will be the first."

And a sixth would say that was enough of that kind of talk, let's talk about something else—like how a young duckling cooked with apples tastes.

And then people would talk about food for a while. They would plan feasts and draw up menus, until the talk turned again to their tribulations and fear forced them to weep by the rivers of Babylon.

But now they were silent. Nobody moved. Until finally Robert erupted angrily, "Don't you know anything? Don't you know what's going on? They're starting transports."

I didn't know about anything. I didn't know what transports meant, but it was most certainly something bad, because they were so overcome by it they could hardly speak.

"Those two who were killed," continued Robert, "they knew what was coming." He seemed to be glad that he could scare someone, that a new person would shortly join the wake. "They put people in railroad cars like cattle and take them east. They tell them it's for work. But they take old people, women, and children. If you can't walk, they take you in a wheelchair. The first transport is leaving tomorrow. It's full of paupers who were on assistance. They can only take fifty kilos of luggage with them."

"I don't even have fifty kilos," I said.

"You wouldn't need them," answered the man sitting next to Robert. "You could go to death lightly."

"A man does not go to death lightly," I said, "because he knows about death. An animal doesn't know about death, so it can go to its death lightly."

"Maybe it's not death yet. Maybe they really do need a work force in the east. They want to build fortifications there."

"They have enough people there. They have prisoners of war and forced labor from all over Europe. They even have radio broadcasts for them in all languages. Programs with popular songs, operetta stars singing about love and little cottages in the mountains."

"The people who were sent in the first transport certainly weren't singing. They were taken away at night, they were caught in their houses. They were all stooped over, because they were old and sick. They had rucksacks on their backs and carried suitcases. They were ordered to hurry because it was night. They were silent; they weren't allowed to talk to one another. The only sound was the stomping of riding boots on the pavement, but people have already become used to that."

"Nobody ran away?" I asked.

"Nobody," said Robert. "Some were sick, others pretended to be sick, but that didn't do them any good. They loaded them all into railroad cars."

"But they're still not satisfied," said a man sitting next to Robert. "They like gold and jewelry. They want crystal chandeliers and silk underwear. They want to walk on thick carpets and drink tea out of Meissen china. These paupers didn't have gold or beautifully furnished houses. There was no profit for them. Now they're disappointed and furious. They'll have to be given a transport of rich people."

"I spoke to Fischel. They're going to change the procedure. They're going to make lists of everything so that nothing escapes them."

"What's left for us?" I asked.

"Only time," said Robert. "But there's not much of it."

I couldn't believe in time. It always flew when I was with Ruzena and crawled when I was staring at the damp circle on the ceiling. I was never a friend of time, and I didn't like to have to think about it.

"I don't believe in time," I said. "Nobody has ever gotten the upper hand with time."

"The rich think they can buy their way out," Robert continued, "but they'll be disappointed. You can't buy your way out. They're too greedy. They want everything—houses, businesses, furniture, rings, automobiles, toys. They love things. They're not afraid to steal and murder to get things. They love all things, even ones that belong to the poor—bare cupboards and worn-out shoes. They want to fill up huge warehouses— at the Community they're already emptying the synagogues so they can store everything there. They want to look at things, to touch fabrics, to plunge their hands into gold, to smell good soap and listen to the rustle of silk. A lot of people will die because *they* like things so much."

"Rich people love things, too," I said, "but things didn't help them a bit. Things can't talk, and it's useless to call on them to help. They're crazy if they believe in things. They won't help them at all when they have to be thrown away on the run."

"They're not running," said one of the group of mourners.

"But they will run," I said. "People who cling to things will have to lose. We lost too when we wanted to save our furniture."

"That's neither here nor there," said Robert. "My advice to you is to get some tin bowls and rucksacks ready and sew some bags."

So now traveling with fifty kilos to an unknown destination was the order of the day. Nobody wanted to guess what happened at the end of this journey. They tried to talk about preparations instead—money sewn into the linings of jackets, jars of lard disguised as marmalade, fake toothpaste tubes with money hidden in them. There were also things that would now be more valuable than phonographs, rugs, or refrigerators used to be. Fights would erupt over them; people would try to hide them, would covet pencils and cloves of garlic. These new objects would become their focus. They would love and protect them the way they had once loved and protected pianos and gold earrings.

"I'm not going to bother about anything," I said. "I'm not going to drag along fifty kilos to God knows what places and then throw them into some ditch. I'm not going to prepare any luggage for them, because you never know if they'll let you keep it. They're much too greedy, and they'll want a frying pan as much as they do a typewriter."

"Do as you like," somebody said. "But remember, no one will give you or lend you anything, not even a comb or a crust of bread."

"After the first transport of rich people there'll be several weeks of peace before they organize things in a new way. First there'll be registration, and then transports will begin again. A lot of people will be needed for that work, and those who do it will be the last to go."

"Body snatchers and gravediggers," I said.

"You won't be one of them. Don't envy them," Robert said sadly. "They'll be people with connections, cousins and relatives. You'll never be among them. I've already tried, but all the jobs have been taken, even polishing the floors in the stolen apartments."

I joined the circle of mourners, too. There was no need for me to tear my clothes or put ashes on my head; all of us were already gray as ash. Like the others, I stared at the dusty floor of the chapel. I could see a line of people being taken to the train, marching in the mud. I saw how they walked, then stopped, to the sound of stomping metal-tipped boots. I heard the squeak of unoiled handcarts and the quiet sobbing and crying. They crouched in the dust I was staring at. Pavel was there in the transport of rich people. He used to be very rich; he owned real estate. They would want him to die soon.

I saw that the line through the dust was meandering. I knew

that the road did not lead directly to death, that there were many stops, full of pain and humiliation. The march continued along this road, marking time at various stops.

I longed for someone to stroke my lowered head. I imagined a woman's hand, Ruzena's hand, hardened by work but still light and smooth. I tore my eyes away from the dust and raised my head. I looked around me and smiled at the mourning trees, dripping with water, and at the marble tombstones with droplets of water caught in the gilded inscriptions.

"I heard a while ago," I said, "that they wanted to sink ships. Maybe that would be a better way to die than after a long train ride through foreign flatlands. I heard they don't have much of an understanding of railroads; it's bound to be a terrible trip. But they don't have much understanding of the sea either. They don't even want to venture out to sea."

The man sitting next to Robert suddenly jumped up and began to shout, "I've had enough! Stop talking about death. I can't stand it any longer—I'll kill myself." We were all silent and stared into the dust.

The day dragged on. No one even thought of leaving early. I could see they were more afraid now that the transports had begun.

I set off to see Pavel. His place was on my way home, but of course everything was on my way home since I lived at the other end of the city. Pavel now lived in the Old Town. I knew his new address, but I had never visited him. I was afraid he would think I wanted something from him.

The house Pavel was living in was old and dark and full of recesses and corners. I walked up the worn stairs to the third floor slowly, with great effort, and stopped in front of an apartment door that had a card with several names on it and the number of times visitors were to ring for each. I looked for Pavel's name among them.

I rang the designated number of times and entered the hall as someone came out to open the door. It must have been Pavel, because I had rung the correct number of times, but I couldn't see his face. Soon I heard his voice, however. It was difficult going, so I let him lead me. We had to make our way through bureaus, baskets, suitcases, and all sorts of junk. The hall was full of things, and only a narrow path was left for people.

We entered a large, dark room, furnished with old, hand-carved furniture whose heavy frames seemed to be looking at us threateningly. Besides the furniture there were numerous baskets, suitcases, and boxes. We sat down at an oak table on uncomfortable high-backed chairs upholstered in leather stamped with a water-lily pattern.

"I'm leaving," said Pavel. "They've called us up. My wife and daughter are looking up friends to get the things we need for the transport. I'm sure you're tired, but I'm afraid I can't even offer you some tea. It's not our hour in the kitchen now."

"There's no need," I replied. "I only stopped by for a minute to say goodbye. You know, I have to be at home before eight o'clock."

"I'm glad I'm leaving," Pavel said, as if he hadn't even heard me. "They're punishing us and torturing us with one another. Five families are fighting over the gas range, space in the larder, who cleans the toilet. They're at each other all day. They cry and complain. It's hard to live among so many people."

"You won't be alone there either," I said. "A person can't be alone. Pavel, have you ever thought of disappearing and just not going?"

"I can't hide in the woods with a family. Anyway, there are no forests; there are only apartments, police registration, domicile cards, work cards, identification cards, household cards, and birth certificates. There's no other way but to become a number."

"What do you mean?"

"A number—hanging around your neck, attached to your suitcase, glued to your rucksack. Then I'll load myself with fifty kilos and go. Don't you want to take some things?"

"I don't want any things. I'm glad I no longer have any."

"I can't give you any money, but you could sell something."

"I don't want to sell anything. I get something for going to the cemetery; it's enough."

"I told André that we're going by train and she's looking forward to the trip. I told her she'll see trees, a big sky, and animals."

"That's good. I always looked forward to taking the train when I was little."

"Look at that wallpaper. It has flowers on it, tulips, roses, and strawberry leaves. They put flowers on everything—on plates, chairs, even on toilet bowls. They had paper flowers, with leaves made of oilcloth, in vases. But they never touched real flowers. They never lay in a field or ran along paths in the rain. We used to ride motorcycles and ski. André looks forward to real flowers."

"Goodbye, Pavel. I have to go. Maybe a messenger with a yellow slip of paper is already waiting for me by my gate. Perhaps we'll meet again soon."

"Nobody will ever meet anybody again, but that's not important."

I walked down the stairs slowly. The staircase was poorly lit. I had to grope along, stepping into the darkness. But downstairs, at the entrance to the house, there was a light. The janitor's wife was standing there trying to get a look at me. She opened the door to her basement apartment so that the light hit me directly in the face. She gave me a long, careful look that followed me as I closed the front door behind me.

"No one is allowed to carry anything away from the apartment of the deceased," I said to myself. "The ravens are croaking and the vultures are flying in. A hyena always follows the tiger. But sometimes the hyena arrives before the tiger."

"Manicka, how about going to the movies?" a young man asked a girl. I stood in front of them on the streetcar. It wasn't full and I could have sat down, but I preferred to stand because it meant I wouldn't have to get up if anybody got on. I didn't like getting up with the whole streetcar staring at me.

"They're showing a great movie. Lojza saw it and said it was sensational."

"Let's go, then."

"And afterward we could go to a wine cellar. They let you have two glasses of wine and everything's without ration cards, but only for friends—you know."

They laughed and talked about movies and good food, and then Manicka said, "And when will we get married? I can't stand all this talk anymore. Our whole class is already married. I'm the only one left. Do you want them to send me into forced labor? If you don't want to marry me there are plenty who will."

"We don't have an apartment. I rent a room and you live with your parents."

"There'll be plenty of apartments. Haven't you heard about those transports?"

"But only they will get those apartments. Even if I joined the Vlajka, they wouldn't give me an apartment. Or they'd give me some hole full of bedbugs."

"I've already told you—either you marry me or I'll marry someone else, but I won't go to work," cried Manicka.

I didn't want to listen to their quarrel, so I went to stand on the platform.

"People know that transports are being organized," I told myself. "Maybe they've sometimes run into them or they've seen flashlights as they've left wine cellars. They hear the commands and the stomping of metal-tipped boots and the heavy, tired steps of people sagging under heavy burdens."

"We'll eat, Tomas," I said when I got home. "We'll fry some slices of old bread in margarine. That's food too. Some people are dying for margarine, and others are heading toward death through the darkness. And below us is the city. People go to the movies and watch human lives entwine and untangle so happily and cleverly—in a way no one can in real life. And they also have arguments because they can't find an apartment and will have to go to work in a foreign country."

Tomas and I ate together and then I told him, "Wait for me. I'm only going to get warm. I'll bring back some bones for you. It's such an amusing game to tear off my star and go visit Materna. It's a good game and a worthwhile one, because I only have one life, and it's unique, while you have nine lives. But I don't really believe that. What would you be doing with nine lives?"

People were sitting around at Materna's place. It was warm, and Materna's mother gave me some tea and a filled bun. I drank the hot tea and ate my bun. The talk was about the war. The war was something far away; it seemed to me I was sitting in the dark and watching a film. People were shooting at one another in it and running across a field. They were lying in ditches, machine guns were barking, and cannons thundered. Towns were burning and flags were flying above destroyed buildings. There were many towns and many flags. They used to hang in our city too, even though it wasn't in ruins, and there used to be a lot of loud music. But I saw only the hands of the clock moving forward slowly. I heard it ticking, regular and relentless.

"What's the matter with you, Josef?" asked Materna. "Are you staring at the floor again?"

"Look at it this way, Franta. People are angry—you have to say that much for them—but nobody wants to put his own neck on the block, definitely not. For instance . . ."

Now they were talking about factories, sabotage, the factory guards, and informers.

"Well, what's the matter with you?" repeated Materna.

"Nothing," I said. "Transports are leaving."

"What's that?"

"They call people up, take away their documents, and hang numbers around their necks. They take them somewhere east."

"Oh, I know. I was at the Radio Mart the other day, and as I was walking along the sidewalk I bumped into a policeman. He said to me, 'Cross to the other side. You're not allowed to walk here.' I said to him, 'So a person can't even walk along the sidewalk when he's going home from work?' But I was already hurrying away because he was shouting after me that he would show me what I could and couldn't do. So I think they're using the Radio Mart in connection with these transports."

"Yes," I said, "there are wooden pavilions, just nailed-together boards really. There's no heating because the place would catch fire. They've brought straw there from the Community. They say they're organizing a circus."

"And you don't feel like joining the circus."

"No, I don't."

I imagined how we would lie pressed against one another on the straw, how we would shiver from the cold and, even more, from fear—because now we would be completely in their power. I sat close to the stove, drinking hot tea and chewing my marmalade-filled bun. I felt good because of the warmth and because I was among people who spoke about the war and about factory work. I felt good even though I continued to hear the ticking of the clock, regular and relentless.

"Does that mean you'll pack up your belongings and go east?"

"When my turn comes."

"Lucky you're pretty far along in the alphabet."

"They don't care too much about the alphabet. They have their own alphabet. I don't know how they invented it. Or maybe they want to play at fishing and throw their nets into the water. I can't even begin to calculate when my time will come. I have to wait until they call me up and that could be tomorrow or in a year. There are still plenty of people."

"And when they do call you up, will you go?"

"I will. I can't imagine doing anything else."

"Wait, then. Something will happen."

Materna began talking to his friends again. These were good words to hear—"something will happen"—and they warmed me pleasantly. I knew that it was nonsense, that no one could

help me, but it was a glimmer of hope, just a tiny glimmer
that a person could cling to. I knew because long ago I had
read, in a book that I was devouring quickly so my uncle
wouldn't catch me at it, that a man descended into a cave
where he met an octopus and struggled with it until he overcame it; it was a good novel and I was very scared for the
hero. Anyway, I had never seen an octopus, only in the picture
that illustrated the scene in the book. I knew that the man had
to win. I wanted him to and I hoped he would. It was very
pleasant to read the book and believe in victory. "Something
will happen," I repeated to myself. "Maybe it will take a long
time before they call me, and until then I can eat, read, sleep,
smoke, and cling to that little glimmer of hope."

I got some scraps of food for Tomas. They weren't very
good, but no one could accuse Tomas of being choosy.

14

I knew all about the circus. My aunt and uncle had taken me
to the circus several times. They probably thought that it was
the right thing to do or that it was their obligation. Or perhaps
it was just an excuse so that they themselves could go. I admired
the ushers' uniforms and watched the circus riders and tightrope walkers spellbound. During the intermissions I looked
at the exotic animals, animals I didn't know. They looked
wretched and sad. I never thought about it, though, because
they were always forced out into the arena (I thought they
went there by themselves), and then everything was different;
they performed only for me. They walked, danced, jumped,
and did all sorts of tricks under the artificial lights, to the
sound of brassy music and the cries of the tamers. I never
thought it was a difficult thing to be an animal in the circus,

since I was sitting on a wooden bench with a canvas canopy above me. I looked at the sawdust that covered the floor and at the braziers full of red-hot coals. When I watched the seals pushing a ball with their snouts I didn't know it was a bad thing to be an animal in the circus. It never occurred to me that it was something seals did not usually do. I had also never seen a dog walk on two feet, with a little hunting cap on his head and a gun over his shoulder. But it was amusing to look at him as he walked around the circus arena. The circus was a wonderful, exciting place, where things happened that I had never seen. It was thrilling to sit comfortably on the wooden bench and watch the acrobats.

But when I myself was to perform in the circus, I didn't like to remember the sound of the whip and the cries of the tamers. I didn't want to remember the horses running around and around or the dog jumping through a large hoop covered with paper. I wouldn't lift my head to look at the ropes under the ceiling when I myself had to walk a tightrope and look down at the gaping faces.

I didn't want to enter the circus with the shaved head of a clown and let myself be kicked in the behind. All of a sudden I knew an awful lot about the circus when I was on the other side of the railing.

I didn't think they could force Tomas or Materna to join the circus unless the two of them wanted to, but I knew they could force me as soon as they hung a number around my neck.

I had to pass by the Radio Mart and I saw a lot from the streetcar I was standing in while the others sat. I even saw a little of the compound over the fence. I also saw the gate that people with numbers hanging around their necks passed through, bent over under the weight of their huge rucksacks. I saw the policeman standing by the gate, his feet wide apart. And I heard the silence when the streetcar passed the Radio Mart. Yes, I heard the silence even though the streetcar was rumbling and the wheels of the car rattled on the track. The same silence showed on the faces of the people tensely watching a somersault on the ropes under the ceiling of the circus tent. I remember the silent, frozen expressions of horror.

The number of people at the cemetery began to decrease. Some of them said goodbye and some simply disappeared. Nothing changed, except that it grew colder.

We sat around the hot stove. We weren't cold, because there was always enough wood at the cemetery. We also burned the church pews when we were too lazy to cut down trees. The pews were old and burned very well. I saw how the value of things had changed when Robert traded a small Persian rug for two strings of garlic. I heard how on the way east jewelry was traded for lemons. It was good to have a sleeping bag, a metal bowl for food, a long-sleeved sweater, ski boots, vitamin pills, a pocket knife with various instruments, a razor, and a supply of razor blades. And one's luggage should be prepared in advance, ready any time of day or night, because sometimes transports were called up suddenly, so that people didn't have time to make preparations and had to leave all their belongings in their homes.

I was standing in front of the villa gate once more, and snow was falling again. I already knew the whole ceremony and there was no need to provide me with information. It was very quiet inside the house even though this time children were there also. Whole families were being registered. Chains of questionnaires had bound them together, made them inseparable, even families whose members hated one another. But I also saw an old husband and wife supporting each other. It was not a happy group. Everybody was thrown together to endure the long, anxious wait. Entire families stood there, holding in their hands papers whose meaning they didn't understand. Their property was listed on these papers, but they were no longer interested in property, which was passing, somewhere, into the hands of foreigners. Tangible property consisted of rucksacks, sleeping bags, strings of garlic, and lard inserted into toothpaste tubes. I stood among families, and I too had papers in my hand. Everyone had to have papers, even if he had no property. But at least I had a sleeping bag and a metal bowl. I had had these things for a long time and didn't have to struggle to get them. Yes, I was better off than the others because I was alone—and, besides, I had, hidden away, a glimmer of hope.

I stood in line at the villa all morning, but I had to leave at noon and kill time for several hours because we weren't allowed on the grounds at lunchtime. It had stopped snowing but was raining instead. The streets were covered with a thin layer of mud. I left with the man who had stood in front of me in line. He was an older, robust man with a wind-whipped face.

"Are you from out of town too, so you can't go home these few hours?" he asked me as we left.

"I live some distance away, at the other end of town," I said. "I wouldn't know what to do at home. It's cold there and there would be no time to start the stove."

"Come with me. Maybe we'll find a place where we can get a bite to eat."

But in this section of the city all the restaurants were off-limits for us. We couldn't go into a house either, because there were only carefully locked and guarded villas. And if we went a little farther, to the section of the city with apartment houses, those would be *their* houses and they might set a policeman on us.

We saw a brickyard in the distance.

"Can't we go to the brickyard?" asked the man from out of town.

"Maybe," I said. "I never read anything about brickyards in any public notice. But I didn't read them all, so I can't guarantee anything."

"Only beggars and tramps stay in brickyards. Why would they turn us in?"

"Search parties go there too, but I don't think anybody will go at noon, when everybody is away and the police are having lunch."

We were cold and the rain kept falling. We went to the

brickyard. It wasn't far. We didn't see anybody. Maybe its inhabitants were off somewhere begging or were hiding inside. We sat on pieces of lumber and the man from out of town offered me some bread with lard. We sat in silence for a time, eating. Then the man from out of town said, "You're better off in the city."

"Why?" I said. It was ridiculous to argue about who was better off, but it made more sense than talking about the villa and waiting for a transport. "Out in the country it's easier to find something to eat. And the air is better. They can't take that away from you."

"Why should they take the air away from us? That's not what they want. They're only interested in property. They came to look at my accounts. I said, 'That's all right. They're nothing. Take them.' I mean, what would I do with accounting books in times like these? But when they took Bruna away, I cried. I reared her with my own hands, you know. I got her when she was still a foal. And when I think that someone will be beating her with a whip . . ."

"Don't worry. They're not bad to animals. They even have laws prohibiting cruelty to animals. They can't be cruel to animals and people at the same time. That would be too complicated."

"To come back to Bruna, you may not believe it, but she really cried. You don't believe me?"

"I believe you. If you told me the stones in your courtyard cried, I would believe you."

"The bread you're eating, that's still from flour ground at my mill. You know, I had a flour mill. It was a family business. We had land too, a nice piece of land. And then they moved all of us who lived in the district into an abandoned mansion. There were lots of families, and everybody argued with everyone else. We lived there like in a prison. They watched every step we took. But that's not the worst of it; you got used to that. During the whole time I was there I didn't get a wink of sleep. You know how it is in a flour mill—all night something is clapping, but that's still not the worst of it. What I missed the most was the mill wheel and the sound of water splashing from the channel. You in the cities can at least walk the streets."

"That won't last much longer, and anyway, there isn't much of a choice." I was no longer in a mood to argue. I saw a village mill. It was nice to lie by a millstream and look at the water flowing into the channel. It was pleasant to listen to the clapping of a mill.

We still had time, but we sat in silence. Then we got up and went back to the villa.

We waited in a long line again, watched over by a policeman. We didn't talk to each other. We had been ordered to be quiet; we even had to walk on tiptoe. In a large room we once again had to answer questions about jewelry, mortgages, gold, stocks, and bonds. The questions were asked quietly, and the answers were quiet too. When the ceremony was over and I was back out in the courtyard, I knew that hell must also be a quiet place. Certainly sinners don't moan there, because that would mean that their pain was not very great. Certainly the horse Bruna cried when she was separated from her master—she didn't like an alien harness. Perhaps she even cried out, as if spurred in the groin, even if her master hadn't mentioned it.

·I don't know what Bruna would have done if she had had to stand for so many hours. Even though we moved through rustling papers and rows of digits, even though we saw ourselves turned into numbers, we were not allowed to weep, writhe in pain, or beat our heads; we were not allowed to sing psalms or play funeral marches.

I was sitting at the cemetery again, by the warm stove. People had left or disappeared. Some people poisoned themselves or jumped from high buildings. They also hanged themselves or drowned in the river. But that did not alter any accounts; one number was simply replaced by another. People had numbers and transports had numbers. In wooden huts numbers froze to death on the straw. The strange thing was that numbers ate—food was brought to them at the Radio Mart from the Community. The food bearers moved about the Radio Mart anxiously: sometimes they too were changed into numbers, when the required total in the account books was not large enough. But enough people were found for all the work. Even watchmen to guard the numbers were found, even maintenance men to collect trash and change the straw that the numbers slept on. There were people to wheel the sick in wheelchairs; there were people who acted as search dogs, looking for those who disappeared and helping to intimidate those who resisted.

The gladiators entered the arena with heavy footsteps and no greeting. The name had been given to them officially. They had special places where they gathered and their own commanders; they were the only ones who received special rations, even meat, because they had to be strong in order to play the role of gladiator in the circus. It was good to be a gladiator, but it was a difficult skill, requiring great strength. It was good to be a gladiator, but one had to have strong legs and a hard heart to be able to stay in the circus until the last performance.

I was helping my aunt and uncle pack their luggage. They had sent a message asking me to come, but then my uncle said, "My blood will be on your head, you ingrate. You got us into this. Couldn't you have pity for two old people? Couldn't you get us out and send someone else in place of us?"

"You were always a bad one, spoiled and envious. If Klara had lived to see this day . . ." said my aunt.

"I work at the cemetery," I said. "In the summer we plant vegetables and in the fall we rake leaves. In the winter we sit in the chapel by the stove and drink linden tea."

"There, you see. That's the kind of work you got yourself and yet you couldn't get anything for your own uncle? All you're interested in is saving your own skin, but your own uncle, who fed and clothed you and took care of you when you were sick, he can be left to die, can't he?" wept my aunt.

I bent my head and looked about the room. Things were scattered around the whole house. I saw a kind of sleeping bag made of quickly sewn together rags. Then I saw worn-out, discarded things, chosen from piles of junk and set aside to be put into bags and rucksacks. They were senseless things: rusty cookie cutters, an old inkwell with a broken lid, a knife without a handle, brass buttons and wooden skewers. Everything was useless, worthless—objects that my aunt and uncle had kept in various corners of the house. I knew many of these objects from my childhood. They were useless and broken even then, and now I was surprised to see them again after so many years, when they were to be taken east.

"What are you taking along?" I said. "These things won't be of any use to you. Where do you have food, warm underwear, bowls for eating, work shoes, and good socks?"

"That's none of your business, you hooligan, you murderer!" my uncle began to scream at me. "As if it wasn't enough that you got us into the transport. Now you want to deprive us of our property?"

"I'm not interested in your things. I'm only telling you you should take your best clothes and underwear so that they'll last. It doesn't matter what you leave here because it will be taken away anyway."

"And that's where you're mistaken," cried my uncle. "They won't get anything. I'll hide everything that's valuable with good people, but I won't tell you their address. You would take it from them."

"I've already told you. I don't want your things. I don't want any things at all. I'll have to go with a transport anyway, so what would I want with a lot of junk?"

My aunt and uncle looked at each other with scorn on their faces. It was obvious to them that I wanted their property, that I was pretending, because I had arranged everything, I had a job that protected me. There was no use trying to persuade them not to hide things with people who were weeping over their fate. I knew that jackals were roaming the desert and that they wept bitter tears. "How sorry we are that people are dying of thirst and exhaustion by the sides of the caravan routes! We curse the sun that dried out their throats; we curse the thieves who wait behind the dunes and kill stragglers. We are the merciful funeral brotherhood, but we don't have picks or shovels to dig graves with. Nor do we have water to wash the deceased, but we can perform the last rites. We can perform a last great service—to gnaw their bones, to make them nice and white, so the sun can dry them." The jackals are polite and kind. They know how to feel sorry and how to weep. They know many beautiful words. They also promise an early return and good luck. No, I have never been friendly with jackals. I was glad they did not seek my company.

"Why aren't you coming with us?" grumbled my uncle. "How come you got out of this when whole families are going?"

"You told me I was not to mention that I was related to you, because I have Tomas the cat illegally. You were afraid you would be responsible for me."

"You got us into this anyway, you and your cat."

I didn't answer. There was no sense answering his reproaches, which my uncle probably didn't even believe, but he had to blame someone and have someone to place the guilt on.

"I want you to know I'll be back in two months. The lady we are leaving all our bedding with told us that within two months it will all be over, and she always has good information—not like you, who are always trying to scare us."

"All right, if you believe it. But why don't you at least take some food with you?"

"That would be a smart thing to do. Then we would have to share with the others. This way the others will have to share with us."

"Can I go home now?" I said. "It's almost eight o'clock. I'll come to help you when you leave. I'll go with you to the Radio Mart."

They had to leave on a Sunday and that wasn't good, because none of us was allowed to travel by streetcar on Sundays. People had to come on foot from all sections of the city with their rucksacks and heavy luggage.

I set out to my uncle's. I would have had to walk across the whole city, so I only walked down the hill and waited there for a streetcar and then covered my star with my briefcase. I helped my aunt and uncle put on their two heavy rucksacks and I myself took their bulky sack over my shoulder. My aunt and uncle had numbers hung around their necks and they walked stooped under their heavy loads. On the outside of her rucksack my aunt had tied a decorative cake pan. I knew the form well; I would always scrape out what was left after she turned a cake out. I remembered how the cakes smelled of lemon peel. I wished I could sit on a stool in the kitchen again and wait for my aunt to turn the cake out on a wooden board. The pan was now swinging on the rucksack. It wasn't fastened properly, so that it kept hitting her in the back. I felt sorry for my aunt and uncle as they lumbered through the streets with numbers around their necks, in run-down shoes and threadbare clothes.

"We'll definitely return within two months. That lady told us so again today."

They no longer blamed me; they only wept quietly to themselves. I too told them they would certainly return in two months. What else could I tell them? I didn't tell them about the circus, although I had a few moments of guilt for not preparing them. But they would not have believed me. Perhaps it was a good thing they did not know what role they had been given in the circus. Perhaps it was better that they didn't know about the straw and the cold in the wooden pavilions.

As we approached the Radio Mart we met streams of people. We saw sick people in wheelchairs and children hung with various pieces of luggage. They too had stars on their coats, and the numbers around their necks swung as they walked. We walked in the road because there were so many of us, and pedestrians looked at us from the sidewalks. We took no notice of them. We didn't know if they felt sorry for us or if they were laughing at us. But doubtless we no longer existed for them, because they wished us not to exist so they did not have to look at us, because they passed by us quickly and mostly with their faces turned away, because it was imperative to forget everything quickly and never see anything.

I saw several people I knew in the crowd, but I didn't want to greet them. They would have had to notice that I didn't have a number around my neck and therefore would not be entering the gate with them. Perhaps they would have envied me. There was no reason I could give, nor could I think of words of consolation. In any case, they would not have listened to consolation. Perhaps they would not even have recognized me, because their eyes already had a glassy film. All they saw was the open gate and the policeman in front of it, standing with his feet apart.

"Goodbye," I said to my aunt and uncle as we approached the gate and I gave them their bag. I could not go up to the gate, because the policeman would catch a person accompanying others and throw him in among them even if the person didn't have a number around his neck. "Come back soon and in good health."

"Goodbye, Josef," said my uncle. "You're not angry at me for all the things I said to you, are you?"

"Goodbye, Josef." My aunt kissed me. "Maybe at least you will survive this."

"We will all survive and we'll all meet again. Everything will be beautiful again when we meet," I said.

I stood on the sidewalk and watched as they entered the gate with heavy steps, but I couldn't watch for long, because policemen were guarding the sidewalks.

I walked home slowly and kept meeting people loaded down with rucksacks, with numbers around their necks. I heard the high-pitched sound of pipes and the low rumble of drums. I thought that Death was marching up front, accompanied by pipers and drummers, the way she is accustomed to. From a nearby park a unit of their army emerged, headed by a man with a horse's tail attached to a baton.

15

The winter that year was mild, but it didn't help the people in the circus much. They still froze on the straw in the wooden pavilions. Some of the transports were sent east, while others went to a fortress town where a menagerie had been set up. A person was very lucky to become an animal assigned to this menagerie, but only a few people managed to stay in the fortress town. The rest were sent to the east. That town too had its circus; there too one had to walk a tightrope without a safety net and jump over high hurdles.

But it was a town that lay in the middle of the country. A river flowed through it and meadows were close by. The wind would bring the fragrance of apricots in bloom; birds perched on telephone poles. It was a good thing to live in the town even though it was a menagerie behind barbed wire. It was a good thing to enter with hope, since there was the possibility that some would stay in the town, if only to tend the dead. News came from the town. It crossed the barbed wire guarded by police, in the bags of trainmen or the baskets of market women. It was said that money had not lost its power in this town, that it even won out over hunger and death. But that required large sums, which none of us had. It was also said that things had their value in the town, that one could stand up to the cold and to sickness with them. It was said that relations and friendships meant a great deal in the town. There were stories about letters of recommendation, about sons who were able to save their fathers, about cousins who were given jobs as food carriers or stable hands. Those who had neither money nor things nor relatives with luck could stay on in the town as draft horses. Many draft horses were required, and they received little food. They had to drag heavy loads, sowing and harvesting machines, moving vans and barrels. Because in this menagerie any animals other than people were forbidden.

We would talk about the fortress town as we sat by the stove. It had its own stamp, on which it was pictured among linden trees; it even had its own money, portraying the creator of the Ten Commandments. The Ten Commandments now applied only to animals, but animals couldn't live their lives in accordance with them. They were given to them only in a picture, where they were held by a man with a long beard, who had long ago led his nation through the desert.

Most of the people at the cemetery were new. Those who had left in transports were replaced by others. There was no difference; the stove was the same; you couldn't see the faces of people as they stared into the dust, through which the same roads led. The fact that Robert had disappeared and now lived in the fortress town didn't matter much. Someone else was always around who knew a lot of news. There was the former owner of a fabric shop who told us about a miracle. It was now possible for miracles to happen, when people took on the form and image of animals, when biblical predators came out of hiding and millstones could sweat blood. Comets could be harbingers of the plague and prophecies could be read as instructions for living through the next few days. Thus it happened that a paralyzed old man was brought to the Radio Mart; for the past twenty years he had spent his days in a wheelchair and his nights in bed. It was difficult now to force such a person to play the role assigned to him. First of all his head had to be shaved; otherwise he could not perform in the circus. It was forbidden for one to be shaved in the stall where people slept. Everyone had to go to the barbershop, which was in a special pavilion. He had to cross a large compound, where onlookers could enjoy his jerky, difficult progress. But this particular paralyzed man didn't want to hop or crawl forward; he didn't want to dance and throw his hands about. He sat on a chair, as he had done for the last twenty years. Thus the barber was forced to report this disobedience to the policeman on duty. The policeman set out for the stall where the paralyzed man sat (he no longer had his wheelchair; he sat on a stool). He ordered him to get up and walk, but the order was not obeyed. So he shot him in the ear and repeated the order. And then a real miracle occurred. The paralyzed man got up for the first time in twenty years and took a few steps. Then he fell down on the straw and died. Not even another shot from a revolver could bring him to life again.

I had no reason not to believe that this miracle had happened, because the former fabric-shop owner was the barber who had been forced to call the policeman. The shop owner was punished by having his own head shaved and he had to participate in several other circus acts, but he was lucky because at the time there were a great many numbers and he did not have to leave for the east. It was not pleasant walking in the cold with a shaved head, but the affair helped him rid himself of the barber job.

I sat on a stool next to the stove and thought about the miracle. At one time we all dreamed of miracles and now we didn't like it when they occurred. We would have preferred to live calmly and simply, instead of on the edge of our seats. So we didn't talk about the miracle; instead we talked about normal things close at hand, about an ointment against lice and about vitamin tablets. Some people also talked about suicides and arrests, but these too were ordinary things. And then we also had arguments about whether all this would be over in two months.

I walked to the streetcar station with my eyes to the ground. There was no sense walking with a raised head; one needed to get used to carrying a load.

An elderly lady stopped me. "Do you happen to know Mrs. Bejkovska?" she asked.

"No, I don't," I replied.

"She was a very nice person. She's in that town now where your people are."

"Yes," I said. "Goodbye, lady. They'll arrest you."

"Jesus Christ is there also, isn't he? He was one of your people, wasn't he?"

"Yes," I said. "Maybe he's there."

"That's good. I knew he would be there. Thank you very much for the news."

"You're welcome," I said.

"When you get there, tell him I pray to him. Please tell him my name is Manakova and my husband works for the post office."

"I'll tell him," I said. "Only I'm afraid I won't catch him there."

"I'm sure you'll meet him. Perhaps he'll be there secretly. I'll pray for you. What's your first name?"

"Josef," I said.

I didn't want to sit at home so I went to see Materna. I went to see him often now, since the cold had set in. I didn't have to take my star off, because the nights were dark and I took paths that ran behind the houses. The Maternas had become used to my coming and also to the fact that I did not talk much. I was content sitting and listening; I was content because it was warm at Materna's and I didn't have to light the stove at home. This time I told them about the miracle.

"A revolver—that's a good thing," said Materna. "You don't know what brand it was?"

"I don't know," I said. "Probably their army brand. They always carry them."

"They have very good army revolvers," said Franta. "We could use some."

They began to talk about arms. I was quiet. I didn't understand arms.

"They haven't sent for you yet?" asked Materna after a while.

"Not yet," I said. "Maybe they put numbers into a hat and

draw them. Or they measure noses to calculate the numbers. Or maybe they look at the stars and study horoscopes. I don't know. Maybe they're crazy. Now they're going to kill animals."

"What animals?"

"Our animals. Any animal in our households has to be killed. It's a good thing they don't know about Tomas. I didn't register him."

"What crime could Tomas have committed?"

"I'm sure something would be found. He certainly breaks laws and regulations. He often goes out after eight o'clock and he walks through forbidden streets. He also doesn't abide by rationing regulations because he eats my bread and your leftovers. And he gets hold of mouse meat and the meat of songbirds even though he's not eligible for meat rations."

"They certainly have interesting things to worry about in this war of theirs," said Franta.

"They're very inventive," I said. "They don't mind the war at all."

Then everyone talked at length about the war and places on a map. Later I crept back to my room and slipped into my sleeping bag. Tomas was not at home. I didn't know what he would be looking for in the cold night, when all the mice were hidden away and the birds had migrated south.

I went to the cemetery one day. It was still winter, but spring was already approaching. The circus was continuing, with intermissions—some shorter, some longer. When an intermission was long, people would say that no more performances would be held and that all those who had not yet been called up would no longer have to go.

But that was a futile hope. The transports began again. Large moving vans took furniture and various objects to storage houses. Every morning groups left the Community with assigned tasks—some made lists of home furnishings, others took belongings away; still others cleaned houses and scrubbed and polished floors for the new tenants.

Groups left in the dark and came back after dark. Nothing

could interrupt their work—not freezing hands or ice-cold water or the weight of huge cupboards. Even objects got numbers; a broken wooden spoon received a number just as a pile carpet did. People went off to the east or to the fortress town, and after they had left, their things were taken from their homes to storage houses and from storage houses to other homes. It seemed that no one could stop this movement and its accompaniment—the swarming, the standing on streets, the squeaking of wheels, the cries and prayers. Orders were given from a great distance, secret orders that often contradicted each other. Sometimes they seemed nonsensical; people would look for a hidden meaning, and they usually found it. All these orders were carried out even though they seemed impossible. At times the work of a week was carried out in a single day and the work of a day in a single hour. People would work day and night without interruption and sometimes without food, because fear stalked their tables and Death marched ahead, to the sounds of pipes and drums. It was *their* music and the people adjusted their steps.

I was sitting on a stool when the former fabric-shop owner said, "The Roubiceks are all going."

"What's that?" I asked.

"Three weeks ago all the Kohns went, now all the Roubiceks. They're already making lists at the Community. What fun! A policeman yells 'Roubicek' and fifty people rush up. They certainly know how to think up amusements."

I knew they knew how to invent amusements so that each performance in the circus was different; suddenly I felt ill and heavyhearted and didn't want to talk to anyone. I sat on the stool all day and stared into the dust through which my own road led. The time had now come when I would have to hang a number around my neck and wait for the yellow letter to arrive with my exact place in the order. I always knew this hour was approaching, but I had kept casting it away to make it bob up and down and then spin like a top. The top was a wooden block from a game called Diabolo. It was a good game because how else could I have continued to wait, eat, sleep, and talk to people? I would have had to shout, weep, and beat my head against the wall, to writhe on the floor. I would have had to call on Death a thousand times a day to hurry up because I couldn't stand the constant uncertainty. I would have had to kindle the hope that I would make it to the fortress town and that there I would be given the uplifting task of sweeping the streets or at least might become a draft horse. I would have had to run about all day and beg someone to have mercy on me, knowing all along that it was no use, because I would never have found the person who could decide my fate. I would have had to pass through dozens of offices, and at each door I would have had to become a supplicant. They would have chased me away everywhere and I would never even have learned where the correct office was. But even if I had learned its whereabouts through some message or secret conversation I had overheard by chance, nothing would have come of it, because I would never have had the courage to enter that office without a letter of recommendation.

I did, however, have one shred of hope. Materna had said that we would see. Materna and his friends walked the streets with their heads high and they looked policemen in the eye. They drank tea and told one another jokes; they laughed and discussed brands of weapons too. They didn't cower, they didn't seek out back alleys, they didn't stand in streetcars or press themselves against the platform window. Could I go to them and ask them for help when I didn't belong among them, when I wasn't their equal in either my stride or my bearing? No, I could never rely on their help. I only took comfort from the hope; I nourished it for myself, for my pleasure.

I waited for the Community messenger. I knew that first a messenger would come to bring tidings, like a herald, and after him other people would come to make a list of my furniture and to give me instructions. Then still other people would come, whose task it would be to check my luggage, to see that it was properly packed and weighed. But the Community messenger did not arrive. I learned, though, that the names of those whose turn had come were announced in the sanctuary. I went to the sanctuary on the designated day.

It was a dark room that had to be lighted all day long. It was below street level, because out of the depths we must cry to thee, O Lord. It had only bare walls and pews; the place where the ark of the covenant had stood was empty. From that spot names were being announced, read from long pieces of paper. They were read by a man dressed in an ordinary manner and seated on a small table. People sat in the pews and listened to the names. They greeted each name with a sigh. The names were called out slowly so that everyone could hear.

The names dripped slowly. Out of the depths we cry to thee, O Lord, from the depths of pain and despair. The Abeles went, the Askenazys, the Bendas, slowly the Anns, Maries, and Hedvigs followed, the Elizabeths and Josefines, the Josefs, Roberts, Egons, Jans, and Pavels went by. Out of the depths I cry to thee, O Lord, because they have already passed, they have fallen into the darkness, and new names appear. It was impossible to tell whether those called were present—there were too many people in the sanctuary. There were no children there, though the names of children were also called. Women mingled with men in this sanctuary, even though a special gallery was set aside for them. There were bloodstains on the walls, which it was forbidden to whitewash. The blood on the walls of this sanctuary had never dried—sometimes it turned black while at other times, when things were very bad, it turned red again. Names continued to fall into the darkness and shadows.

The wall was covered by people's backs; nobody could see whether the wall was bloody. I stood by the wall because I couldn't find a seat in the pews. I was glad I had something to lean on. It was a good thing the wall with the bloodstains was behind me so I couldn't see them. I looked only at the man reading the names. The Roubiceks were still up ahead—

there were a number of stops—Kohn, Kraus, Kopecky, Langr, and Lederer. The names had to be read slowly so that there were no mistakes. One had to listen carefully for the addresses. There were many people with the same forenames and surnames; some were relatives and others strangers. There were also unusual names, for which it was not necessary to read the addresses slowly. I listened as the names changed into the words of the prayer for martyrs. They were only the names and addresses of ordinary city sections and streets, but they rose from the pulpit to fill the room all the way to the blackened traceries of the ceiling. I waited for my name. I waited a long time because my name was toward the end of the alphabet. Out of the depths we cry to thee, O Lord. The sheets of paper rustled as they were turned in the hands of the man reading, and the rustling sound of the turned sheets of paper changed into the rustling of leaves driven by the wind just before spring arrives. They rose up to the sky and fell to the ground again, far away. They were trampled into the mud and became mixed with soil and ash. The Poppers went, with the Porgeses, Prazaks; soon the Roubiceks would come. The first was Abraham Roubicek. I imagined him an old man, with a long gray beard, on crutches. I could see him dragging himself along on his crutches, lagging behind the others, urged on with kicks. I saw his sweating face bowed toward the ground. I saw him swallowing his curses, stumbling into a ditch, and I saw his tears fall on his beard. Abraham Roubicek fell into the darkness, along with his address, and behind him marched other Roubiceks, whose addresses were read according to the sections of Prague they lived in. Many Roubiceks were read and many Josefs; then the letter of the alphabet changed, and they read Salus, Stamic, Stein, and Steiner, and no other Roubicek appeared in the rustle of the pages. I took a deep breath and suddenly felt dizzy. I could no longer stand it in the sanctuary. I could no longer listen to the slow dripping of names. I repeated nonsense words to myself again: "kukureke," "tucivod," and "floor wax." I walked through a dark corridor to the street and suddenly I was blinded by the daylight and staggered. I would have fallen if someone hadn't caught me. It was a fairly high official of the Community whom I knew a little because the administration of the cemetery was under his jurisdiction and he sometimes came for inspection.

"I left with you," he said. "I was there too; my brother-in-law is among them. His name is Frantisek Roubicek."

"I . . . ," I stammered. "I wasn't among them, was I?"

"No, you're not. You're very lucky. It's incredible, unheard-of luck. An accident, one in a thousand. I saw those lists at the Community. All the Josef Roubiceks are there except you. You'll be the only Josef Roubicek in the whole city, though there may be some Josef Roubicek who is indispensable and will be the last to go. Believe me, you're very lucky—you don't even know how lucky. Now you have at least half a year, maybe even a year."

"But how did it happen?" I asked. "I don't understand."

"Well, you see, they took all the Roubiceks out of the file. They thought they took them all, but they missed your card. They won't look for a Roubicek for a long time. You'll stay in the card file until the final selection is made, when they'll go through the file card by card. But that won't happen until the very end."

I went out into the street. I wasn't careful and kept stepping in mud. Since everyone knew that the Roubiceks were going, I could do anything with the day, but I didn't know what to do with it. It had been given to me, along with many more days, if the Community official was right. I knew he was right, because Community officials knew a lot—they just didn't have the courage to tell ordinary people about it. They guarded their secrets because they were afraid they would be discovered and put into a transport themselves. I knew I mustn't tell anyone about my magical luck because many people were envious and wouldn't want me to have it. The other Roubiceks would surely not be happy if they knew that I was not among them by sheer accident; they would certainly want me to give up my name and take on the form and image of a number. The Roubiceks would never learn that one of them had been lost, that by mistake he had stayed behind in a file cabinet. Perhaps this Roubicek ducked as a hand reached for him or managed to fall to the bottom of the drawer, stayed underneath the other Roubiceks, and thus escaped notice. It was good to rise up from the depths of despair, from the blackened walls that had never been whitewashed because they were stained with blood. It was good to come out into the street, into the cloudy early spring day, and to breathe fresh air, clear of the irritating smoke of candles. It was good to walk out the gates of death, to rise up on the day of resurrection, to leave the depths for a high mountain, and to cry "Hallelujah" to the wind.

But I did not cry "Hallelujah," because I had come out of a sanctuary where they had read the names of men, women, and children—and at that moment all of them were preparing their shrouds and awaiting death. They had looked at me with empty eyes and had motioned me to join them. I didn't join their procession. There was infinite joy in not having to join them. I simply left the sanctuary, the valley of death, lit by flickering candles, for the muddy street. The man from the Community had said there would be no more Roubiceks. The Roubiceks would no longer walk, eat, sleep, make love to their wives if they had them. Only I, Josef Roubicek, would live for a time, perhaps half a year, perhaps a year, because someone had made a mistake in pulling the Roubiceks out of the file. I would never learn why I wasn't read among the others, yet this nonsensical error, unbelievable and impossible, had given me this day.

"Ruzena"—I spoke to her for the first time in a long while— "I must tell you that my life has been given to me though I was already on my way to the bottom of the abyss. A hand has caught me in midair and has cast me up on a high mountain, where I am standing now and telling you about it because I know that it will make you happy. I want you to be with me now as I walk through the street and step in mud, as I watch the ice flowing down the river, as I inhale the cold air and put my hands, in their torn gloves, into my pockets. These hands still belong to me. A great deal belongs to me because a miracle occurred as the Roubiceks entered the darkness in shrouds, with candles lighting their way, and I was left out in the street in the bad weather."

I was waking after a long illness and Ruzena was standing at my bedside. She had brought me a bunch of violets and she sat on the bed. "Ruzena, the doctors said I would not survive the operation. It was a difficult operation—almost no one survives it. The doctors said I had one chance in a hundred. Ruzena, it's good to be able to look at you."

"You're pale," said Ruzena. "You must take care of yourself. You're not over it yet."

"I won't die, Ruzena. We'll go somewhere out of the city and we'll lie in the grass. We'll go somewhere where there's a high hill, so that we can look down on the city, and I'll show you the hospital where I was dying when they took me for the operation."

"You mustn't talk so much," said Ruzena. "Lie still and sleep. You must get a lot of sleep and eat a lot so that you grow stronger."

"I will sleep, Ruzena, and I'll dream about you—how we're walking in thick grass and going up a hill. I'll show you chimneys rising from the bottom of the city; we'll watch smoke rising to the sky. I didn't die, Ruzena."

"I have to leave. You mustn't talk so much. You must be quiet because you've escaped death."

I walked along the street without knowing where I was going. I was talking to Ruzena and stepping in mud. My hands were freezing in my torn gloves, and when I wanted to shove them deeper into my pockets my right hand touched something cold. I remembered that I had an onion in my pocket: I had been given it the day before at the cemetery by the man who told me the Roubiceks were going. I knew now that I had no right to this onion, because I wasn't joining a transport. I tried to remember if I had heard any familiar names being read in the sanctuary, and finally I recalled the name of a man with whom I had spent a night on stand-by duty. Now I knew where I was going—to give him the onion.

16

I kept touching the onion until it was warm. I held my hand over it as I entered a dark apartment house and, with my other hand, rang the bell several times.

"It's nice of you to come to say goodbye to me," said the man. "A lot of people have been here and all of them wanted me to leave them something as a souvenir. There were also people who took things by themselves."

"I don't want anything," I said. "I've brought you something. It's a small thing, but I think it will come in handy. It's an onion."

"It's not going to come in handy, because I'm not leaving with any transport."

I didn't know what to say. Maybe he didn't want to go; maybe he wanted to run away, live under a false name, hide. But if that were the case he wouldn't have mentioned it. He didn't know me well enough to trust me. He certainly knew I would not turn him in, but he couldn't know if I was talkative. Such things had to be done secretly and with great care.

"Oh, so you don't have to go. They exempted you as an indispensable person."

There were such people, but they had to have a lot of friends at the highest levels of the Community. I didn't believe he was that type of influential person since he tended the furnace at the Community offices and gave orders to no one. It would be very difficult to consider such work indispensable.

"Oh, no," he said. "I'll kill myself. The silly thing is I can't get hold of any poison. There's a big demand for poison on the black market. I don't have enough money to afford it. I'll try to do it with gas, but that's difficult too because they often shut off the mains. I'm afraid I'll have to hang myself or jump in the river or cut my veins. But that goes wrong too sometimes. They might cut me down or pull me out of the river, or I won't be able to find an artery and the doctors will sew me up again. What would you advise?"

"I've never tried it," I said. "But take the onion. It'll be valuable even in the fortress town or in the east. Doctors say onions are very healthy."

"You don't believe me, but I'm serious. I don't want your onion."

"Don't be angry. I've heard a lot of people talk about suicide. I think about it too, but if the worst happened I probably wouldn't go through with it. If I had poison, yes. Somebody told me that with cyanide death is easy."

"Don't believe it. It's a nasty, ugly death."

"Look," I said, "maybe there's still hope. Not everyone will die. They say that some people are pretty well off even in the fortress town."

"I didn't think you would try to dissuade me and it's no use. I don't know if anyone told you—a lot of people know about it. My wife divorced me and joined them, but she still finds it a nuisance that I'm alive. They blame her for it. She sent me a message that it would be best if I committed suicide. I wouldn't mind that, but my daughter wants it too. They wrote to me that I'm a selfish bastard, that I never think of the family. But they didn't send me any poison."

"Maybe they don't want you to have an easy death. Maybe they want to punish you for your selfishness."

"Yes, that's probably true. People are very righteous now, and they like playing judge. But really, I want to give you something if you'll take it. How about a cigarette?"

"You'll need all the cigarettes you have when you make that decision."

"I have enough. Take at least three."

"I can't accept gifts from you," I said, "unless you take the onion. Maybe it will come in handy as a last meal. That would be a good trade for me."

"I'm not going to trade anything. You must admit I have the right to refuse. When I'm dying your onion will be no help to me. Eat it yourself if you stay alive."

"I can't do that. I only got it because people thought I would be in the transport. But they didn't call me up. I'm not on the list."

"So keep it. They'll call you up sometime."

I lit one of the cigarettes. It seemed to be made of grass, but it was thick and I wanted a cigarette badly. We sat in silence for a while.

"We lived quite happily," he said. "I worked for an international shipping company and we had enough money. We traveled abroad and to the seashore. I have a lot of albums full of photographs. They show us at the seashore; there are ones of us with lots of friends, standing in the water and throwing a ball. I didn't know it would end like this. And I'm not surprised at my wife. We lived well and now she wants to keep on living well. When we were getting a divorce she said she only wanted to save our money and property. Then she joined them and they let her keep everything. We had a house in the country and they let her keep that too. I can understand her wanting to keep our property. She was always a practical woman, and if now she thinks I should commit suicide, she must have good reasons. She wouldn't want it if it weren't necessary. Believe me—you don't know her. But what I can't understand is that my daughter wants it too. I always loved her and I never harmed her. She's had everything she's wanted ever since she was a little girl."

"Maybe she's ashamed of you," I said.

"Yes, that's probably it. She's ashamed of me. She goes out a lot and they probably laugh at her. I think she was always ashamed of me. She also didn't like my name, Robitschek."

"But you still shouldn't kill yourself. They can't force you to do it."

"No, it's been decided. I'll kill myself, but it all makes no sense. I lived just like other people lived. I had a home, we went to the theater and to the movies, we went abroad and we met people we had our pictures taken with on the beach. And suddenly I'm alone and have to kill myself. And the others keep on living just as we used to live. Of course they're a little worse off because there's a war going on, but afterward they'll go on living like before and only I have to die. Tell me, is there any sense in it?"

"I don't know," I said. "I keep thinking that too. Maybe I'll hit on something. Once I thought it was because we covet things too much. But the others covet them even more. So I really don't have an answer for you."

I carried my onion away again and warmed it with my hand. The joy I had felt earlier as I staggered through the streets had now disappeared. I walked again as I always did, with my head bowed. I looked about me once more, to see if danger was lurking anywhere.

I decided to go to the cemetery. It was warm there and it gave me a place to go.

But first I had to get something to eat. I didn't want to go to the tavern I had been to with Wiener some time ago. I hadn't been there since. But there was a place where I could have lunch, even if a lot of questionnaires had to be filled out first and I had to ask for permission in several offices. But I hoped I would get permission to eat if I gave the chief a cigarette.

The dining room was full of officials and clerks from the Community, eating a watery soup and potatoes cooked with vegetables. It was the only food the dining room could offer. The vegetables came from our cemetery. Each person had to carry his own food from a window, where it was given out. There were rough wooden tables covered with linoleum that nobody seemed to clean. But the food was warm and it was pleasant to sit on a wooden chair in safety and peace.

The clerks from the Community who were sitting at my table talked about transports and about packages sent to relatives in the fortress town. I wasn't interested in their conversation: I had no one in the fortress town. I read the newspaper that was posted in the dining room, the only newspaper I was allowed to read. It was the official Community circular, which had one page of announcements and another of death notices. It wasn't pleasant reading. I didn't know which page was more important. I couldn't find anything informative in the announcements, because they were all new prohibitions and threats addressed to people who hadn't yet dutifully given up their property. There was also an announcement threatening death to anyone who helped people in hiding and another announcement promising death to those who didn't come forward to be registered. The third announcement was mild; it explained how and when gas could be used and the punishments for those who exceeded their quotas. These were the only announcements that pertained to all the others too. The death notices didn't give the causes of death, but there was no need for that. The deaths of those who had gone in the transports were not noted, because they no longer had names. Only those who still lived in their homes could die with names. Perhaps it was a good thing to die in your home, because then your name was cited in the circular and your body was buried in the cemetery.

I couldn't stay in the dining room for long. Other guests were waiting for free places at the tables. I had read the whole circular anyway.

I left the dining room and saw people with stars come in carrying bundles of carefully pressed rags tied with string. I saw that none of the property of the dead was lost, that every rag could be used. I knew that *they* did everything with the care of diligent landlords, that they took good care of all their property, which until recently had warmed the bodies of the dead.

I got on a streetcar, pressed myself against the window of the front platform, and thought about an answer to the question asked by my friend Robitschek, whose name would make its way into the circular.

It still didn't make any sense, even if bundled rags were brought to the storage house to be transformed into military cloth. It made no sense that the outcome was death, even if the booty warmed the heart and soothed the soul. People could be robbed without being killed if the lust for things was so strong.

I thought about the victims. Plucked clean, people entered the circus with numbers around their necks. They were subjected to hardships. They were forced to jump, perform, and listen to the sound of a whip. What sort of martyrs could they be!

They didn't want to accept suffering, but it never occurred to them to struggle for a martyr's crown. They would be satisfied with plain noodles, run-down shoes, and patched clothes. They had burned the pews and would have burned the ark of the covenant if it had been available. They would walk on their heads if they were ordered to, and they would change their faith three times a week. They only wanted to live, and not long ago that had not been asking too much. But they had been selected to be sacrificed, to die for something, for a cause that wasn't their cause. I belonged with them and I too didn't really know what I was to die for. It would have been easier if I had known. I might have been proud of my death. I could have dressed it in a purple robe and accompanied it with songs or cries of farewell.

I was no longer surprised that people at the cemetery didn't want to listen to me. It no longer surprised me that they didn't want to find ways of escaping. They were watching an earthquake; they saw their houses destroyed and their property go up in flames. They were watching a flood as it swallowed the ground they were standing on. They were numbed by the endless waiting, by the waiting day after day to be called up. It was ridiculous to summon the dead to rise; they could not respond.

But their sacrifice and mine had to have some meaning. It was difficult to imagine that you could change people into animals merely by confiscating their personal documents and registering their property. Ludvik Porges died for reciting *Hamlet*, not because he had some tasty meat; others died for Beethoven, not for fine furs. Some people r.aved as they lay on the straw; others recited poems they had learned in school; still others studied English, and some stuffed cotton in their ears. It still made no sense even when they were reduced to animals.

I finally arrived at the cemetery and sat on a stool with the others. Nobody asked me about anything; no one spoke. After a while the former fabric-shop owner said, "You're lucky. You're not in the transport."

"Yes," I said. "I was in the sanctuary today."

"Don't worry," said the man sitting next to me. "Everyone's turn will come."

"I really don't understand," I said. "Why do we do everything for them? We call people up, print numbers, transport the sick, move everything to storage houses. It seems pretty clear that everyone doing those things ends up in a transport too."

"You know," said the former owner of a fabric shop, "when I was still in school I remember reading a book. It told about how a tyrant or a military commander captured some people, ordered them to dig graves, and then had them all murdered. I always asked myself why those people worked so hard when they knew they were going to be killed anyway. Now I know."

"If there were no hope," I said, "we would probably fight."

"And people always think there's hope, even when they're standing over an open grave," said the former owner of a fabric shop.

"Stop this talk," said the man sitting next to me. "It leads nowhere."

We started talking again about ordinary things and about food. We began to play cards. We could play cards that day

because we knew there wouldn't be inspections when transports were being organized. We pulled down the blackout
blinds and slapped the cards down hard on the table. It was
good to play cards when it was warm in the chapel and we
didn't have to worry that someone would barge in. I still had
the onion in the pocket of my overcoat. I remembered it as I
was taking some cards. I decided I would cut it into thin slices
and put it on bread. It was good, that onion, even if Tomas
probably would not want to eat it.

But I had not been able to save Robitschek with that onion.
Nor could I save myself. I sat by the round stove and tried to
warm my hands. Tomas lay under the stove. He had become
lazy and loved warmth. He had stopped wandering and was
always waiting for me when I came home from the cemetery.
He had even grown fat, and his coat was smooth, but it
couldn't have been because he had better food: I had nothing
for him but the scraps from the Maternas and bread. I couldn't
even give him blood, because I was never home when my
shopping hours came around. But I didn't seem to be hungry
and neither did Tomas. We probably got used to things, and
then, too, we lay still for long periods of time, not doing
anything, to save coal and to kill time.

I didn't feel like eating the onion. I kept thinking of Robitschek sitting on his chair with his head in one hand, running
his other hand up and down the green table cover. But it was
silly to think about Robitschek when all the other Roubiceks
were willingly going to the circus and to the east.

Suddenly it occurred to me that one Roubicek would not
be going. Not a Roubicek really but a number. And because
the numbers had to be correct, someone would have to go in
place of Robitschek, some other number. As soon as Robitschek killed himself he would have to be replaced by another
number. Because the dead Robitschek would no longer be a
number—in death he would change into a person and have
the right to be listed in the death notices.

It could easily be me who would cease to be Josef Roubicek
when Robitschek killed himself; for a moment I was full of

fear again, but no, it wouldn't be me who would go in his place. They had passed me over, and besides, there were surely alternates since they always assumed a few suicides, which were even rewarded with death notices.

And so it became clear to me that a person who killed himself or didn't go bore the guilt of pulling someone else down. Of course that other person wanted to live too; it wasn't right to take someone's life, but you could always say that person would have had to go anyway. If only one word did not exist.

That word was "hope." Digging their graves, they counted every minute separating them from death. As long as they held the handles of their shovels, as long as their fingers held a handle, as long as their fingers were freezing and the skin on their hands was raw, they were alive. I turned off the light, pulled up the blackout shade, opened the window, and looked out. It was very dark; not a single ray of light shone anywhere even though people were still up. The windows are dark and blind when a procession passes through the night, the stomp of metal-tipped boots accompanying the dragging footsteps of stooped marchers. People sit behind those windows, read books, put children to bed, and play cards. They drink and laugh too, tell one another jokes and listen to dance music from phonographs and radios.

I looked into the darkness. I knew that in my street, on the outskirts of the city, no procession would ever march by. There were no stars in the sky, but a fine rain was falling. I heard its fall as a quiet rustle, like the turning pages of a book. Perhaps it was a hand running along a table covered by a green cloth with a leaf design; perhaps it was the rustle of those leaves being touched that I heard. Perhaps Death too has a friendly, kind voice and perhaps she too caresses one's hair with her hard, callused hand.

My name had not been read in the sanctuary when the names of the others had fallen into the darkness and red stains had appeared on the wall. I rose from the depths to a high cliff to see the beauty of the city in the rain and mud.

I pulled down the blackout shade and turned on the light.

The onion was shining on the washstand that served as my table.

17

I rang the bell at an ordinary house. It was a run-down old house that had not been painted in a long time, but all the houses in that street were run-down. It looked like the other houses. One could easily picture that it was rented and imagine its tenants looking out the windows at the sad street. There was no sign or marker on the house, but I knew it was a hospital and that Robitschek was lying inside.

I had learned that his suicide attempt had been unsuccessful. He would probably have succeeded if he had had enough gas to inhale, but gas was scarce and had to be rationed. Robitschek might still have succeeded, even with the little gas available, if officials from the Community whose task it was to make lists of furniture and possessions had not barged into his apartment. They had the keys to the apartment, and that too contributed to Robitschek's lack of success, because he had hoped to die before a locksmith was found.

An attendant came to open the door for me. First he looked at my star and then said curtly, the way attendants usually do, "What do you want?"

"Is Robitschek here?"

"Which Roubicek?"

"No, Robitschek. You spell it and pronounce it that way."

"I'll look on the list," said the attendant.

"You don't have to look on the list. He's the person who poisoned himself with gas."

"There are a lot of people here who poisoned themselves with gas."

"They brought him here the day before yesterday," I said. "Community clerks found him."

"Hmm," said the attendant. "Of course. That was just before the transport. That's when they all poison themselves. We always prepare new beds when a transport is due. That's when we always have a lot of work."

I knew that he knew well enough which Robitschek I was talking about, and I knew that he knew which room he was lying in.

But some bureaucratic activity was required of him, so he carefully looked down a long list of names and then said tersely, "Room 35, on the third floor."

The third floor was the top floor. It certainly could not have been convenient to carry failed suicides up so far when there was no elevator in the building and the morgue was in the basement. But perhaps they were supposed to be near the roof, or perhaps ordinary patients weren't supposed to see them die. But Robitschek was alive, and there was no danger now that they would have to carry him down the steep stairs to the morgue.

I knocked and entered the room. It wasn't large. At one time it must have been part of an apartment—a pantry or a bathroom perhaps—an apartment that had long since disappeared into hospital smells and whitewashed walls. The beds were packed in, one next to the other, with no room for even a chair between them. I had to sit on the edge of the bed. Robitschek was pale, but he spoke quite easily.

"I had bad luck," he said. "They saved me. I'm damn unlucky. I shouldn't have tried gas. I should have known what would happen with those economy measures. But I didn't want to jump in water when it's still so cold and I didn't want to hang myself. I read somewhere that a hanged person sticks his tongue out and is all blue in the face."

"You're alive," I said. "It's good to be alive, isn't it?"

"No, you're quite wrong. It's not good. You know, the mistake I made was that I believed the public notice. Because according to it the gas is supposed to be on full blast at lunch-time, so that women can cook, but instead it wasn't. I'm afraid they're going to prosecute me for using too much gas; I went over my quota. That's in the public notice too."

"They can't prosecute you. You're only a number now. What can you take from a number, when it doesn't have documents or property?"

"You're right. You've made me feel good about that. But that isn't my only bad luck. The worst of it is that now I can't kill myself. They watch me here. They're responsible for me, for putting me back in order for the transport. I can't get out of here to go home or anywhere else. They're going to keep me here until the next transport. They took my clothes away too, so I can't even go out on the street."

"Look," I said. "You don't have to commit suicide. I'm telling you—there's hope."

"I don't want your onion or your hope. My wife was here yesterday. They didn't want to let her in, because they had just pulled me through the worst and I was still unconscious, but she shouted and threatened, so that they had to let her have her way. She was furious. She said I did it on purpose, that I didn't really want to kill myself. She complained that I'd made things very difficult for her, because she had gone to a lot of trouble to get a black dress and she'd had her best pair of stockings dyed black. She could have forgiven me for the black dress, because that can be worn at other times, but she couldn't forgive me for the stockings."

"But she could still make a widow of herself when you leave with the transport."

"That's what I told her, but she wouldn't listen. She said she needs to have it in black and white that I'm dead—a death certificate, signed by a district physician, and so on."

"You'll feel better if I tell you about my cat, Tomas. Forget about this stuff. I'm secretly keeping a cat named Tomas. The other day he caught a mouse and offered it to me, quite se-riously. But I haven't yet learned to eat mice, so I refused his gift. He ate it himself, but I'm sure he was very disappointed. But Tomas has the kind of disposition that never worries too long about anything. I envy him his disposition."

"I like animals too. I once brought a dog home. You know, a mutt. But my wife said, 'Get rid of that thing. It'll do nothing but eat and make a mess,' so I had to let it go. She believes in keeping things neat and clean. You have to hand it to her. Everything in our house sparkled like in a store window. But maybe you could give me some advice on how to commit suicide. They watch me here, and it's no good doing it inside the Radio Mart because then my wife wouldn't get a death certificate signed by a district physician."

"I can't give you any advice. I'm not familiar with things here; I've never been here before. I only go to the outpatient clinic and for check-ups where they're interested in whether I can work. They call me for that every three months. They seem to think in three months I might turn into someone strong."

"You shouldn't be surprised. They have to show they're doing something. Otherwise they could be fired and sent to dig air-raid shelters. Or be sent off in a transport."

"Who shares your room with you?" I asked quietly. "These are all suicides?"

"Only one of them," said Robitschek. "He swallowed around twenty sleeping pills, but he probably wasn't serious about suicide. I think he just wanted to put off the transport for a few weeks. There are other suicides in the big room next door. But I don't think they're genuine suicides. You wouldn't believe all the schemes. There are people here who break a leg on purpose or cut off fingers. They think up all kinds of things just to gain a few days. They think that their transport is the last one, that they might win if they manage to stay out of it. Sometimes, of course, they miscalculate and actually die. While I, who was serious, have to stay alive. But I'm telling you, they won't be able to stop me. I'll commit suicide anyway."

"Visiting hours are over," said the nurse.

"I'll come visit you again," I said. "It's on my way home."

"Well, make it soon if you still want to find me here," Robitschek called after me.

I didn't feel well in the hospital; it was warm, but the air was too close. I had a dull feeling of defeat: all the people lying there were glad to be sick and didn't want to get well. It was better to lie in the close air of the hospital and eat gruel than to walk the streets with a star or perform in the circus.

But, just like the patients, I knew that escape led nowhere. They took the dying to transports in wheelchairs; it was all the same to them whether they took people from the hospital or from their homes. There were people who pretended to be crazy, or who really were crazy, and they forced them to go too, even in straitjackets. In fact, they liked madmen, because their acts in the circus were unusually amusing and their acting quite natural. Maybe Robitschek was right, after all; it was better to save oneself the trip and having to pack one's baggage. But for the time being I was alive, and it was good to be alive and to bank on the hope that it would take a long, long time for them to call me up. A lot of things could happen in the meantime. They could lose the war or have to stop the transports because of a shortage of railroad cars. "Some will be saved," said the people at the cemetery. Why couldn't it be me, Josef Roubicek, who wasn't called up when the other Roubiceks went?

Soon it would be spring. At the cemetery we would plant vegetables and warm ourselves in the sun. I would no longer have to freeze in my house or cope with my broken-down stove. Perhaps I would survive until summer and then things wouldn't be so bad. If they called me up in the summer I wouldn't have to shiver in the straw at the Radio Mart. Everything would be different if I survived until spring and summer. Maybe I would find the courage to run away. I would have enough time to conquer my fear and to stand apart from everyone who went off docilely. I had to learn the courage to accept guilt; I had to push away the outstretched hands inviting me to join their procession of stooped backs.

About a week later I learned that Robitschek had killed himself after all. Stupidly and senselessly. He had jumped out the third-floor window when they had come to take him to join the next transport.

I went to his funeral. I didn't have to go far. It was held at our cemetery, and it was just as stupid and senseless as Robitschek's death. There was no ceremony. Robitschek was Catholic, but he wasn't allowed to be buried in a Catholic cemetery, because one of the official decrees forbade it. And besides, he had committed suicide. When the coffin was lowered into the wet spring earth there were no relatives—his wife and daughter didn't come. Only we stood there, leaning on our shovels and hoes, a few people who had left their gardening work. We had just been turning over the soil when they carried Robitschek's coffin by on the cemetery path, and we walked behind it to the open grave. We had time. We didn't mind taking part in his funeral; we were glad to interrupt our work. The people carrying Robitschek's coffin put it down on the ground for a moment to rest. They told us that Robitschek didn't have an easy death. He lay dying a long time, with his broken limbs. It was stupid that the hospital had only three floors. It was too bad he had jumped to the street; he should have jumped into the courtyard. His fall had called attention to the hospital and caused a lot of people to gather, and the doctors were worried the hospital would be closed or relocated to wooden huts on the outskirts of the city. They looked at Robitschek's broken body with distaste and angrily gave him a morphine injection. They threatened to have the nurses responsible for watching Robitschek fired. The nurses were extremely afraid because they knew that losing their jobs meant being sent off with a transport. They took Robitschek's bloody clothes off nervously. In the evening Robitschek's wife arrived and was nasty to the doctor on duty, who knew nothing about the case. She had wanted her husband to die a quiet, inconspicuous death. The doctor listened to her in silence and didn't answer: she spoke a foreign language and was one of them.

He resisted her only when she ordered him to put an end to Robitschek quickly because she didn't want him to suffer long and she wanted to get the whole thing over and done with.

"We don't kill people here," said the doctor quietly. "We only try to save them."

"To save your people?" cried Robitschek's wife. "Who ever heard such nonsense? You'll all go to the devil, including you, you quack, you fraud."

The doctor said nothing. He knew that she was waiting for him to say something rude so she could call a policeman. He knew not to cross her. She carried on for a long time, until she was out of breath, then she left, stopping to spit on the floor by the attendant's window. So Robitschek died a death as unlucky as his life had been in recent years. His question kept echoing from his grave as we helped fill it. The only answer I could give him was a shovelful of earth that made a dull sound on the coffin, a miserable wooden crate our workers had made. They knew nothing about the art of making a coffin, and this one was rough and lopsided—not even like the simple coffin a country carpenter might make for a local pauper whose funeral was paid for by the government. It was just a clumsy box, and Robitschek's broken limbs clattered about in it.

The people who made it had never in their lives wished to make coffins. They didn't love the craft; they worked at it because they were forced to. They were bank managers, shopkeepers, a musician who had played in a string orchestra and was afraid that rough work would ruin his hands. They all cursed the work on Robitschek's coffin: it came at a bad time and they had to do it after hours, without pay. They had enough work as it was, because so many people were dying. Maybe their anger and hatred showed in the shabbiness of Robitschek's coffin.

Robitschek was dead now and probably didn't care that his death had cost his nurses sleepless nights, infuriated his doctors and his coffin makers, and fueled his wife's hatred. It was probably all the same to him that he was buried without cer-

emony in a corner of the cemetery, that the people who carried
his crate of a coffin put it down on the ground, lit cigarettes,
and made rude remarks about him by the open grave. None
of us took our caps off. When we had filled the grave, we went
to drink tea and get warm in the chapel. The coffin bearers
went with us, glad to take a rest. Like the coffin makers, they
hated their work, and they didn't get along with one another
either. Each of them had had a different occupation. One of
them had been a judge, another a watchmaker, a third a bookie,
and the last a teacher of the Talmud. They were angry—it was
clear they would soon be sent off with a transport, because
the work of coffin bearers was not esteemed; it was considered
a kind of punishment for those who had been unsuccessful in
some other type of work.

"That was irresponsible of Robitschek," said the former
fabric-shop owner as we sat on stools by the stove. "It was
irresponsible to jump out the window of the hospital. Everyone at the Community was furious. The Council of Elders had
to hold a special meeting, and its chairman had to beg for-
giveness and listen to all sorts of insults, and they may even
have beaten him. They could punish us by stepping up the
transports or taking away our ration cards and restricting the
hours we can walk on the streets even more. All of that could
happen because of Robitschek's stupid death. Was he a relative
of yours?"

"No, he wasn't," I said. "He was an acquaintance of mine.
I offered him an onion and tried to talk him out of suicide.
He didn't want to take my onion and he wouldn't let me talk
him out of suicide, because he loved his daughter and wanted
to please her since she wanted him to die. He said he'd always
done everything she wanted, ever since she was a little girl.
She was his only child. You're right. He should have died
quietly. He tried to, but he wasn't successful, because the
authorities don't obey their own rules. He had to kill himself
in the hospital, because at the Radio Mart his suicide would
have been no use to his daughter. She wouldn't have got a

death certificate signed by a district physician. I am not trying
to excuse him; I'm only explaining that Robitschek didn't have
bad intentions and didn't mean us harm. He was just unlucky."

"We're all unlucky—that's no excuse," said the man sitting
next to the shop owner. "He should have been more considerate of others. He should have known the damage he could
cause."

"Look," I said. "The other day someone here was saying
that there are times when a person takes only himself into
consideration. I would probably curse Robitschek too if I had
to suffer because of him, but that wouldn't help. Maybe Robitschek is to blame, but they are much more to blame. Robitschek kept saying he didn't understand how it all happened
to him. He lived an ordinary life. It never occurred to him
that something he did as a private person could affect thousands of people. If he had stolen some money and then killed
himself, it would only have affected his wife and daughter.
Robitschek wasn't used to thinking about things any other
way."

"No, what you're saying doesn't excuse him," said one of
the coffin bearers, the Talmud teacher. "People act like wolves
toward each other these days. Why should I have to sweat
over his coffin? It started when we had to drag it all across
town in a handcart. When I was pulling, the person who was
pushing would say I wasn't doing enough, that he had to work
harder because of me. And when we changed places, he started
cursing me because he said I was only hanging on and letting
myself be pulled with the cart. Can I help it if I'm no gladiator?
I've never done any physical work."

"Be quiet," interrupted the bookie. It was clear that he was
the coffin bearer the Talmud teacher was talking about. "If I
were you I wouldn't brag so much. You're a good-for-nothing.
You want others to do your work for you."

"Sir," said the coffin bearer angrily, "I was a Talmud teacher
and that's a distinguished occupation. People who study the
Talmud don't do dirty work. Everyone considers it an honor

to provide for them, because they serve a noble cause, you racetrack bum, with your horses."

"Who are you calling a bum?" shouted the bookie. "I've always worked honestly for my living while you were getting fat on somebody else's money, you parasite."

"And who bit Stern?" The Talmud teacher had jumped up from his stool. "Who did they have to kick out because he bit Stern?"

"Yes, I did bite Stern, if you want to know." The bookie jumped up too. "But they didn't kick me out because I didn't want to work. Stern was my boss and he was on my back all the time. He was a louse who cared only about work and nagging me. So one day I got really mad and started to pretend I'd gone crazy and bit him. They didn't believe I was crazy, but they kicked me out, and now I have to work with this parasite."

"Who are you calling a parasite?" screamed the Talmud teacher. It looked as if they were going to fight, but the former judge stepped in. "Stop, stop this nonsense," he said calmly. "What's the sense of arguing who did what? Don't you know it makes them happy when you argue? They'd love for you to fight and hit each other; that would be nice for them. It'd save them the work of beating us themselves. That's enough now. Let's go home."

"Excuse me for asking," said the former fabric-shop owner respectfully, "but how did you get into this group?"

"I worked in the registry," said the judge irritably. "We issued birth certificates and compiled family trees. It was silly, boring work. You had to read through dusty old documents, which I wouldn't have minded—I was used to old documents—but we worked in a basement and it was dark even in the daytime. My eyes were constantly watering, and I was afraid I would go blind altogether. I have weak eyes, you see. And so I asked them to transfer me somewhere else. They gave me this work. Well, at least I'm out in the fresh air a lot, and I don't have to strain my eyes, and I would have to join a transport in any case, so it doesn't really matter one way or the other. Goodbye. I'm glad to have met you, gentlemen."

The coffin bearers left, and we were alone in the chapel again. We went out too, with our tools, and walked slowly along a lane of trees to the end of the cemetery, near Robitschek's grave, where we were turning the soil and preparing vegetable beds. We passed proud monuments of black and white marble. Gilded inscriptions declared the rank and standing of the deceased. None of the graves even had wilted flowers—it seemed that no one was caring for these distinguished stones. But they didn't require care. Solid and strong, they were erected for eternity; they stood there watching us indifferently as we walked to the end of the cemetery. There mounds of thin soil lay on new graves marked only with wooden tablets inscribed in a language no one understood. All we could read were the dates, and they were recent ones, the very years we were living in. They were bad years, and so we walked past those poor graves quickly. It was better to bend over the earth, to breathe its dampness, and to shovel it than to look at the graves. It was better to use a hoe and to shovel earth than to carry a crude coffin with Robitschek's broken body. A shovel and a hoe were simple things a person could get used to and grow to like, and the soil didn't resist; when it was loosened by the rain it could be turned easily and it breathed dampness in your face. There was no need to argue over the soil, because there was no need to rush this kind of work, and it wasn't possible to pass your work on to someone else, because each of us had his own bed. It was good ordinary work. The past occupations of the people who did this work didn't matter. One could be a judge or a Talmud teacher or Josef Roubicek.

We didn't talk about Robitschek again. He was buried and his grave was filled. Robitschek would never be again. Perhaps he had never even existed: tomorrow a wooden tablet would be stuck on top of his grave with an inscription written with tar, giving his name in letters that nobody knew how to read. Nobody would notice when the rain washed the inscription away, and there would be no need for anyone to notice, because the people who knew Robitschek would no longer be at the cemetery. They would all have left for the fortress town or for the east.

It was good to turn the soil and prepare a vegetable bed, because soon we would be planting and nobody would think about Robitschek. Everyone would have forgotten that he had jumped from the third floor and that a special meeting of the Council of Elders had had to be held. The meeting would have been forgotten, new public notices would have been issued, and new dangers would threaten. It was good that we were turning the soil with shovels and hoes, because this was real work and the fact that Robitschek was buried nearby no longer mattered. Soon nobody would know Robitschek, but the vegetables that would grow would be eaten by us or by others. *They* would not eat them, because they didn't like vegetables grown in a cemetery. Vegetables that grew near graves were not to their taste. They liked death and vegetables, but not vegetables that drew their nourishment from buried bodies.

18

We felt good at the cemetery when the spring sun shone. We planted vegetables and used wooden sticks to make furrows for seeds. We felt good when we saw how the plants, full of energy, pushed through the earth, sometimes cracking it. We were happy to see the force of the plants and their desire to live. We watered them and happily watched the streams of water loosen the earth. We watched the drops on the leaves happily and felt good when we came to the cemetery and saw that our plants were growing taller all the time. We were free.

It was a good feeling to be free and to be able to decide which plants would grow. We pulled out weeds and burned them in between the vegetable beds. We were happy when the soil had been cleared and our plants didn't have to compete with parasites. We were powerful because we were making decisions about life and death; we were bent over the soil and the sun was beating on our backs. The tombstones, with their gilded inscriptions, didn't bother us at all, nor did the freshly dug graves with wooden tablets at their heads. We felt fine when we smelled the heavy odor of compost. It felt good to have our hands dirty from the soil.

At noon we would lie in the sun, even though the earth was damp and the grass wet. We lay next to our vegetable beds and looked at our work. It was good work and we were proud because the rows were straight and because our plants fared well at the cemetery. We didn't think that it was to the credit of the dead; we didn't think of the dead at all, though funeral processions often passed us and we sometimes helped the burial detail fill in the graves. We didn't think of death even when we talked about transports to the fortress town and to the east. We didn't think of death even when people kept leaving to join the circus, even when, eventually, only three of us were left of those who had worked in the cemetery during the fall. We got to know the new gravediggers. The judge and the Talmud teacher were no longer among them; nor was the watchmaker. Only the bookie remained. There was much more harmony among them now. It was fun to sit on the grass with them and listen to their stories about the Community. They were always full of news since they picked up bodies from all parts of the city and from the hospitals. They went to the Radio Mart as well; those people too were buried in our cemetery, but without death certificates. They didn't like their work, but when they sat resting by our vegetable beds with us they laughed and told us jokes. They also talked about women, their own wives and other women too. We enjoyed listening to the various stories. We often lay by our vegetable beds, with their straight, neat rows, and showed off our work, because the burial detail couldn't brag about theirs; instead they bragged about their lives—the different sections of the city they went to and their many adventures. And they bragged about their closeness to death because they had to brag about something. Yes, they were a brave lot, especially when they lay in the grass and ate bread spread with lean cheese. They went to mortuaries and to dark morgues, and they saw a lot. They knew a great many secrets they were not allowed to talk about with anyone. They were proud of these secrets, even if giving them away carried a death sentence. These were very powerful people who now lay in the grass and talked about various things; of course, the lives they led were very colorful, with their corpses and coffins, lives full of adventure and suspense that couldn't be compared to the lives of gardeners digging up the earth all day. We were like moles who never left the cemetery, while they accompanied Death and served as her assistants in dark morgues and on biers. We didn't envy them—we just liked to listen to their tales. We felt good because the sun was shining and because it seemed to us that their stories were made up, that they had read them in books that someone had been writing in secret. We were glad to be at the cemetery all day because there we never saw *them*. We could even imagine that they didn't exist, that they were only characters in books written by someone. We could even imagine we were very good gardeners who diligently cared for their vegetables and destroyed all weeds, because we were free, because we could decide matters of life and death, because we could light cigarettes without being afraid that someone would tear them out of our mouths, because we could talk out loud without having to whisper, because we could walk the paths freely and listen to anecdotes, because we could love the soil and not worry about its being cemetery soil since we were at home on our soil, which we were tilling with our own hands. Above us birds were singing in the tops of trees, ordinary trees, chestnuts and lindens, that bloomed like other trees did, like the ones that stood in village squares or behind garden fences and next to ditches along the sides of the roads.

We felt as if we were lying next to a river, watching the water as it flowed over rapids; we felt as if we were lying behind a fence in the noon stillness, listening to the sound of a wagon with creaking wheels approach as we lay hidden in the damp grass. We listened to stories: horrible stories about cruelty and hardship, stories full of adventure and suspense. We were close, quite close, to death on the wet grass and wet soil where parsley, cabbage, and carrots grew, where celery stalks were pushing their way up and tomato plants stood tied to neat rows of stakes. We were behind a fence on the green lawn, and we were glad that the fence was a high cemetery wall. We didn't think about the fact that we weren't growing asparagus—we were glad not to have to grow asparagus, because it took a lot of work. We were glad that we were forbidden to eat asparagus and therefore were not allowed to grow it. We were glad that we were allowed to eat only those vegetables that grew at the cemetery and no others, that we didn't have to eat vegetables grown in fields or in suburban gardens irrigated by river water. We didn't mind at all that our vegetables were fertilized by nutrients provided by the dead; we didn't think about the dead, the suicides—those who killed themselves with gas and barbiturates, who were run over by trains, who drowned in the river, and who were dying on the sidewalks. These were good vegetables, maybe better than those grown in suburban gardens and fields. We looked forward to eating these vegetables, cultivated with our own hands, in regular rows, in cleanly weeded beds.

"If we had a car," said one of the gravediggers, "I could forget the corpses. If I were driving down a road, I could look at shop assistants opening the shutters of their shops or at children going to school; I could look at women hanging their wash and watering flowers in their windows as I drove through the town. I would check my speedometer, so that I stayed within the speed limit, but I would still have time to take everything in: the people walking along the sidewalk to work, dogs playing at the edge of the road, smoke coming out of chimneys, and the milkman putting bottles of milk in front of doors, and open windows, with pillows and blankets hung out to air. I saw all those things when I passed through towns on the main road, but I never thought about them before, only now that I deal with dead bodies. Maybe I passed cemeteries too. I don't seem to remember them, though I often had to wait for a funeral procession to pass. But I never thought about the body, because those funeral processions were part of the landscape. Up front the musicians would march and, behind the coffin, the relatives dressed in black, the women with veils over their faces, heads down, and the men, upright, forcing themselves to look serious. I always looked at the people when I had to wait a long time for a procession to pass, but I never noticed the coffin. Sometimes I came on wedding processions and had to wait for them too. I also had to wait for Corpus Christi processions and for harvest processions. I didn't like them at all, especially when they included a lot of wagons, because then I knew I would have to wait a long time for the road to clear. But if I had a car now and could drive along a road or through a town, I would never think about corpses, even if I had to wait for a funeral procession to pass. If I could hear the music I would never be sad."

"I had a car too," said the bookie. "I could afford to have a car; those were good times. I had a lot of arguments with policemen and delivery men and people who would curse me from the sidewalks, but it was still good to have a car, to go out in the evening when we felt like it to one of those places outside the city and make a night of it. There were some nice places. And the things that went on there!"

"Once I was with some people in a car," I said, "and we saw a dead motorcyclist by the road. It was horrible, but we didn't stop, because the people who owned the car didn't want to get blood on it. Then we sat in the garden of a restaurant drinking coffee with whipped cream and didn't even think

about the motorcyclist lying there in the dust by the side of
the road, and it was only after I had gone to bed at home that
night and turned out the light that it all came back to me, as
I was falling asleep. The broken motorcycle and that man with
the broken skull. I had to get up and light a cigarette, and it
took me a long time to fall asleep."

"Yes," said one of the gravediggers, "we weren't used to
dead bodies in those days. I wouldn't even hear of going to
a hospital—the slightest sight of a little blood took my appetite
away."

"You get used to it," I said. "That's the problem. We
shouldn't become used to it. Is it supposed to be normal to
carry corpses? Did you ever in your lives think that you would
be going to morgues and mortuaries?"

"A person can do anything if he's ordered to," said the
former owner of a fabric shop. "I've seen people do even worse
things."

"A horse will also do all sorts of things if a man forces him
to," said the bookie. "But there are things a horse won't do,
even if you whip him from morning till night. Man is powerful—he'll do anything."

But we didn't want to talk about what a person was capable
of doing. It wasn't necessary to talk about that. Instead, we
asked the bookie to tell us stories about the horse races and
about people who bet on them, about the stands and the big
wins, about favorites and long shots, about fixed races and
close finishes. Because the sun was shining and we were lying
on the wet grass, because a high stone wall separated us from
the road, because we heard locomotives in the distance and
streetcars screeching as they went around a bend, because the
sky was high and the trees above us were about to bloom,
because none of us wanted to think about having to go home
in the evening and about our stars casting a yellow sheen in
the streets and squares of the city, because we had met strangers
who had been chosen to carry corpses but who didn't like that
occupation and would rather have been driving on roads or
placing bets at the racetrack. The gravediggers got up when

the lunch hour was over, but we remained lying in the grass because we didn't have to hurry. Only the soil was waiting for us, and the soil was patient. We didn't have to struggle with it. It was fertile soil that anything grew in easily. It was soil without stones or silt.

When the sun began to get warmer, other people came to the cemetery or were brought there. They had advanced cases of tuberculosis and had been told to lie outdoors in the woods, but since the woods and forests were forbidden to them, they had to lie in the cemetery. They weren't allowed to move about or to lie in the sun, so they lay quietly, some of them reading, while others looked at the marble statues with their gilded inscriptions. They didn't mind lying in a cemetery; they were glad not to have to lie in the close air of the hospital, and they liked to look at us as we bent over the earth and hoed the soil. Doctors and nurses came as well, and we sometimes talked to them, as they always had news, something that we, who were at the cemetery, surrounded by a high wall, did not know. The doctors and nurses liked coming to the cemetery because they longed for the air and the sun. When it rained nobody came, but those days we didn't do much work at the cemetery either. Instead, we sat in the chapel and drank tea. But when the sun returned, they would bring the sick again, only the sick would have changed because many of them would have died and new ones would come. Many also left with transports when their time came. On our lunch hours, we would sometimes sit with the sick; we felt sorry for them, lying still all day, unable to move about. They had no amusements other than to stare at the sky, read books, and talk to one another. Some of them were accompanied by their wives or relatives, but most were alone, among them Karel Kauders, whom we often went to see. There was nothing special about Karel Kauders except that he was old and dying, but in fact everyone who lay on the wooden deck chairs next to the marble statues was dying. Nobody ever came to see him. He was alone and very bored.

"How do you feel today?" I said. "Here at the cemetery

you're sure to get better. It's quiet with only the dead here, and the air is good; they never come here."

"I've never actually seen any of them," said Kauders. "They go everywhere, but they've never come to my place. They don't like people with advanced tuberculosis."

"Be glad you've never seen them," I said. "You're very lucky not to have seen them."

"I hope I don't ever see them. I hope I die before they call me to the Radio Mart. Where I'm going, I'm sure they won't be."

"I think you're right. Their power isn't so great they can think up a life after death for us. Though they would if they could. But they're modest; they're satisfied with having thought up a life for us in the here and now. They can never really succeed, though. I remember my uncle once gave me a building kit made in their country. I could never build anything proper with it. Just dumb things. The worst of it is that we have to live the life they've thought up for us. It's difficult to live a life someone else has thought up for you."

"Yes," said Kauders. "I'm happy. Before, I would have envied healthy people. Now I'm happy to live the life my disease has determined for me. I used to work for the income tax bureau, and I've always liked things to be in order. I didn't even get married, because it probably would have disturbed me—I wouldn't have been able to stand it if my wife had arranged things according to her own ideas and if all sorts of silly things like cosmetics were all over my apartment . . ."

I interrupted him. "I'm beginning to be fed up living a life someone else made up. I don't know how to get out of it, but I will. I was in the sanctuary when they read the names of the people for the next transport. I thought they would read my name. But they didn't. And it occurred to me that I really should lead my own life. It seemed to wake me up. But I still haven't hit on a way to do it."

"My way isn't much good."

I told Kauders all the new stories I had heard from the gravediggers and the doctors and nurses, and Kauders told me old ones, dating back to his youth. We often sat in the garden when the sun was out and the sick could lie in the shade, close to the tombstones.

"Come see me Sunday morning in the hospital," said Kauders.

"I'll come," I said, "but I won't be too happy about it. I was in a hospital once, when someone I knew was there."

"You'll like it this time," said Kauders. "This hospital is different. They never come there. We have a wonderful thing there that nobody else has, a piano. They didn't take it away from us; they were afraid it would be full of germs. And every Sunday morning there are concerts only for us, who aren't afraid of death, because we're dying anyway, but other people might not want to take the risk."

I had to walk all the way across town, but I didn't mind, because it was Sunday and I wouldn't have known what to do with my time. I would have had to lie reading, then cook my lunch, and read again. I had never been to a concert and was never interested in serious music, but still, it was entertainment. I looked forward to it, because at least I would be sitting in a chair. I would look and listen.

When I finally arrived at the hospital, the dining room was full. The patients were sitting at their tables and the concert was about to begin. I heard the musicians tuning their instruments. It was good to hear those sounds and to look forward to music I didn't know.

I sat next to Kauders. No one noticed me. The people sitting at the tables didn't look as if they were dying, but I knew that with tuberculosis appearances meant little and that the patients would never have been admitted to this hospital if it hadn't been clear that they were going to die.

"Beethoven is on the program," said Kauders. "The three men who are going to play are great musicians. Two of them are professionals; the one at the piano is an amateur but a great musician nevertheless. He's quite their equal. He was a very well-to-do lawyer."

"They probably wouldn't like it if they found out that

Beethoven was being played here. They play him themselves.
I heard at the cemetery that they killed someone named Utitz
because he wanted to listen to Beethoven."

"But these three performers are all going to die. It's spelled
out for them in black and white. Their X-rays tell the whole
story. They're not so crazy as to kill someone who's going to
die anyway."

The dining room grew silent and the concert began. I sat
on a chair and listened. It was good to sit quietly and listen.
It was good not to think about the chapel, about the circus,
or about the transports to the east; it was good not to think
of bread spread with lean cheese or of barley cooked in water;
it was good not to know about the decrees and prohibitions,
about being thrown out of streetcars, or about processions
and the sound of metal-tipped boots. I knew that now everything had disappeared. I knew that everything was absurd and
unimportant; I knew that there were no hardships and dangers,
no strangulations, no beatings, no having one's teeth knocked
out. I knew there was no jumping and fetching or tightrope
walking. I knew there was no gate that people entered,
weighed down by rucksacks and with numbers around their
necks; I knew that there were no numbers, that there never
had been any numbers and never would be until the end of
time. I knew that bloodstains would not appear on the walls
of the sanctuary. I knew that people would not writhe when
fear caught them by the throat. I knew there was no huddled
and trampled city and there never had been. I heard the wind
snapping the flags; they rustled in the wind. I saw their colors,
different from those of the flags that hung on buildings now,
buildings I was not allowed to enter. I listened to what the
colors on the flags had to say. There was no sound of piercing
pipes and thundering drums in their words. They told of a
country I knew well. I knew now how happiness awoke; I
knew that happiness was quiet, that it hid in crevices but could
not be destroyed by shouting and whipping. How ridiculous
Death now seemed in her bloody shroud, how wretched and

pathetic she seemed as happiness rose slowly and quietly, climbing ever higher from the depths, forcing Death to flee with her drums and pipes. How ridiculous her horse's tail, her pride, her epaulets, and braid trim were. I saw her standing there like a scarecrow, and everyone was laughing at her. I saw how her servant faltered, how her majesty disappeared; nobody listened to her commands or to the drum rolls that announced them. I saw a mouse, an ordinary gray mouse, run around her and laugh in her fleshless face. No, the world devised by Death had never existed. No, she would never be able to force anyone to bow to her or honor her. As long as this music was heard, as long as joy was heard, she would never be able to win. She could not chase away joy with drums and pipes, with decrees and prohibitions and torments. She couldn't, after all, prevent a blade of grass from making its way through rocks; she couldn't force trees to stop blooming. This Death of theirs, which they honored, was ridiculous, a stuffed scarecrow that schoolchildren were shown to scare them. Bells could be heard now, slowly building to full pitch. At first they rang a death knell, but slowly the ringing became louder, until the hall was full of their sound, rising ever higher, up to the heavens.

"Thank you very much," I said to Kauders when the musicians finished playing. "It's a good thing, this music. I never knew that before."

We stayed at the table and waited for lunch. We ate some thin soup and cooked peas, drank rose-hip tea, and talked about everyday things until the time came for the patients to lie down and I had to leave for my long walk to the outskirts of the city, where Tomas was waiting for me. I took him some leftover peas that the cook had given me.

It was a spring day and there were a lot of people on the streets. I had to avoid the main streets and squares, which were off-limits for me on Sundays. I took a roundabout route through side streets, quickly slipping through alleys. I didn't look at people dressed in their Sunday best, and I took no notice of policemen or of their official badges. I was still listening to the music, and it accompanied me for a long time, until I reached the river and the bridge. And as I slowly climbed the hill I looked down at the city lying in the spring air on this Sunday when chimneys weren't smoking—lying quietly, as if cringing before blows. I noticed pigeons flying across the city peacefully and quietly, seeming not to see what went on under them as they headed to some faraway place and disappeared from my sight.

19

One day it was the former fabric-store owner's turn.

"I'm leaving," he said. "I won't be working with you anymore. You'll get a lawyer in my place."

We were silent. We couldn't lament with him or comfort him. The spring sun was shining, and that was good; we all felt much better when the sun shone, but we couldn't very well console the shopkeeper with the sun.

"We'll miss you," I said. "I don't know whether a lawyer will be the right person. Because you really know something about this work."

But it would have been stupid to praise the shopkeeper for his work. It wasn't really work hoeing the soil with us and planting vegetables; it didn't require any special skill. He had sent reports on our work to the Community, which had perhaps passed them on to *them*, but it was clear that nobody read the reports. They weren't interested in the work at the cemetery, because it didn't bring them valuables or furniture. And they weren't at all interested in the vegetables grown at the cemetery; they had enough vegetables from gardens on the outskirts and from distribution centers. But it was good to be able to praise the shopkeeper for something; he needed the praise, since he was leaving. In the circus he could say how important he had been, he could say that without him our dining room would not have had any vegetables. It would please him to be able to put himself above all the clerks and all the looters' assistants. It was a good thing to feed the hungry; it was a good deed that might be written into the book of honor. It was much better than drawing up lists of furniture and moving boxes of clothes. It was much better than shining the floors of apartments for them, better even than being a locksmith, a plumber, or a coffin maker. Coffin makers and gravediggers got no credit for performing acts of mercy; it was still better to feed the living. The former fabric-shop owner was flattered.

"I'll give you a coffee mill," he said.

"Thank you," I said. "I don't need a coffee mill. I can hardly remember what real coffee tastes like, and the acorns they give us are already ground. I wouldn't know what to do with a coffee mill."

"There's nothing else I can give you to remember me by. They've made lists of everything, but they forgot the coffee mill. It would be a pity to leave it for them; it's a good mill. You can also use it to grind corn, if you don't have any coffee."

"I don't know where I would get corn unless I stole a few ears from a field. But the fields are watched and you can get the death penalty for stealing from them. I'll take your coffee mill so I have something to remember you by. At least I'll have something to put on my list when it's my turn to go."

I took the coffee mill home and turned the handle idly. I thought Tomas might like it, but he paid no attention to it. It was pleasant to turn the handle; it was a nice big, old-fashioned mill, like one I remembered my aunt having. I used to watch her fill it with coffee, which she scooped out with a special measuring spoon. I remembered the smell of coffee, a wonderful smell that had filled the whole kitchen. I had also liked to watch her spoon the ground coffee into a large china pot that steam rose through as drops of coffee dripped slowly down. The smell would grow even stronger throughout the kitchen.

As I turned the handle of the empty mill, I suddenly realized why I was doing it. I wanted to summon Ruzena, who had dissolved long ago and to whom I no longer spoke. It was Ruzena who used to sit on a kitchen stool when I came to see her. She wore an apron over her dress, and I always studied the apron so I could guess the shape of her young, firm breasts. But now the mill was clicking emptily and I couldn't summon Ruzena—I had lost her forever. I would never be able to call her forth again to help me fend off despair and overcome fear.

So I was alone, and that wasn't good. I didn't feel like staying home turning an empty coffee mill if Ruzena wouldn't appear.

I went to see Materna. He wasn't surprised by my visit. None of his guests seemed surprised. They had become as used to me as they were to a piece of furniture or to the coal bin. I never spoke when they discussed plans or argued. Nobody asked me anything and nobody sought my advice. I always sat quietly, drinking my tea and eating the buns that Materna's mother had baked. I would leave earlier than the others, and sometimes I took leftovers for Tomas with me or cigarettes that Materna had got for me. This time, too, I was silent, but I was impatient. I waited for them to stop talking.

"I'm not going to go. I won't join the circus."

"That's good, Josef. I was afraid you were a chicken. That's the way," said Materna.

"I would be lying if I said I wasn't afraid," I continued. "I'm afraid—and how. But I think I have to come to a decision. That mill made me see it."

"What mill?"

"Oh, it's not important, just a figure of speech. I got a coffee mill from a man called up for a transport. It's a silly thing when there's no coffee."

"Yes," said Materna, "but do you know what's in store for you?"

"I do," I said. "I've thought it all out. Now it depends on what you say."

"It's not that easy," said Franta. "This business of hiding is nothing to fool around with. You might have to sit all day in some hole without being able to clear your throat. You might have to sleep on the floor or lie in some damp cellar."

"That's nothing," I said. "I've gotten used to all sorts of things. Materna here knows how I live."

"You're right. Do it!" said Franta.

But then I remembered something. It came to me suddenly. I must have realized it for a long time but managed to deny it. I probably hadn't wanted to think about it.

"There's another thing," I said. "The people who hid me— they would be killed if I were caught, wouldn't they? There's a law about that."

"Well, what if there is, what of it?" said Materna.

"You know," said Franta, "nobody wants to die. But without taking risks we would never get anywhere. And who says they have to catch you? Lots of people are hiding, and have been for a long time."

"Wait a minute. I have to think about it. I can't really ask a person to stick his neck out for me that way, can I?"

"If we're genuinely offering, you can. Why not?"

"Wait. There's still a lot of time. They haven't called me up yet. I have to think about it. I only came to the decision as I was turning the coffee-mill handle, but now I see it has several sides."

"Well, nobody's forcing you," said Materna.

They continued discussing their work and the war. I was quiet again. Then I went home with some food for Tomas and settled into my sleeping bag, but I couldn't sleep.

It was all so easy when I was listening to the music, with flags waving in the wind and bells sounding, Death crawling into a crevice and a small mouse laughing in her face. It was so easy when I was turning the coffee-mill handle; it clicked emptily, but it seemed to me to crush my fear, grinding it into a fine powder that the wind would blow away. It would be so simple to tear off my star and leave my house, which was almost collapsing in the spring wind, to say goodbye to the damp circle on the ceiling and leave them nothing but a silly little table and a round coffee mill.

But I knew it wasn't at all simple. If a replacement for me had to join the circus, if someone else had to hang a number around his neck, he would lose all hope. Hope was a great thing, and it wasn't right to take it away from someone; it was wrong to steal a week or a month from an unknown person. But maybe it was possible to avoid responsibility, because hope didn't weigh much when you put it on the scale, and, in any case, it was somebody else's hope, that of an unknown person, a private hope that was unimportant in the end, because it would never be realized. And when the throngs passed by blacked-out windows to the accompaniment of stomping metal-tipped boots, it was possible to close your ears and not listen to their sighs. They passed by in a distant section of the city, bound for the freight station, where a long train of cattle cars awaited them. When you opened the window on a dark night you couldn't even hear the shunting of the railroad cars or the whistle of the locomotives, that's how far that section of the city was. And when a train departed for the fortress town or for the east, nobody noticed, because it was an entirely ordinary freight train moving slowly along the tracks with closed cars that might have carried cement or gun mounts. I too would not have had to notice it; I would not have had to think about my replacement, who was on it, heading east.

But the other thing was not simple at all, and there was no way around it. I thrashed about in my sleeping bag thinking about it. No matter how I approached it, I couldn't resolve the problem. Long ago I had done ordinary things; I went to the bank, I ate and slept, I made love with Ruzena and waited for her on street corners. I went to the movies and to coffee-houses. I didn't have to decide anything. Everything was clear and established. I had superiors whom I had to obey, there were rules and regulations, there were box offices where I could buy tickets, a waiter to whom I paid my bill. There was no need to assume responsibility when I hung my hat up at the bank or when I lay in the grass by the river. Of course, there was that time with Ruzena when we sat in the restaurant above the city and she tried to convince me that we should run away, escape abroad, but I avoided making a decision then; I fled downtown, to things that were familiar to me, to the news-stand, the coffeehouse, and the tobacco shop. It was bad to run away, but I didn't know then that it was.

One had to assume responsibility as it came; one had to cross the frontier and tumble down a steep hill without a single bush to break one's fall. I couldn't figure things out. But finally I told myself that it would be a long time before they called me up. I still had enough time. I didn't have to think about making a decision now. There would be enough time. I could chase the decision away and be rid of it for a while. I hoped that the summer would be mine and that a decision could wait until the fall, when I would be raking leaves at the cemetery again. No, now was not the right time, not when the sun had begun to warm everything and I was no longer freezing by my broken-down stove.

It was still damp in my garret. The sun had not yet had time to dry it, and it was unpleasant to lie around in the dampness and breathe the moist air. It was unpleasant to have to make decisions about other people's lives. I didn't want to play that game, because I had lived a simple life, in which nobody had ever forced me to play such games. Of course, I was afraid for my own life too, but that was not a decisive or important issue. My life was lost in any case. Fear was no help and I didn't want to contaminate other people with it. I couldn't hang my troubles on somebody else's peg, and in my garret I had only three pegs, which my clothes hung on—though they were actually hooks that I had hammered into the wall when I burned my bureau. It wasn't difficult to decide to abandon a garret with three hooks on the wall, but I couldn't think of anything with which to pay for the lives of other people.

I didn't go to the cemetery the next day. I had to go to the Community to have my streetcar permit renewed. The procedure was complicated, because each time they had to measure the distance from my house to the cemetery. It took four officials to establish the distance correctly and write up a document, to which a small map was attached. My house was quite far from the cemetery, and it was impossible for the distance to have become shorter, but I still had to renew my card every month. I had nothing against this official procedure: I could spend the whole morning at the Community because the procedure took that long. I had to wait in the corridors outside various offices, submit to a strict interrogation, sign several documents. But it was a change from the comfortable work at the cemetery. I just had to be careful to sign the correct things.

As I was leaving the Community building, I saw a truck with two horses harnessed to it out on the street. Next to it walked my acquaintance the village miller, whom I had met during the registration.

"I'm glad to see you again," I said. "So you got a job. You're lucky not to be in that wreck of a mansion anymore."

"I don't know whether I'm lucky," said the miller. "I have horses to take care of, and it's nice when you can groom and feed a horse. But I'm alone, completely alone. My family was taken away to the fortress town. They're still there, but what if they're sent to the east without me? What if I never see my wife and son again?"

"How did it happen?" I asked. "They don't usually separate families."

"They ordered everyone to take off their shoes and gave them clogs. They took away their warm underwear and winter coats. It was just after the holidays. Then they forced them to walk to the main town and locked them in a school there for three days. It was right after Christmas, and there was snow on the roads and no heat in the school. Then they loaded them on trucks and took them away. The train stopped at the fortress town and several people were told to get off, and then it continued on to the east. My wife and son stayed in the fortress town. She was supposed to be taken east, but there was a problem with the papers because there's an order that families are supposed to stay together. The local officials couldn't come to an agreement with the head of the transport, so in the meantime they left my wife and son in the fortress town."

"But I still don't understand why you didn't go with them."

"I'll explain in a moment. Once, when I was filling out about the tenth questionnaire, they asked if I knew how to work with horses. I know how to work with horses. So I wrote that down without giving it any thought. There were so many questions, like whether I used the force of the wind in my occupation. I no longer had an occupation and the wind was no use to me, and now it was blowing through the broken windows of the mansion, but I liked horses. When I think of Bruna and how she said goodbye to me, I could cry. Then suddenly the transport was announced and they gave my family clogs and drove them through the snow, and I remained in the mansion by myself. They told me I should report to the capital because they needed a person who understood horses. There aren't a lot of us. As you know, our people hardly ever do that kind of work. I had to stay another week in the mansion by myself, without a single living soul. It was terrible. I carried a photograph of my wife and son in my hand and walked from one room to the next, crying. I can tell you, this time I was the one who was crying, not Bruna. If an animal can be excused for crying, I'll have to be forgiven too because, let me tell you, there were still pots and pans and straw mattresses in those rooms. All that stuff was lying around, because people didn't know they were going to have to walk through the snow in clogs, and anyway, even if they had known, they still would have had to leave their things behind. So I walked around among those things and thought about my wife and son and how they were walking along the road with the others, and I kept thinking about what would happen to them, because, you know, we heard a lot of things in that mansion. Bad news ignores locks and doors. I thought I would go crazy. Several times I wanted to smash my head against the wall, but then they sent for me, and now I have these horses and I move things to warehouses."

"What kind of things?" I asked.

"Look for yourself," said the miller. "I don't like it a bit." I looked in the truck. Things were stacked high, and I could understand the miller's not liking to move them. There were dolls of various sizes, from rag dolls, all shabby and worn, to fancy life-size dolls with eyelids that moved. There were building kits, children's abacuses, dollhouses and tiny kitchen sets, model trains with tracks, tunnels, and bridges. There were tin soldiers of every era and all nations of the world. There were all sorts of games, Ping-Pong balls, foldout picture books, and toy animals. Sheep lay beside lions, rubber giraffes beside antelopes and lizards. Wooden horses hitched to wooden carts were stacked next to rocking horses with elaborate harnesses. And one couldn't miss the angels that had once decorated Christmas trees or the stars made of glimmering glass.

"I don't like carrying such things," said the miller. "I'd rather carry furniture or rugs. These things are alive. They keep saying something; they keep complaining. Suddenly a teddy bear will growl, or a doll will say 'Ma-ma.' I'm telling you, even the horses don't like carrying these things. They're not at all happy, even though I take care of them as best I can. They get oats, and you know how scarce they are nowadays. My old neighbor brings them to me secretly. I told him I needed some for myself, that I grind them, but I think he knows I give them to the horses. They should be happy I give them oats. They should be neighing with pleasure. But these horses are sad. They dawdle, and they hate pulling. I'm telling you, they know what they're pulling. God knows you can't fool horses; no one can tell me otherwise. I saw the way they moved when we carried grain to the mill. And they were only fed straw then. These things think we're to blame. I can tell you that the poor horses and I aren't guilty, but you can't tell that to these things, can you?"

"They're just objects," I said. "Dead things. They can't talk. And they can't blame you. You're certainly not responsible for the work you've been given."

"No, there you're mistaken. These things are crying. I'm telling you, they're reproaching me for helping *them*. Those horses are innocent. They can't talk back. But I shouldn't be doing this work; I should refuse to do it. I should let myself be killed rather than carry toys that have been taken away from children by force."

"There are worse things they've made us do. Not long ago someone at our cemetery said that man was so powerful he could be forced to do anything but that nobody could force a horse to do something. And yet look, they've forced the horses, so why should you blame yourself?"

But the miller wouldn't listen. He said goodbye to me. I watched him as he slowly walked beside his horses. I saw that they really did move unwillingly, both the horses and the man.

20

That summer Kauders died. He no longer came to lie outdoors at the cemetery. He had succeeded in never encountering *them*. The burial detail brought him and buried him in a new grave. There were no mourners except us, who stood by the grave again, but this time without shovels or hoes because we were no longer cultivating the soil; now we were harvesting our crop. We were very prosperous. We could eat as many vegetables as we liked and could even give some away or trade them with the gravediggers for cigarettes.

We lay in the grass again and the gravediggers told us stories about their adventurous lives—frightening, secret stories that they bragged about. And as usual the bookie was the most talkative.

"They sent us to get a body from one of those shantytowns on the outskirts. We thought that was strange. None of our people has ever lived in one of those places. And even if they had lived there before the war, they wouldn't have been allowed to go on living there, because all sorts of people who want to lie low, as they say, live there, and even a Chinaman would go unnoticed in a place like that, not to mention one of us. But since they told us to go there, we decided that they probably knew what they were talking about. You can't imagine how strange it was when we got there. Everyone ran out of their huts to look at us. We had stars, of course, and these people probably weren't used to them. They couldn't figure out what we were doing there, since we weren't policemen or officials. We asked for the house where we were supposed to pick up the body—it had a nice name, the Rosebush—because the huts didn't have numbers, only names. 'Oh,' said one woman, 'that's the house where the shooting was.' 'Shut up, woman,' a man standing next to her yelled. 'Don't you know you're not supposed to talk about it?' We found the house; it was a wreck, like a pile of matchsticks, and there weren't any rosebushes, just empty cans and junk. The door was pushed in, feather beds were ripped open, there was blood on the floor, and things strewn everywhere. The windows were broken and there were bullet holes in the walls.

" 'Well, I'll be damned,' I said to Egon here. 'This is a hell of a mess. What happened?' On a bench was the body, shot full of holes like a sieve. And without a star. 'I don't like this at all,' I said to the others. 'We've seen a lot of things, but never a body that didn't have a star. We're not allowed to touch anybody that isn't one of us.' But then I looked at the dead man's face. It was more or less whole. 'He's ours,' I said. 'Let's take him. Don't worry—we can always sew his star on, or he can go in his coffin without a star. Who would care?' So we carried him out of the house, put him on our cart, threw a blanket over him, and started off. But I was curious. 'You go on ahead slowly,' I said. 'I'll ask someone what this was all about.' There were a lot of people around, and I came up behind the woman who had showed us the way. Her husband wasn't there; he'd probably gone off somewhere. 'Ma'am,' I said to her, 'what happened here? The place looks like a slaughterhouse.' 'Don't you know?' said the woman. 'One of your people was hiding with the Sejkoras. They kept him in secret and somebody told on them. People are full of evil nowadays. Sejkora got some money from him and kept rabbits and, as you know, people are jealous. When they came for him, Sejkora tried to run away. His wife was out somewhere gossiping, so your man was there all alone. He bolted the door and refused to open, and they shouted at him in their language. All of a sudden he pulled out a gun, and then it started. I don't know if he killed any of them. They say he got two of them, but nobody really knows for sure, because they chased us away and we had to sit behind closed doors until it was all over. And then they went away and told us to keep quiet or they would arrest all of us, and they arrested Sejkora. He hasn't returned, and his wife didn't come home either. They say she was caught somewhere downtown. Then some others came for the rabbits, and they left the body here. People say Sejkora and his wife will be hanged, and it's probably true, because they certainly have the power to do it.' The woman didn't know anything else, but that was enough. Then I learned at the Community that the man's name was Froehlich, that he had run away from a transport half a year ago and hidden with this Sejkora, who was one of his employees when he still owned a brickyard."

We were silent. The story was too awful even though the bookie told it matter-of-factly. But then, the gravediggers were used to death; death didn't mean much to them when they carried dead bodies as part of their everyday work.

Then the lawyer who worked with us now, in place of the former fabric-shop owner, said: "I think it was wrong for this Froehlich to make other people suffer for him. What will people think of us? How can they feel sorry for us when a scoundrel like that causes two people's deaths just to save his own skin?"

"Wait a minute," said the bookie. "You've got it all wrong. Froehlich paid the Sejkoras. It was a business transaction, like when somebody bets on a horse."

"You're very much mistaken there," said the lawyer. "How can you pay for such a service? That kind of contract is unethical and therefore invalid."

"What ethics are you talking about? That won't get you anywhere nowadays," said one of the gravediggers, the man the bookie had called Egon. "But he shouldn't have done it. No one has the right to ask someone else to risk his life for him."

"Even if that person offers to do it?" I said.

"Not even then," replied Egon.

"Anything can be done for money," said the bookie, "because then it's a different story." But our group had joined Egon. They all spoke out: money had lost its value, and they didn't like to think it could be equated with life. I was quiet. I couldn't defend the bookie because I didn't trust money either. I didn't trust money or objects, but I was still prepared to do what Froehlich had done. As I listened to the argument, I knew I was in a quandary again that I couldn't resolve. Maybe things were the way they said, but maybe it was all different. Maybe these people were afraid; maybe each of them wanted to do what Froehlich did. Maybe they envied him because they didn't have the same opportunity. Maybe they were afraid they might have to stand with a gun in hand—or without one—face to face with death. And so they said: Decent people don't ask other people to risk their lives for them; we would rather die than accept such help—people would stop feeling pity for us. It's very fine to conceal your fear with nobleness. Then you can say we're dying because we are noble, because we are decent. What are we dying for, Josef Roubicek?

No, this wasn't the way it was. We were lying on the grass, and we felt good lying there, listening to the bookie's story. It was a terrible story about blood and death, but where was this shantytown? It was somewhere far away, written about in books and made up, so that people could lie on the grass and listen to a story with shooting in it. They had forced us to call everything a dream or make-believe, because how else could we live? We would have to lie with Froehlich on a bench covered with blood if we admitted that Froehlich could run away from the transport. So many people disappeared each minute that it was better to think that they had never existed. It was better to believe that, so we could eat, work, and sleep.

But it wasn't true. It wasn't easy to take the blood of others upon yourself, and now I knew why. Because our death was worthless. Nothing changed when people departed by the thousands for the fortress town and for the east. They didn't serve as warnings or examples. They went stooped under a load of useless things; they walked to the gates of the circus with clumsy strides, their jerks and starts serving only as amusement for *them*. And because their death was worthless, their lives had been worthless too.

But, as Robitschek had said, the lives of the others were the same. Robitschek didn't want anything more than the others did; he only wanted to live. He didn't care about his life being worthless—he knew it was unique and could never be repeated. Everybody knew that, because there were very few people who believed in life in the hereafter or justice in heaven.

We had carrots, cabbage, and green peas. We lived well at the cemetery. We had fresh air and easy work that we enjoyed doing. We were very rich and everyone envied us, even those who worked in the cellars or moved property to warehouses. Even the gravediggers envied us, though they bragged about their life of adventure. We would never have admitted that our lives were worthless, because they were our lives, our unique and unrepeatable lives.

It was clear that everyone agreed with the lawyer—our cemetery group as well as the burial detail, with the sole exception of the bookie. But how could his words have any value when he talked only about money, bets, and the good old days when it was possible to buy even a clear conscience with money? Froehlich was buried and condemned. There was nothing to do but accept the judgment. In his day, Robitschek too had been judged and condemned.

But it wasn't right. It meant admitting that the truth was on their side. It meant making a worthless life even more worthless.

Yes, I already knew, even if I didn't want to admit it, that almost everyone was conceding the truth to them, that people obeyed their laws, not only by joining the circus at their command and helping them with their plunder, but also by damning those who no longer wanted to serve, to jump, to walk a tightrope without a safety net. Perhaps everyone already believed that they were right to send us to our deaths in the fortress town; perhaps we cursed them only out of helplessness and futile anger.

It was much easier to believe in being helpless and obey them, to let oneself be driven to death, than it was to stand up to them, face to face, with a gun or without one. It was true that there was nothing to die for, but it was also true that there was nothing to live for. If not for Ruzena, probably everything would have been different. I would have been like the others at the cemetery or like the gravediggers. I wouldn't have had anyone to talk to and trust. But now there was no more Ruzena, and not even the coffee mill helped. But, still, I had stepped out of line and there was no returning.

I ran into them often even though I tried to avoid them, even though I used alleys and side streets. I couldn't avoid them entirely, because they were all over. They walked along the streets and through the squares, full of confidence, talking loudly. I never thought that they too might be afraid, but perhaps they were; otherwise they wouldn't have yelled so much. The word on our stars was in their language, foreign and sharp, so that they could understand the distorted letters. It was clear they were not afraid of us. It was also clear they were not afraid of death, because they celebrated and loved it. But they were afraid of the city, of the alien, hostile city, which they had not succeeded in subjugating. They loved objects; they were capable of filling warehouses and stolen apartments with them, but I knew they were uneasy among alien things and alien people.

They kept thinking up new laws and regulations for us. Maybe it was fear that made them so diligent, but I couldn't understand their fear, because there were so few of us and, after all, we hadn't defended ourselves. Perhaps they had thought up this life for us only so that we would let ourselves be driven toward death quietly and peacefully, so that they wouldn't have problems when they called us up to join the circus. Perhaps they did it so that, like them, we would fall in love with death, after a life of hardship.

Sometimes they also appeared in our section of the city. They never spoke to us, and we didn't want to speak to them. They spoke to us only in the circus, when we were already on the threshold of death. They could only speak to us when Death was present as a witness. Otherwise they had no wish to speak to us.

If I could be somewhere by the water, I told myself, I would be fine. I knew that the water could break their spell. I preferred a river, but a stream would do, perhaps even a small spring. If I lay in flowing water, if I swam in water that gushed in rapids and overflowed its banks, that constantly renewed itself, I would be fine.

They didn't like water. They knew that we would ignore their laws and regulations if we had water. They walked the length of the river catching people. They caught them with motorboats and asked to see their identity cards. They forbade us to walk by the riverside, because they thought we wouldn't be afraid of them if we saw water. They forbade us to take steamers, rowboats, and skiffs, so we couldn't swim in the water or dip a paddle into it. They allowed us to look into the fire, to breathe the air, to walk the earth, but they did not permit us water. I said to myself that they were afraid of water.

I went to see Materna early that day. It wasn't a good idea, because now, in summer, it was still light and Materna's neighbors sat in their gardens or in front of their doors. They would be certain to see me when I went to his house, but I didn't care now. I had to speak to Materna even though I knew he wouldn't understand me.

I found him alone; his friends hadn't come yet.

"What did you mean?" I asked him. "If I don't want to go with the transport, would you help me hide?"

"But I promised you that long ago," said Materna. "It's all set, but we couldn't do it here—you know that. There are people here who know that we know each other. But I have plenty of friends in other sections of the city. Of course, it wouldn't be easy, but it could be done."

"And would these people know what would happen if they caught me?"

"Of course they would know. In this kind of thing you have to tell the truth."

"And they would still do it? Why?"

"How can you ask such a silly question? If I tell them it needs to be done, they'll do it. I've hidden people too. It's understood."

"But they won't know me at all. What do they care about some Roubicek? There's nothing I can do for them in return because I don't have anything."

"Do you think such things are done for money or some reward?"

I told him about Froehlich and the Sejkoras.

"That was bad," said Materna, "bad from beginning to end. Except for the gun—that was good. It's absurd to think a person can hide in one of those shantytowns. They breathe down one another's backs in places like that. Even that wouldn't be so bad, but a lot of lowlifes live in these places, and those types would sell their own brother. I'm not saying that decent people don't also live there, but there's more of the bad kind. An apartment house, that's what you need, a place where a lot of people live and someone is coming and going all the time."

"But that's not the main thing I wanted to ask you. I don't know how I could live with my conscience if I got people I don't know into trouble."

"My God, what kind of a person are you, anyway? Here I am, offering you a way out of this mess, and you babble about conscience."

There was no way I could make myself understood to Materna.

"At the place where I work, everybody said we don't have the right to do such things. They condemned this Froehlich."

"Don't listen to that claptrap. Those people made their living off other people's work. How can they understand anything?"

"I don't know," I said. "I'm one of them, even if I've never lived off anybody else's work."

"I see there are still a lot of things you need to understand," said Materna. "When the time comes, you mustn't take too long to make up your mind."

I promised Materna I wouldn't. But I went home in a bad mood. I knew that my visit to Materna had not been successful.

These were great times for Tomas, now that it was summer. He went wandering for long stretches again, but when I came home in the evening he always welcomed me at the gate. He would have dinner with me but then go out into the night. I paid no attention because toward morning he always came back. The window would be open, and he was able to climb up to the garret. I wasn't afraid for Tomas, because I knew he was experienced and wasn't afraid. I envied him his courage and carefreeness.

But one day when I came home from the cemetery he was not at the gate. I had come home late. It had been a bad day. All the streetcars had been packed, and I wasn't allowed to get on a full car. When I finally did get on one that wasn't full, it filled up along the way and the conductor, who was either a Vlajka member or simply afraid of them, threw me out, so I had to wait a long time until a less full one came by.

I waited and waited at the stop. Streetcars passed, but they were all full. I was hungry and wanted to get home, because it was a summer evening and I could have read by the open window until it grew dark. Later I would have to close the window so I could pull down the blackout shade and then, when it was late, I would have to turn off the light, crawl out of my sleeping bag, pull up the shade, and open the window again. It wasn't pleasant lying in the garret, which was very hot after the sun had been shining through its closed windows all day. But it was a good feeling to open the window again and feel the cool night air fill the garret, and it was better still when there was a wind outside and I lay quietly in my sleeping bag listening to the rustle of trees in neighboring gardens. It was even better when the wind brought the smell of flowers from distant gardens, and sometimes—not very often—I could even hear the whistle of a train in the distance. At dawn Tomas would always return home and wake me by jumping on my sleeping bag, and I would look out the window and see the sunrise and know a new day was beginning. I was sorry that the day was beginning and that I would have to go out in the street and wait for the streetcar and have to stand when it went through the downtown area, but I was also happy that the sun was rising, because it was cool outside and the air was damp. And Tomas would come to warm himself by me; he would be cold after his night's prowling and sniffing. He would slip into my sleeping bag, his fur smelling of the fresh air, and begin to purr with satisfaction. We would both fall asleep again by the open window in the cool air of dawn. We wouldn't sleep long, because I had to get up early for the long trip to work. And I had to cook my breakfast on an old hot plate that I had bought from the electricians at the Community and constantly had to repair because its wires kept breaking. We were warm lying together in the sleeping bag; Tomas's fur warmed me. It was good to have him as a companion. He listened to me patiently and never argued back. It was good to have him lying next to me. He warmed me and purred softly because he had never learned to purr properly; he was afraid he would give himself away if he purred too loudly.

I came home late that day. It was already past eight, and when I got off the streetcar I covered my star, afraid that an informer might see me. But I didn't have far to go from the streetcar stop. I was glad to get home finally, tired from the long wait and all the standing around on the sidewalk. This time Tomas didn't welcome me, but I wasn't angry at him. He had probably waited until the hour when I usually came home from work and then had become impatient and set out on one of his journeys. It was a beautiful evening, and it would have been silly to expect Tomas to lose so much valuable time. So I went up to my garret and had my dinner without him. Then I had to close the window so I could pull down the blackout shade. Doing that meant Tomas couldn't get in, but he would be sure to meow so I could hear him and open the door of the house since he couldn't jump in the window.

But I didn't hear any meowing even though it was quiet out, so I lay down, put out the light, and opened the window. I thought perhaps something had kept Tomas and that he would be back at dawn. But Tomas wasn't back at dawn or later in the morning as I was leaving for work. I said to myself that he was probably too tired and had fallen asleep in an attic, as he sometimes did, and now was afraid to come home in full daylight lest people throw stones at him. At the cemetery I thought about him several times. I was a little worried that something had happened to him, but I consoled myself with the thought that he was an experienced stray, that he knew how to take care of himself, and that I would surely see him in the evening when I came home from work.

But when I got home Tomas wasn't there, though I called

him. Sometimes he played jokes on me and hid in the bushes, but when I called him he always came. I was beginning to be really worried, because it was unlike him to be outdoors for so long.

I had to go to the pump to get water for cooking and washing, and there I met a neighbor of mine, the one who had once asked me about the house. I tried to avoid her whenever I could because I was afraid she might remember me and turn me in, out of greed, in order to have the house empty sooner.

But this time I didn't notice her, probably because I was thinking about what could have happened to Tomas.

"I heard you calling a little while ago," she said. "Are you looking for your cat?"

"That's not my cat," I said. "You know we're not allowed to have pets. But he does come to visit me at this time of day and I've gotten used to him."

"Well, it doesn't matter whether he was your cat or not, because he's dead, dead as a doornail, and old Burianek from the brickyard came to get him so he could skin him and bake him with garlic. He likes cat so much he claims that with garlic it's better than rabbit."

"So old Burianek killed him?" I asked, forcing myself to speak calmly. I didn't want my neighbor to see how it distressed me to hear that Tomas had been killed.

"Oh no, that cat was much too smart for him! He's been after him for years, but he's never been able to get him. He only took him from the garden where he was shot. He came and took him."

"But who shot him?"

"Oh, that man with the badge who lives in that big villa by the streetcar stop. The one who sometimes wears a uniform. Who else could shoot nowadays except them?"

"Thank you," I said. "I must go home. Good night."

I carried my water pail slowly. Some of the water splashed out and immediately disappeared into the ground. I wasn't careful with the water, because they had killed Tomas. They had killed him just as they wanted to kill me. Whether Tomas was guilty or innocent was not important. They killed him because they had the right to shoot. They had guns, and they were bored when they didn't have anyone to kill. Maybe Tomas had gone into their garden to hunt for birds, and that was why they killed him. They were sure to like birds better than cats, but Tomas couldn't have known they lived there. He hadn't learned to distinguish people by their badges and uniforms. He hadn't even known that I wore a star; otherwise he certainly wouldn't have made his home with me.

I was alone again and depressed, now that I was without both Ruzena and Tomas. I had liked Tomas and Tomas had liked me. He had decided to live with me, even though I fed him only bread crusts and leftovers from the Maternas. Even if he didn't have to wear a star, he had to suffer many wrongs. He was persecuted, and people he had never harmed threw rocks at him. We had a lot in common and we felt affection for each other. I was sorry for Tomas, being eaten now with garlic by old Burianek. He was sure to be disappointed because Tomas's meat was bound to be tough and have no more fat than I did. But his fur was very nice, soft and warm, much better than my skin. It always smelled of the fresh air when he slipped into my sleeping bag at dawn to warm himself and purred quietly so he wouldn't give himself away. He had learned long ago not to call attention to himself and not to trust anyone. But in the end that didn't help him. They killed him without mercy or sorrow. They killed him without knowing anything about him: the fact that he knew how to creep, hide in the bushes, climb trees, and walk on rooftops didn't do him any good. They had guns and the right to shoot at anything that moved and lived.

I couldn't fall asleep for a long time, and I tried in vain to read. Everything in my room seemed ugly and hateful, even the damp circle, which was smaller now, in the summer.

Then I turned out the light, pulled up the blackout shade, and cried for Tomas, out of sorrow, anger, and helplessness.

21

Now that I had lost Tomas, there was nothing to make me glad. It was not so bad when I was working at the cemetery, but I felt worse when I sat at home in the evening by the open window or when I lay in the garden on Sundays. Sometimes I wished that I had finally been called up for a transport, and sometimes I wanted to leave everything behind, crawl into a hole, and hide there until the end of the war.

And then I said to myself that only water could save me. Water was forbidden to me, and their patrols watched over the river. But that was in and above the city, where the water was still clean and had not yet reached the residential areas. At the other end of the city, beyond the outskirts, where I lived, the water was dirty. No one went in it except a few boys, and there were no patrols there.

"That water will do," I said to myself. "It doesn't matter that the whole city's sewage is in it. Nothing can harm it and it will rid itself of the waste as soon as it leaves the city. It's still the same river that has its source in the mountains, makes its way through rocks and forests, takes on streams and small rivers, and keeps growing until it comes to the city, where it's inundated with dirt. The dirt isn't important; dirt can be washed away with water from the pump and soap, though I can't buy it and have to use clay. The dirt won't stay with me, even if I have to scrub myself with sand, just as dirt doesn't stay in the river when it flows through fields and forests again. The dirt settles at the bottom and the river is clean again and can laugh at those who scorn it."

I set out on a Sunday. I walked along the river—in this section of the city, the banks were lined with warehouses. I could walk there because the water was stagnant and dirty. Where sewers emptied into it or factories stood on its banks, it smelled bad. There were no fishermen; fish would surely avoid this part of the river. I walked for a long time and the road seemed endless. I stopped meeting people—nobody went for walks in this dirty, run-down part of the city, with its factories and wooden fences. Of course people lived here too, but they had gone to higher ground or to the other end of the city, where the water was clean and the banks were full of people bathing because it was a beautiful day, the kind that drives people out of their houses and to the river or to parks. I was sure our cemetery was also full of people, but I didn't want to go there. I was glad that at least one day a week I didn't have to look at the marble statues and their gilded inscriptions or at the freshly dug graves with their wooden tablets. I thought of Tomas as I walked. I would have taken him with me; he had certainly never come this far in his life, and he would have found much of interest in places where I saw only wooden fences, dirt, and garbage dumps. But Tomas was dead and all I could do was look for water that was less dirty and stagnant and a bank with a little grass that wasn't choked with silt or grazed bare by goats.

I had come to the city limits, and beyond them lay a district I was not allowed to enter. There were no longer streets, only roads patrolled by guards, and it was possible that they would check all pedestrians. I was afraid to cross the border.

Since I hadn't found any grass, I had to make do with rocks and dirty sand. The water still wasn't clean, but there was no factory on its banks and no sewer flushed into it. I took my clothes off and went into the water. Several people were bathing there already. I wasn't afraid of them, nor was I afraid that someone would steal my clothes. I had nothing in them, and they were old clothes. I was glad I had a tan and didn't look different in any way from the others, though I did have a white spot on my breast because at the cemetery we worked in shorts, with the star hanging around our necks. Only then could an exception be made, since we couldn't sew the star onto our skin.

It felt good to be in the water again after such a long time, and I thought of Ruzena once more, how we had swum across the river together. Ruzena was a much better swimmer than I was, and I had not wanted to swim across, because the river was wide at that spot and I was afraid I wouldn't have the stamina. But Ruzena laughed at me and promised she would help me if I sank. I felt good when I had swum across the river and we lay in the grass, close to each other, our swimsuits dripping. We felt good as we lay, tired, drying off in the sun.

This time I didn't swim across the river. I didn't feel like it. The opposite bank was even dirtier, and there was no grass. Instead I let myself be carried by the current. I floated on the water and looked up at the sky; I felt good floating on the water, looking at the sky. I didn't think about the fact that the water was dark and muddy and that it smelled of kerosene.

I felt good as I warmed myself in the sun, even though I wasn't lying on grass, and as I swam in the river once more and put my clothes on again. I went home slowly, feeling blissfully tired; I felt as if I were returning to the city from the beach on a summer evening. If I could have, I would certainly have finished the day with a good movie or a good dinner or have gone to a coffeehouse or to listen to music. But I had to finish the day at the garden gate, where Tomas was not waiting for me.

It was silly to mourn Tomas when so many people were dying. I told myself as much, but it didn't do any good. I told myself Tomas would long before have died of frost and exposure if he hadn't found a home with me. He would not have survived long as a stray. He would have been killed by a stone or died of hunger; it was only by chance that he was killed by a gun. I would never, of course, have cared for a stray cat if I had still been working at the bank. I couldn't imagine that

I would have shared my food or slept in the same bed with him. But it was useless to wish to comfort myself with such excuses. I felt sorrier about Tomas than about Robitschek.

That night the wind howled, and it felt good to sleep by the open window. I dreamed about Tomas. He was in animal paradise, a real paradise, where he was pushing a swing with mice on it. He was swinging them and smiling at them. He was very happy, and I was glad that he was happy. I was glad there was a paradise for animals to go to. He wasn't at all sad, and there were no wounds to be seen on his fur. He was more joyful and playful than I had ever seen him in life. He was no longer wary, suspicious, or sulky. This was a Tomas from a book of fairy tales, a Tomas from a picture book for little children, a Tomas from my childhood, with upturned whiskers and a happy, good-natured face. I knew he was in paradise because even in the dream I knew he was dead.

"How come," I asked myself, "they manage to instill fear in everyone? How come everyone obeys them, when death is so easy? A person can die only once, but we are dying a thousand deaths. They have taught us to fear death because we have become ensnared by laws and regulations, because we have tried to use them as a magic formula to chase death away. Tomas laughed at their laws and is dead. Materna doesn't laugh at them, but he is alive; they couldn't make him fear death."

I was sleepy the next day and didn't feel like going to work. Though it was summer, it had taken me a long time to fall asleep. I had heard shooting in the night. I often heard shooting, but I never paid attention. Their shooting was none of my business. I knew they never shot us, because they considered such a death too honorable. They had badges in the shape of skulls because they honored death, worshiped it, loved it. There was a shooting range near my house and everybody had become used to the sound of shots. Nobody was interested—the people in the surrounding houses bred rabbits, weeded their gardens, fed their chickens, and gossiped in their doorways. Sometimes I ran into soldiers who were getting on a streetcar. I never got on with them, because they had once thrown me out of one, and if I saw them at a stop I always waited for the next car. They were happy and in high spirits. It seemed that they enjoyed shooting a great deal. They hadn't even pushed me off the stairs; they had only pounded the butts of their rifles on the floor and shouted "Out" in their language. I wasn't at all sorry to leave them. I was glad to be rid of their company. I didn't like the fact that they were so happy. I knew the ways their happiness could express itself. Perhaps they were drunk too, because they were loud, yelling at one another in their language.

But this time I listened to their shooting and couldn't fall asleep. They were no longer shooting Tomas—he was already dead—but they were shooting other Tomases. They weren't shooting at any of us, because such a death was too noble for us, but I felt as if they were shooting at me. I couldn't sleep. Shots in the night were none of my business. I shouldn't have been interested, just as those who cared for rabbits, cleaned their pens, went to the movies, and had a glass of wine with a black-market dinner weren't interested. But now, with Tomas dead, I knew the shots were aimed at me. I would have to think about them even if I was permitted to breed rabbits or go to the movies.

That day we took our vegetables to our canteen in a hand-cart. It wasn't bad work, because it gave us an opportunity to walk through the whole city and to kill an entire day at it. It was enjoyable pushing and pulling the cart, standing at street corners and waiting for the policemen to give the signal, joining the stream of vehicles. We took turns at the job, and this time it was my turn and that of a former shop assistant. I pushed the cart because the assistant wanted to pull—it reminded him of the old days, when he used to pull a cart as an apprentice. We were in no hurry. We had the whole day before us; it was still morning and we were making good progress downhill. It was nice to push a cart full of vegetables—it was ordinary work. We felt good as we made our way through the streets and maneuvered among the streetcars and trucks. There was a lot of traffic and naturally we were slow. Now and then their black limousines, flying flags, would pass us, and their faces, superior and satisfied, could be seen looking out. We ignored the cars. They were none of our business, because we were carrying vegetables that would be eaten by people, the only vegetables they were allowed to eat, vegetables from a cemetery, which we had cultivated with our own hands. We ignored them. We had nothing in common with them; we worked and pushed a handcart while they were on their way someplace to kill. We had no respect for their occupation, just as they had no respect for ours. We had to obey them and to perform in the circus for their amusement, but we were not their slaves, because we never acknowledged them as our masters. They were alien. They had forced themselves on us. We didn't understand their insignia, their epaulets, their fringes and flags. We went along the roadway with our vegetables, good vegetables that they would never eat. They could eat all the asparagus they wanted; we weren't allowed to grow it or to eat it. We weren't interested in asparagus, just as we weren't interested in their cars, because they had taught us to stop loving things—and that was good. Instead of things we had vegetables that we ourselves had made grow.

Part of the way we had to go down the main street, which was full of fancy shops and of restaurants and coffeehouses. We had to take that route to get into a side street; there was no other way. We didn't look at the sidewalks as we went. We knew that they walked there, that they were overeating behind the open windows of restaurants and coffeehouses. We only attended to our vegetables, but we knew that even here we might be envied, because they were greedy, insatiable, and couldn't know that we were coming from the cemetery. But they didn't notice us. They were so engrossed with the shop windows and the good food that we passed through the street unobserved. Of course we had stars, yellow stars with crooked letters in a foreign language, but we were in the roadway among clanging streetcars and honking automobiles. Who would look at the roadway and at our cart?

But as we passed a corner, a group of people came out of a restaurant in a lively mood. It was only noon, but they were already in high spirits. They shouted and laughed, probably after some good food and a lot of wine. These people weren't *them*, because I didn't notice any badges or uniforms and because one was a young woman whom I recognized from a photograph. She was in a movie that I thought Ruzena had gone to see, a young woman whose picture I had seen in showcases. She laughed with the others when she saw the two clumsy oafs with a cart—and clean stars shining on their dirty jackets. We must have been a comical sight, because our cart was a pitiful, clattering wreck held together with pieces of wire, and it screeched with every move it made. It was in constant use and never lay idle: it transported the sick to the Radio Mart, corpses to the cemetery, stolen property to warehouses, and who knew what else. We couldn't lubricate it because we weren't allowed to buy lubricating oil. We were a funny sight for people who had just come out of a restaurant and were probably planning to go swimming in the river; it was amusing for the plump young woman standing on the sidewalk, carefree and content on this summer day. We ignored their laughter—we had enough to do with the cart and the vegetables. We couldn't stare at them the way they stared at us. We ignored what they said, their silly, tipsy talk. Well-dressed people with lots of money, they could laugh at us because we were poor, skinny, and alone.

"There are people who are still well off," said the shop assistant when we reached a side street. "They never worry about anything, and they even have things to laugh at."

"They're in movies," I said. "I recognized that young woman. They provide amusement for people, so they too have to have a good time. There are only rich, happy people in her movies, so she has to live well if she's going to play them. And she has to laugh at bums with bright yellow stars because we're clowns."

"I never laughed at people in distress."

"Neither did I," I said, "but I did in movies. Those people have to enjoy themselves and laugh. Today they're laughing at us; one day they'll laugh at *them*."

There was no point continuing our conversation about the lively group of people. We had to pull the cart, and we couldn't take forever. And we were hungry and looked forward to eating.

But it took us a long time to unload the vegetables and put them in the cellar of the canteen. Only after we had done that did we go to the kitchen to eat; because it was late, the mess hall was already closed. It was hot in the kitchen, but we were glad to be there, because we knew the chief cook, a former corset maker who had also worked at the cemetery for a time before he was promoted to cook. Everyone envied him his work because a cook always had enough to eat, even if it was only beggars' rations. We took off our jackets and sat down, without stars, to eat at the wooden table with the other cooks and the waiters. We enjoyed eating vegetables that we had cultivated. We couldn't overeat or get rowdy, but we felt fine, as if we were at home sitting on wooden stools by the kitchen stove. We were surrounded by pots and pans, we got our water straight from the faucet, and we could take as much as we liked from the bowls of food, even if it was miserable stuff, fit for beggars.

Then we had the whole afternoon to ourselves—we had done our work, and didn't need to return to the cemetery. I didn't know what to do with this summer day. I couldn't go swimming in the river or sit in the park, and in earlier days I would have looked forward to going home, lying in the grass, and reading. But now that Tomas had been shot I didn't look forward to anything at home. I always thought of him when I searched in my pocket for the house keys, and I was restless when I lay in the garden, as if I expected Tomas to make an appearance from the bushes at any moment. But I couldn't think of anything better to do if I didn't want to go back to the cemetery, so I walked through the streets and decided I would only wait for a streetcar when I was good and tired. I walked through the streets in our quarter of the city slowly. They looked shabby and bare in the afternoon sun, gray and indifferent, listless and brooding. Groups of people with stars were standing in front of the Community building. People were excited and ran from one group to another. A transport was probably being organized; there were always groups of people in that street when a transport was being organized. No doubt they were looking for ways to save themselves at the last minute, or trying to comfort one another and to tell one another amazing stories, or searching for food or belongings.

I thought of the flowers we had passed as we pulled and pushed our cart of vegetables, heaps of flowers, masses of flowers whose names I didn't even know, bunches of flowers to put in vases, flowers in pots and in wreaths, with ribbons. Drops of water dripped off their blooms and stems; they were so fresh, so lively and spirited, they seemed to grow on the sidewalks. They were all flowers for cemeteries—not for our cemetery but for ones in our area, where people were allowed to bring flowers. They were all for decorating graves; they would wilt there to celebrate Death, the comforter and deliverer. Or perhaps they were only a way to bribe Death and adorn her with a beautiful shroud, to flatter her with a sacrifice so that she would smile and be kind.

I thought of the flowers so extravagantly massed to please Death as I watched the groups of people standing and running about in the dirty, gray streets. Death was deaf to pleas. It was impossible to bribe her with flowers; it was impossible to make her smile and be kind. Nothing could disguise her ragged shroud. She was plain, a beggar, and only the fact that she was all bones prevented her from fastening a star to the place where she should have had a heart.

I walked through our quarter to its boundaries, where the ordinary sections of the city began. I had to cross one of the streets that formed the border. It had an insulting name to remind everyone that it kept watch over our quarter.

There were loudspeakers on the lampposts, but I had never paid attention to them and I tried to avoid them. When I did come across them, they were always blaring out marches and unpleasant voices reading the news, to the accompaniment of static and drumbeats. This time groups of people were standing under the lampposts, but they weren't at all similar to the groups standing outside the Community building. They stood silently; they didn't come together and split up to join other groups. They were probably waiting for news to be announced over the loudspeaker, most likely something important. Otherwise they wouldn't be wasting time on a summer afternoon that was so ugly in the gray dust of the street with the insulting name.

I stopped too, but I didn't join one of the groups. I pretended to look in the window of an antiques shop. There wasn't a lavish display, only some Meissen figurines, a wooden statue of a saint, and a piece of heavy furniture. I studied the faces of the figurines. They conveyed nothing: they had the fixed, stupid smiles of ladies who wear wigs. I didn't like their faces, but I had to keep looking at them. I didn't want to turn toward the street, because then people would see my star, and I didn't want anyone to know I was waiting for the announcement with the groups gathered by the lamppost. I didn't quite know why I was waiting, but I had enough time. I didn't feel like going home, and the announcement might be important after all, though it would certainly be something I wouldn't like, because they always announced their victories and played their marches over the loudspeakers. Their marches and songs were no business of mine; they were loud and shrill, like their language. They always used them for celebrations, when they seized something—a city, a country, or a piece of furniture.

I listened to them now as I stood in front of the shop window looking at the fixed smiles of china ladies. The dancing figurines ignored the music, but they ignored me too. It was a good thing they ignored me because I was making a painful face at the sound of the marches.

Then words were spoken, but not in their language. It was the announcement that the groups of people had been waiting for. The announcer had their accent. I learned what the waiting groups already knew; I knew now that he would celebrate death because they always began in that tone of voice when they intended to speak about death. They spoke softly, admiringly, about objects, cities, gold, and jewelry, but death they always celebrated in strident tones.

"Shot to death," said the announcer, exultantly, as if he were offering a prayer of thanks. "Shot to death," he repeated in a hard, arrogant voice, adding some words of explanation. The names did not drip slowly, the way our names had as they were read out in the sanctuary. Here they followed one another in rapid succession. They were shouted abruptly, and after each name, the announcer slowly and ceremoniously called out, "Shot to death." There were a great many names. I didn't recognize any of them, nor was I waiting for any. I kept looking at the china figurines and listening to the shrill voice on the loudspeaker. It was quiet in the street, even though cars and streetcars passed, even though many people went by the lampposts without pausing to listen to the news. Yet it seemed to me that everything stopped, that even the water in the nearby river and the clouds stood still, because silence was set on people's faces and their hands and feet were paralyzed, immovable, as they listened by the lampposts. "Jaroslav Pospichal," said the voice. "Ruzena Pospichalova," it continued, as if pronouncing names in a foreign language, and then, like the peal of a victorious trumpet, "Shot to death," and then, again, indifferently, more names.

I stood in front of the shop window and looked at the figurines in their wigs. I already knew each feature of their faces by heart. Even closing my eyes didn't help. I could still see their rigid faces, with their indifferent, stupid smiles.

"Ruzena," I said to myself. "Is it possible that Ruzena—it's absurd. There are hundreds of Ruzena Pospichalovas and hundreds of Jaroslav Pospichals, just as once there were lots of Josef Roubiceks, before their names were called out in the sanctuary. I'm getting everything mixed up in my mind, because this morning I was pulling that cart and that fat young woman who's in movies laughed at us, and then I saw groups standing in front of the Community who were probably waiting for a transport, and now I've been looking for a long time at the stupid faces of china figurines. I seem to keep looking at things that aren't alive, that aren't moving. I should have paid more attention to those people standing on the sidewalk who were laughing so happily and heartily from an abundance of good food and wine. I should have noticed how happy they were with the beautiful day and the excitement of life. Because Ruzena belonged among those people on the sidewalk. But no, she would never have laughed to see me pull a cart. It was me Death accompanied with drums and pipes; it was for me that the gates of the Radio Mart were open. What did Ruzena have to do with it?"

I couldn't budge from the shop window. There was nothing left to do but stare at the dead faces of the elaborately coiffed figurines. I was unable to leave and had to go on listening to the shrill voice on the loudspeaker, reciting indifferently because now he was only repeating the words "hanged by the neck." That was us at the end of the list and in the indifferent voice; that was us, the unnamed. It wasn't worth it to read our names, since we were only numbers sentenced to death. Then the voice stopped, and the groups slowly dispersed. Each person went his or her way. People left the lampposts and shuffled quietly along the sidewalks as marches blared from the loudspeakers. They were gloating over cities and objects again; once again they were calling on their own people to march, with pipes and drums, on other cities and countries, for more silk, fine wines, and rich food.

I passed the lamppost and had to listen to the marches. They followed me all the way to the bridge, where there were no more loudspeakers. I walked quickly and overtook some of the people who had been standing by the lamppost. They didn't notice my star. I kept pace alongside them across the bridge, which had a narrow walkway that prevented one from passing. Now I longed to be home. I didn't even have a stool there to sit on and look at the floor. Dust was all there was enough of, and I didn't need to tear my clothes—they were already threadbare.

I knew it was Ruzena that the voice on the loudspeaker had named. It was pointless to pretend that it wasn't. But what was I, Josef Roubicek, now? Why should I lie in the grass by the cemetery wall and listen to the streetcars clanging and the cars rumbling over the road? Why should I eat my soup and count the bits of fat in it? I had lost Ruzena a long time ago, but now she was here again, to exchange roles with me. Now Ruzena was dead and I was walking across the bridge and the river was below me.

I was alive, and I knew I was alive, because my feet obeyed me, because I walked next to people and wasn't different from them, though I wore a star. I paid no attention to them and they paid no attention to me, but I knew I belonged among them. They had listened to the voice on the loudspeaker just as I had and, instead of looking at china figurines, they had looked at the ground. They were stifled by the shrill voice and the blaring marches.

I began to understand Materna.

22

I hardly knew how I got home that day. It took a long time, because I walked the whole way. I was soaked when I got there, but I hadn't been aware of the rain. Then I looked out the window and saw that the rain was slowly stopping. I heard the gurgling of water as it ran down the rain gutter and into the drainage ditch in the garden and off somewhere. I was sorry it didn't soak into the ground, and then I remembered the voice on the loudspeaker. But I didn't cry for Ruzena. I couldn't cry for her the way I had cried for Tomas. I simply sat on the windowsill and breathed the damp air. I sat there, dull, and didn't think about anything. I imagined I heard shooting again, but I didn't think of shots; I didn't notice them. I just repeated the words "kukureke" and "tucivod" to myself. They were the words I was trying to cling to. And then I went straight to the wall and began to bang my head against it. I wanted to feel pain. How I longed for pain. How I longed to beat my head bloody, to pound a wound onto my forehead, to wake up! I hit myself with my fist to make the pain come quicker, and then I awoke from my frenzy. I washed and went to see Materna.

My clothes were still wet, and I was covered with plaster. Even the star was smudged, though it was supposed to stay clean. But I no longer cared and I paid no attention to the star as I went out the gate and walked, without noticing the route, to Materna's place. I sat on a stool as usual and received my cup of tea. I was silent. Materna was engrossed in conversation with his friends and only nodded to me. But then they realized that something had happened to me, because my wet clothes hung limply on me and began to steam in the close, dark room.

"Where have you been?" said Materna. "You look like a scarecrow and you're dripping wet. You haven't gotten a summons for a transport, have you?"

"No," I said. "I was passing a lamppost—I heard them read a list of the executed. My friend was among them."

"Where have you been all this time?" Materna shouted. "Probably on the moon. They've been reading those lists every day. Don't you read the papers?"

"No, I don't," I said. "And I don't listen to their radio. I'm at the cemetery all day and there are no lampposts or loudspeakers there. There are other cemeteries all around us, and there are none there either. It's quiet, and nobody mentions these things. People are only concerned with the transports, and nothing else interests them. Sometimes some of our people are buried there and then the burial people come and tell terrible stories. They told us about people who were hanged, but they tell so many stories and such strange ones that you can't even remember them. At the cemetery we think they're made up, that they read them in a book and then show off for our benefit."

"It's high time you did something about that cemetery of yours," said Materna. "You live like a horse with blinders. You'll have to confront things head on, or do you want to duck out again and just wait until they come to get you?"

"No," I said. "I understand that. I see there's no other way."

"Well, let's not talk about it anymore."

I went home. I went to bed. I no longer had to beat my head against the wall. It felt strange to have decided so easily, now that Ruzena was dead and I had no reason to live. I would never see Ruzena again, even when the war was over and even if I survived, but I still decided that I would try to stay alive. I smiled because they couldn't get me now, when my life no longer had any meaning for me. I had to laugh at myself for taking all their laws so seriously and for adhering to all their regulations. I laughed for the first time since I had destroyed all the furniture and damaged the house, when I knew they couldn't take any things away from me. I had got the better of them then and could laugh when I imagined how surprised they would be at getting nothing from me except a useless little table and a broken-down house they wouldn't want to live in. I laughed at them again now, when I imagined that the only thing they would get from me, if they caught me, would be my life, which had absolutely no meaning for me. Now I could laugh at their skull and crossbones, their drums and pipes, their circus, and their metal-tipped boots. How ridiculous they were, doing so much work, using so many papers and questionnaires, to deprive one Josef Roubicek of his life. Josef Roubicek wouldn't be worth their effort; all their work was pointless.

I imagined what would happen if I ran into the plump young lady from the film and her friends again. Now I would be the one to laugh at them. I would raise my head from the handcart. "How ridiculous you are, standing there on the sidewalk in your ironed clothes, with satisfied faces and full stomachs. You're afraid they are going to take all that away from you— there is no certainty that your names too won't be read out from the loudspeakers. But I no longer have anything to fear. I no longer have a name or a life. I wouldn't change places with you on the sidewalk, because down here in the road I'm free." They wouldn't understand me. They would think I was crazy. But they would stop laughing, because it would never have occurred to them that I might lift my head and look them in the eyes with laughter. But it would be a waste of time. Why should I talk to mere lackeys, people capable of laughing even when the names of their friends were heard from the lampposts, capable of laughing only because they had good food, wore fine clothes, and slept in well-furnished homes?

I felt good as I lay in my sleeping bag. I didn't have to think about whether they would pull my number out from the bottom of the file cabinet drawer, about how they would read my name in the sanctuary, about how I would obtain everything needed for the transport. I didn't have to worry about a metal bowl or about vitamin pills; I didn't need to envy anyone for having a lemon in his rucksack and cotton in his ears. I felt good not having anything more to worry about, no longer even hoping that by some miracle I could survive in the fortress town. I remembered how I had once walked along a road with the spring wind whipping against my face; I remembered not knowing where I was going, because I had taken the wrong road in attempting to find a shortcut. And it seemed to me then that I was returning to where I had started from; yet I didn't care that I was walking down that road, because I was pushing against the wind, because I felt it tearing my cap off my head, wanting to blow me away. I didn't mind the wind. I was properly dressed and had a bag over my shoulder with everything I needed. Nothing could happen to me on that road, whatever direction I took. I would arrive somewhere finally and I wouldn't be at all tired. I didn't care about the wind or the road or even the direction I was going in.

When I got up in the morning I began to whistle. It had been a long time since I had whistled because it was a long time since I had last had a bathroom. Now I whistled even though I didn't have a bathroom, and I looked forward to going out on the street and waiting for a streetcar. Now I could look people in the eye and calmly get on the streetcar—even if someone threw me off in a little while—because now no star mattered to me. I actually laughed when I was thrown out of the streetcar at a stop in the downtown area and had to wait a long time for a streetcar that was empty enough. And I didn't care at all that some people waiting for the streetcar looked at me with scorn and others with pity.

"It was a beautiful apartment," the bookie was telling us as we lay stretched out on the grass again, with the gravediggers. "There was a large dining-room table, all set for dinner. Everything was the way it should be. There was a vase with flowers and Carlsbad china, nice silverware and napkins. A half-finished bottle was on the table and under the table were several empty ones. There was some food left on the plates; you could see it was a magnificent meal. And the whole family was sitting at the table. They were all nicely dressed, in their best clothes, and they were rigid as statues. Instead of place cards they had their transport numbers by them. It was clear that they were used to living in luxury and extravagance, that they cared about proper behavior, and that was why they'd decided to die in good taste. They were so polite they left a letter apologizing to us, the undertakers. And what was most terrible, all those people sitting at the table were laughing. Yes, they had laughs on their faces, and they stopped laughing only when their jaws fell. And then Egon here said, 'Let's have a drink, fellows. We can't leave this wine here. Look, it's a Tokay and a very good year. I know about wines. I used to deal in them.' We all said, 'But, Egon, it's poisoned,' but Egon insisted that no, these were decent people—they put their poison in their glasses. Why would they put it in the bottle and spoil good wine? And so we all drank, and it really was wonderful wine. It made you feel all warm inside, and then everything went better. We cleaned up, but the only problem was we couldn't straighten them out properly. They were stuck in a sitting position."

"Were they wearing stars?" asked the lawyer.

"Yes, and they looked very elegant on those dark clothes. They were new stars, which they had been given for the transport, and they were sewn on neatly."

"Did you say they were laughing?" I said.

"Yes, they were laughing, and that was the worst thing. They weren't grimacing; they were actually laughing, like people who are satisfied because they've just brought something off. Maybe the poison has that effect, but the doctor said it was no special poison, just something that's very expensive and rare these days."

"I envy them their courage," said the lawyer. "I wouldn't be capable of doing it. To poison yourself perhaps, but your wife and children? How could they laugh?"

"I don't know," said the bookie. "In our work you see all kinds of things. There are still people in the world who know how to laugh. In our detail we had a man who laughed when he remembered that he was still living in an apartment with central heating and that they hadn't found out yet. And as he went to the transport, he still laughed when he thought of it. There are all sorts of people. You learn that at the racetrack."

"Well, I had to smile too," said Egon. "You know, when you're a traveling salesman with things that are difficult to sell, you have to have a knack with people. I used to know so many jokes all the other salesmen envied me. But with these corpses I seem to have forgotten them all. This is quite another thing."

"There are fewer of us again," said the lawyer. "Your group, and ours too."

"This was a bad transport," said the bookie. "I don't wonder that those people did what they did. Maybe they were right to laugh. That transport went straight east and didn't stop anywhere. They say it had something to do with those executions they're carrying out now."

"But they don't shoot our kind," said the lawyer.

"No, they don't, but they have to make up for it some way. They call these transports punishment."

Everyone was silent. Fear had made its appearance once again, and people could no longer speak. But this time I wasn't afraid. For the first time I wasn't afraid. But I couldn't speak. I wouldn't have known what to say. I knew that I was alone, that I couldn't make anyone understand me.

I knew that the leaves would soon begin to fall again and that we would rake them. I knew that the damp circle in my room would grow again. I knew that different people would come to the cemetery but that they too would talk about the circus, transports, arrests, and food. In the winter I would sit with them by the stove again and drink tea made of linden blossoms or rose hips. Or I would no longer be sitting with them because there would be so many fewer people that the card at the bottom of the file cabinet drawer would finally be found. But when the card made its appearance, I wouldn't join the circus. I wouldn't be their clown. *I* would laugh at *them.*

Suddenly I was standing in the street, laughing to myself.

I only came to my senses when I saw the puzzled looks of people around me. They certainly thought it strange that a man with a star was laughing to himself for no particular reason. Perhaps they thought I was crazy.

Ruzena came to see me in the night. I noticed she wasn't dressed very appropriately. She had on a winter suit, even though it was summer. She must have been hot in that outfit. I knew it well. It was made of fine-quality English wool, and Ruzena liked to wear it. She always liked her clothes to be practical, well made, and simple.

"I came to see how you are," she said.

"I've learned to laugh again," I said. "There's nothing left for me to do."

"You're no longer afraid?" asked Ruzena.

"No," I said. "I was standing in front of an antiques shop when I heard your name on the loudspeaker. And then I hit my head against the wall. Everything is all right now, Ruzena. I understand you now and can talk to you calmly. I can't change anything. They're crazy, and they don't understand a thing. They're scarecrows who love death and objects. They're as dead as those objects of theirs. But we're alive, Ruzena—at least you're alive."

"Yes, I am alive, Josef," said Ruzena. "I don't know how you found out, but it's true. That's what I came to tell you, but you already knew. That's good, Josef. You'll feel better now."

And then she left, disappeared. I didn't even know how, and I woke up and looked out the open window at the quiet morning.

I remembered it was my birthday that day. Ruzena had probably come to congratulate me, but then there was no time. It happened quite often that we forgot to say some important thing when we met because we had too little time, but we didn't care—we knew anyway. How pleasant now if someone were to bring me a large cup of coffee and a piece of cake in bed, like my aunt used to do when I was little. I would always pretend that I didn't know it was my birthday, that I had forgotten, even though I had been looking forward to this breakfast since the night before. My aunt was glad I had forgotten, but in a little while a whining tone crept into her voice and she began to talk about Aunt Klara, her younger sister, whom she had loved most of all and who had died at sixteen. I had never known Aunt Klara, but now I knew that she wasn't spinning in her grave, even though in recent years my aunt had told me, at every possible occasion, that she was.

I didn't even know where my aunt and uncle's grave was, if they had one. I had received no news from them, although a long time had passed since their departure. I asked about their transport—I had written down their numbers—but nobody knew anything. I learned that their train had stood for three days on a sidetrack in the station of the fortress town and then had continued to the east. Nobody was willing to investigate where the transport of old and sick people had ended. Nobody was even willing to talk about it. So perhaps the bloodstains in the sanctuary wouldn't surface again. Nobody wanted bloodstains when the process of getting some extra lard took so much time and energy. Only the numbers, which I had written down in my little notebook, remained, but I didn't know what to do with them, and they just stared back at me. I wished they would at least turn into gravestones, even without gilded inscriptions, but that was impossible. I would have been satisfied with wooden tablets at the far end of the cemetery; I would have been satisfied with a mere dandelion. I didn't have to care for Ruzena and Tomas, who were alive, but I did need to do something in memory of my aunt and uncle so that I could show them the respect due to the dead. I couldn't show my respect to numbers.

I went out into the garden, took a shovel, and began to dig a hole in the ground. I thought I would plant a flower in their memory, but then I realized that a flower would not survive the winter. I stood over the hole and didn't know what to put in it until I saw a chestnut lying in the street. Probably some boy had lost it there. I took the chestnut and planted it in the hole and imagined how it would grow. It was not important if I never saw it, nor was it important if anybody knew in whose memory I had planted it. The main thing was that a new tree was going to grow, that I had replaced numbers with something living, which would grow according to its own laws.

Then I remembered that it was my birthday and that nobody was going to give me a present. I needed someone to give me a present, because I had always received presents on my birthday, except for the years when *they* ruled over me, but I didn't count those. Now, when I had finally rid myself of them; now, when they no longer existed in the world as far as I was concerned, I certainly had to receive a present, because my birthday came only once a year, because birthdays measure the passage of time. Since I knew that no one was aware it was my birthday—and that even if someone had known, he would not have given me anything anyway—I had to give myself a present.

I couldn't give myself anything to eat, even if I managed to get some delicacy on the black market. That would be no gift, because I was constantly hungry and I would simply have gulped anything down without feeling festive. There was nothing I wanted and nothing I needed. I had become too choosy; I didn't know what would make me happy and what I would be glad to get. I had seen family albums, knickknacks for decorating homes, china figurines and deer antlers, embroidered tablecloths and carved wooden castles taken to the warehouses. Now all these things lay battered and useless in trucks, waiting to be thrown, scornfully, into cellars and sorted as rubbish. I wanted nothing of the kind.

Then I decided I would at least give myself the gift of a pocket mirror. All I had was a splinter that I used when I shaved. It didn't show much, it was dull and full of scratches, but I didn't mind. I could have shaved without it, but needing a mirror to shave was a habit. If I had a pocket mirror, though,

I could look at myself. I wanted to see what I looked like. Also, it was possible to buy a small mirror at the kiosk nearby; there was no need to go to a regular shop. So I decided to buy one. Immediately I felt happy because I had thought of a birthday present that was amusing and pleasant. I bought the mirror when I changed from one streetcar to another. The purchase was simple: I went up to the kiosk, covered my star with my briefcase, chose the mirror from among the ones lying on the counter, and paid for it. It was not much of a mirror—small and round, with black paper glued to its back—but I held it in my hand and I could put it in my pocket. Now I was impatient to look into it. I wanted to enjoy it, just as I had always enjoyed my presents on my birthday.

I went into the entryway of a house and looked at my face. And then I knew I shouldn't have. The mirror shouldn't have been used to show me my image. I should have used it instead to reflect sunlight onto the cracked walls of my room. Because at that moment I saw for the first time what Josef Roubicek looked like, and it was not a nice sight. I saw sunken cheeks, with a large nose protruding between them; I saw two deep furrows painfully framing a mouth; I saw grayish skin, a wrinkled forehead, and sunken eyes behind glasses. This was getting me nowhere, being able to look at my face on my birthday. There was nothing in it for me. I shouldn't have looked forward to it, nor should I have bought the mirror. I had no need for it. It slipped from my hand and broke into a hundred pieces on the tiled floor. I left the house without even looking back at the slivers, and then I began to laugh at myself, at my vanity and longing. No, this was not the way back to life.

But I was happy because I was able to laugh. It was good to laugh on one's birthday. I didn't need a cake or a birthday present. I was so rich there was nothing I could give myself. I kept smiling to myself as I pulled carrots out of the soil at the cemetery.

"Has something amusing happened to you?" asked the lawyer. "Or have you received information that the transports have been stopped?"

"I don't know anything," I said. "Nothing has happened. It's only that it's my birthday today."

"But that's not amusing," the lawyer said with contempt.

"No," I said, "but why shouldn't I laugh at it?"

The lawyer turned his back to me and I bent over the bed again and pulled carrots out of the dry, crumbling soil. I still had to smile.

23

Now the passing days all seemed the same to me. Now, when I was no longer afraid, I was a poor listener to the stories about the fortress town and the journeys to the east. But I took a better look at the city. I looked at its streets and passageways. I imagined myself running away through its streets. I looked to see how the boats on the riverbanks were fastened with chains, and I imagined the kind of stone that would be needed to break their locks. I dreamed of underground passages and caves. I remembered the brickyard, but I rejected it even though it would be warm. Someone would surely find me there and turn me in. I preferred to imagine a hole dug into the slope above the river, hidden by shrubs, from which I could look out at the people sunbathing on the beach. But dogs that roamed the thickets would sniff me out. I didn't want to think about a hut somewhere in the woods. Materna had said that was not a good idea, because everyone would notice that the hut was occupied when smoke rose from the chimney.

I knew that at first I would probably not be able to go outdoors. I had become used to enslavement; I moved uncertainly, my face to the ground, and I couldn't look anyone in the eyes. Now I knew how we differed from other people. I knew that no star was needed for us to be recognized. I had to learn to walk confidently, to push ahead in the streetcar, to keep my head raised on the sidewalk. I mustn't be scared of uniforms or of insignia. I had to recall my old way of walking— I thought I could still do it. I remembered how, after a long illness, I had learned to walk again, and how quickly I had learned. I was returning home, to earlier days, but it was difficult to go back because I had to let go of the habits of recent years. I was no longer Josef Roubicek, bank clerk. I no longer knew quite what I was and what I would be.

"I can't make it," I told myself. "I'll be lost, because I won't have regular office hours, I won't go out every day with a briefcase under my arm, and I won't buy the newspaper on the corner. I'll be a ghost with a borrowed name.

"I'll make it," I told myself. "Everybody is a ghost of his former self. It doesn't matter that one more will join them. Nothing is certain when the loudspeakers blare, and yet people walk the streets and push baby carriages in the road."

It began to rain and we spent more and more time in the chapel. There were fewer people at the cemetery, because fewer people remained and those who did remain were needed for taking stolen things to warehouses. The burial detail also remained, because now they had more work than ever. We were raking leaves again, but we knew that we would not be using them for compost; we knew that by spring there would be no one at the cemetery. But we went to the cemetery every morning anyway and left after working hours, and inspection officers still came, even though there was nothing to inspect. We still had to go to the Community to obtain permits to use the streetcar; we still filled out questionnaires and went to the labor office for medical checkups. There was still a demand for strong, healthy people, but there were few of them. They had to be created out of the sickly and the weak, by redesignating their work category. People who were pronounced strong built roads, dug holes, quarried stone, mixed concrete, and carried bricks. Yet they were still called up for transports; their hard labor didn't save them, and their places were taken by even weaker people. Anything could be done with numbers. A person could be transformed from someone weak into someone strong; a person could be changed into a circus animal. But I was no longer interested in numbers. I knew that now no one would turn me into a number. Not even the doctors at the checkups could make me into a strong man, though they tried. And so I remained at the cemetery, among the old and the infirm. I didn't like being with them, because they remembered only the old days and talked about their illnesses, rare illnesses that had stumped learned professors, famous diseases that were the subjects of articles in medical journals. I would have preferred talk about food now, but the old and the infirm didn't talk about food. They had bad teeth and stomachs; imaginary meals had no appeal for them, because they wouldn't have been able to eat the fantasized delicacies. Nor was there anything interesting in their talk about the good old days. All of them had lived very ordinary lives, which only they considered unusual and exceptionally interesting. They talked a lot about the first war; they would smile as they recalled the marches and the furloughs. Only the stories told by the undertakers were amusing, but now they had too much work to do to spend much time at the cemetery.

Snow began to fall, and we could no longer rake leaves. We sat by the stove again and drank linden tea and looked at the dusty floor. There was no longer anything to keep me at the cemetery. There was nothing I had in common with the old and infirm men who sat huddled by the stove. I was somewhere else—in the passageways, caves, and alleys. I was living with other people, and I spent long hours in my sleeping bag, reading books; since I no longer had Tomas, I had no one to take care of and no one to talk to. I went to Materna's more often and paid more attention to the conversation. I became interested in the war and in trying to figure out how much longer it would last. Because now the war and how long it would last were important; now I had to follow the progress of the fighting with lines drawn on a map; now, when I knew that the war was also being fought for my life, it was also my war—now, when I kept returning to the same people and had linked my fate with theirs. But the life I led at the cemetery had grown more difficult. I had trouble talking to the people there, borrowing their spoons to mix my tea, and listening to their memories of the old days. It felt good to leave the cemetery, even if I knew that I would be coming home to an ice-cold room and that it would take me a long time to get the stove going. I secretly took home wood chopped from the pews. There was no regulation forbidding us to carry wood, but even if there had been, I wouldn't have cared. I borrowed newspapers from Materna and tried to read important information between the lines; I looked at the faces of people in the streetcar for signs of good news.

But I had to get used to this life. I had to talk myself into this other Josef Roubicek, who would not even bear that name. It was necessary to force his legs not to run when he passed a man in uniform; he had to be forced to walk casually by Vlajka members' shops, with their insulting photographs and slogans in the windows. So far I had learned to laugh—that was thanks to Ruzena—but my laughter wasn't true laughter. I had to pull the corners of my mouth up. It was forced, desperate laughter. There wasn't a bit of joy in it.

Among the old and the infirm even death had lost its glamour. They clung to life but weren't able to hang on to it with their weak hands. They never spoke of death. They were afraid to pronounce the word. Those who had sat by the stove earlier, before they left for the east and for the fortress town, had spoken the word often, with uncertainty, with sorrow or with hollow scorn. But these people never spoke of death. I didn't speak of it either. Death and I had squared our account. I was no longer its slave.

We no longer even had to wait for messengers. They no longer came, because all of them had already been deported. I had to be my own messenger, to pick up and deliver the summons myself; I had to perform the whole ceremony alone.

There were no longer mysterious knocks on the door to finish the act. Smoke was rising from chimneys when I took the summons home, when I carried it with me on the streetcar, in my breast pocket. Smoke was rising from stoves where dinners were cooking, meals that would soon be eaten by people sitting down to them in peace and quiet. It was a winter day. There were no lights in the streets, and on the streetcar only a blue blackout light was blinking. Faces looked like those of corpses, and I couldn't even read the summons. But there was no need to read it. I knew its contents by heart; it wasn't any different from those delivered by special messengers to hundreds of people. It was a good thing that I was my own messenger, that I didn't have to look the herald in the face; it was a good thing that I wouldn't have to see him. Nor would people come to bring me stars and help me prepare my luggage. Only the people who made lists of the furniture and the movers would come, but by that time I would be gone and wouldn't be able to see the surprise on their faces as they took my little table out to the large moving van.

And at that moment, when I came home, adjusted the blackout shades, and put the summons on the washstand; at that moment, when I was thinking about whether I should start a fire if neither cold nor warmth would exist any longer; at that moment, when I looked around my bare room to see if there were things I could destroy or take with me, I began to hesitate. I knew I had to start the fire, not because I needed warmth but because I had to burn the scraps of paper with my scribblings and my English vocabulary words, absurd invitations from years before, and expired permits to use the streetcar. There were no letters from Ruzena; I had burned those long ago. I began to hesitate because suddenly I felt very tired. I was no longer afraid, but I was tired. It would have been much simpler to leave with the others; it would be better to give up, to disappear, to submerge myself among the hundreds of others going to their deaths. I would be all right; I would have peace; I would accept extinction without fear or shame.

Instead, the freedom I would now have to bear would be a heavy load. It was too much of a burden to be a different Josef Roubicek, to be a rebel who had a price on his head, who would go into hiding and have to prowl at night. Perhaps it would be better after all to become a number, a leaf carried by the wind until it falls to the ground and is trampled into the mud.

But I overcame my hesitation and rejected the temptation. I knew that the moment would never be repeated and that at this moment, at this crossroad, I must come to a decision. It would have been easier to leave the decision to others, but there were no others. There was only myself between the cold, bare walls, placing meager scribblings that I had once thought so highly of into the stove. There was no one to ask for advice and there was no one to pray to, because now I had to cross the line.

But at that moment I already knew I would cross it. Because I had overcome death, and it was a good thing to overcome death. At that moment I already knew whom to ask for advice. It was Ruzena who came to advise me that night, Ruzena whose advice I had rejected long ago. I knew I would accept it now. I knew it was good advice, just as it had been then. I knew that it depended on me, just as it had then, and that now, at this moment, which would never be repeated, the only moment of decision, I must not retreat. Now I must follow Ruzena, as I should have done then. We would never again have to stand on the riverbank and say goodbye at the streetcar stop. If I came to a decision now, we would go on together. Ruzena would always accompany me, and with Ruzena there was nothing to be afraid of.

It was then, when the last sheets of my scribblings were burning in the stove, annulling the name of Josef Roubicek, that I understood that the Josef Roubicek who wanted to make excuses, to evade, and to dodge, only to avoid freedom, no longer existed and would never exist again.

"Yes, Ruzena," I said. "Now you can depend on me."

✻

Jewish Lives

THOMAS BLATT
From the Ashes of Sobibor: A Story of Survival

IDA FINK
A Scrap of Time

LALA FISHMAN AND STEVE WEINGARTNER
Lala's Story: A Memoir of the Holocaust

LISA FITTKO
Solidarity and Treason: Resistance and Exile, 1933–1940

PETER FURST
Don Quixote in Exile

SALOMEA GENIN
Shayndl and Salomea: From Lemberg to Berlin

RICHARD GLAZAR
Trap with a Green Fence: Survival in Treblinka

ROBERT B. GOLDMAN
Wayward Threads

HENRYK GRYNBERG
Children of Zion

ERICH LEYENS AND LOTTE ANDOR
Years of Estrangement